CAM B♥Y

QUINN
ANDERS♥N

Riptide Publishing
PO Box 1537
Burnsville, NC 28714
www.riptidepublishing.com

Cam Boy

Cover art: L.C. Chase, lcchase.com/design.htm
Editor: May Peterson, maypetersonbooks.com
Layout: L.C. Chase, lcchase.com/design.htm

ISBN: 978-1-62649-697-2

First edition
February, 2018

Also available in ebook:
ISBN: 978-1-62649-696-5

CAM BOY

QUINN ANDERSON

RIPTIDE
PUBLISHING

I dedicated the first book in this series to my beta and the second to my best friend. But this one? This one's for me.

TABLE OF CONTENTS

CHAPTER 1

"**S**omeone call for a plumber?" grunted a burly man in blue coveralls that barely contained his bulging muscles. "I'm here to snake your drain."

A smaller blond man batted his eyelashes at him. "You've come to the right place. My pipes are in desperate need of a good snaking."

"Well, bend over, and let me take a—"

"Joshua!"

Josh shrieked and dropped his phone. It landed on the granite countertop with a clatter, but thankfully didn't break. He snatched it up again, scrambling to hit the Home button in the hopes of closing the video before—

It was too late. His boss appeared next to him, and judging by the sour look on her face, she was pissed. "Are you watching *porn* at work?"

"No, Sana! I swear." Josh flashed an innocent smile.

Sana plucked the phone out of his hands. "Then what do you call this?"

"Hey, give it back!" Josh swiped for it, but Sana held it above his head. Thanks to the heels she was never seen without, she was as tall as he was. He couldn't reach it. "Damn your treelike stature."

Sana glanced at the screen. "Not porn, eh? Look, I know gay smut when I see it. Either that hairy bear is about to bend that twink over, or I'm the Easter Bunny."

"I'm telling you, it's not porn."

"You're such a liar."

"No, really. They're just porn *intros*." He stood on tiptoe and managed to finagle his phone away from her. He angled the screen so she could see the title of the YouTube video he'd pulled up.

"I'm watching 'Top Ten Cheesiest Gay Porn Openers.' Let me tell you, some of these are *bad*."

One of Sana's thick eyebrows rose to the top of the bright-purple headscarf that covered her hair. "You know what else is bad? *Watching porn at work*."

"I already told you, I'm not. And besides—" Josh waved a hand at the near-empty coffee shop around them "—it's dead today."

Sana muttered something familiar under her breath that—after a day of extensive googling—Josh had identified as an Islamic prayer for strength. "Joshua. We need to talk."

Uh-oh. Now I've done it.

"What about?"

"You and your recent obsession with the porn industry."

"I'm not *obsessed* with—"

Sana held up a hand, silencing him. "I don't know why you think this behavior is acceptable, but it's not. It's not appropriate for a workplace. I don't care how long you've been working here. If I catch you on your phone again, I *will* write you up. Customers or not, there is plenty around here to do. Busy yourself." With a swish of her long black dress, she disappeared into the stockroom. Probably to do some breathing exercises. Josh had that effect on her.

When he was certain she was gone, he puffed his cheeks up and exhaled, making a rude noise. Sana was a good boss on most days—fair, flexible, and not too demanding—but she never let him have any *fun*.

For a brief moment, he considered going back to his video, but Sana wasn't one to make idle threats. If she caught him on his phone again, she'd probably send him home. He couldn't afford to lose half a day's pay.

Being broke sucked.

Grabbing a clean dish towel from one of the cabinets, Josh wiped spilled coffee grounds and milk from the counters. Sana was right about one thing: there was always something to do around here.

The Globe, where he'd worked for the past three years, was one of few independent coffee shops that had stood against the march of time and Starbucks. Probably because it appealed to a very specific demographic, which Josh could only term "liberal as fuck." There was a rainbow flag undulating outside the door, and the walls were covered in local abstract art. The front of the counter had been layered with bumper stickers over the years that bore pride colors and catchy slogans. The smell of their organic, locally sourced coffee beans was thick in the air.

Josh glanced out the large entryway windows at the aluminum sky. It was an unseasonably cold and gray day, befitting his mood. Summer was normally the time when Los Angeles came alive. The sun seemed to energize the millions of people who lived here, like fields of sunflowers. But the sun was buried beneath leaden clouds, and it reflected in the hunched backs of the people walking down the streets.

The stormy sky added to the ennui that settled over Josh like mist. Sana might not understand his sudden "obsession," but he knew exactly where it'd come from. Well, if he were being totally honest, he'd discovered a healthy interest in porn a *long* time ago, but his recent interest in the *industry* was another matter.

It'd started when one of their long-time employees, Pete, had quit a couple of months ago. That sounded innocuous enough, but Pete had left after it was revealed that he'd been working as a porn star on the side for over a year. Talk about moonlighting.

Not that he'd left because his secret got out. If this were a small town, that might have caused a scandal, but this was LA. The land of starving actors doing whatever they had to do in order to survive.

No, the revelation had been a whimper as opposed to a bang, excuse the pun, to most everyone. Everyone except for Josh. He didn't know for sure why Pete had quit, but he had to assume it was because the money was incredible. LA was the porn capital of the world, after all. If you wanted to star on Broadway, you moved to New York. If you wanted to become a famous porn star—a Jenna Jameson or a Ron Jeremy—LA was the place to do it.

Famous. Damn, he liked the sound of that.

It'd certainly gotten him thinking. And thinking had led to googling. Googling had led to a fever Josh couldn't seem to sweat out. Especially when he'd seen how much porn stars *made*. Jesus. The numbers refused to exit his brain no matter how many times he shooed them out. He was no math whiz, but he didn't need to be: he could get paid more for an hour of sex than he netted in a week at minimum wage.

The bell above the door jingled, startling him back to the present.

Josh shook off his thoughts like water and plastered a smile on his face. "Welcome to the Globe! Let me know if you need any help." He poured extra solicitation into his tone, in case Sana was listening.

The woman who'd walked in barely glanced at him in favor of consulting the baked goods display. After a moment, she jabbed a finger at one of the rows. "I'll take an orange-vanilla scone, um—" she adjusted her glasses and squinted at his name tag "—Joshua. You don't go by 'Josh'?"

"I do." Josh opened the case and used a pair of silver tongs to grab her selection. "With family and friends. Joshua is my professional name." He puffed out his chest. Going by his full name *totally* made him sound like an adult.

"Sounds kinda pretentious if you ask me."

He deflated like a punctured hot-air balloon. "Anything else I can get for you?"

"Glass of water, please."

He grumbled under his breath as he filled a to-go cup from the tap. He plunked it down on the counter, rang her up, and sent her on her way with a smile that had shifted from cheerful to manufactured. When the door closed behind her, he collapsed dramatically on the counter, his face tucked into the crook of his elbow.

"Still slacking off, huh?"

He peeked to the side. Sana had reappeared, and if her voluminous eyelashes were any indication, she'd touched up her makeup.

"I literally just finished with a customer."

"Uh-huh. I believe you."

"I did! And I was the epitome of service with a smile."

"Sure, and Schwarzenegger is gonna run for president next." She frowned. "Although I guess these days that would be a marked improvement."

"I can't believe you. When have I ever lied to—" Josh stopped as half a dozen examples popped into his mind.

Sana pinched the dirty dishcloth between two manicured fingers and held it up. "Get back to work, please."

Josh snatched it from her and, tongue pressed between his teeth, excused himself to the milk station. There, he spent the rest of his shift cleaning up spilled cream, refilling sugar packet dispensers, and topping off cinnamon shakers. Truly, he was living the dream.

The sun had sunk beneath the morose horizon by the time he hung up his apron, clocked out, and said good night to Sana, who usually stayed late to close up. He hauled two bags of trash out to the dumpster behind the Globe and then began the trek home. Twenty minutes of walking and one bumpy, smelly bus ride later, he was in Lincoln Heights, one of the worst neighborhoods in all of LA.

Home sweet home.

The streets around here glittered not with gold but with broken glass. The buildings were run-down at best and collapsing at worst. He wasn't sure why, but he'd always thought the area smelled like . . . beige, somehow. Not the benign, sterile beige of hospitals and dentists' waiting rooms. But of colors that had been bright once, before they'd been beaten down by the sun and grime and decay.

Depressing as it was, it was all Josh could afford. He rented a single bedroom in a derelict house that he shared with three other guys. It wasn't much, but it was his. If nothing else, he always had something to bitch to his friends about.

As he approached the ratty house, he noted for the hundredth time that its yellowing edifice looked like an old man with a squashed face. The gutters sagged like a bad comb-over, and the windows were his clouded, beady eyes. Every time the front door was opened, it swung loosely on its hinges like a single crooked tooth.

"Another day in beautiful California," he muttered to himself as he dug his keys out of his pocket and unlocked the dead bolt. He eased the door open—always concerned that one of these days it would topple right over, bringing the house with it no doubt—and shut it behind him. He flung his shoes off in the entryway and noted two other pairs there: A.J.'s Birkenstocks and Chris's knockoff Vans. Great. He'd have to fight for control of the TV.

After making his way down a short hallway, he poked his head into the living room. Sure enough, A.J. and Chris were piled on the threadbare sofa they'd salvaged from a friend's shed last year. It had been rained on, judging by the watermarks, and what might have once been a pattern of roses now looked like angry red blobs, but free was free.

The blue light from the ancient TV flickered over his roommate's faces, illuminating how incongruous they were from one another. Chris looked like he'd fallen out of a Hot Topic display, and A.J. could have been a page from an Abercrombie catalog. Between hair gel and eyeliner, they probably put the same amount of time into their appearances.

"Hey," Josh greeted them. "Will's not home?"

"Nah." A.J. dug his hand into the bowl of popcorn in his lap and crammed a fistful into his mouth. He chewed for a moment before a wad appeared in his cheek. "He's shacking up with some girl. Said he won't be back tonight."

"Word. Is anyone making dinner?"

"You volunteering?"

"Fuck no." Josh grimaced. "Unless you want three packets of ramen served in a plastic mixing bowl."

"Better than what I've got." Chris flicked black emo bangs out of his eyes. "If I have to eat canned beans and rice one more night . . ."

"You'll what?" A.J. punched him, the sleeve of his salmon polo shirt rising up over his bulging arm muscles. "Finally gain a pound? Be careful, or you'll split your skinny jeans."

Chris opened his mouth—perhaps to deliver an acerbic retort—but Josh backed out of the room before he could hear it. He wasn't in the mood for their squabbling tonight.

His stomach growled as he bypassed the kitchen and made his way to the second bedroom on the right. He'd left his door unlocked, not because of some sacred bond of trust he had with his roommates, but because he had little worth stealing. It opened with a horror-movie-esque creak, revealing an unmade twin bed that took up half the room, a pile of dirty laundry, and a battered dresser that was covered in crap, including his laptop.

He flopped onto the bed and immediately shot up again with a yelp. Fuck, his keys. He dug them out of his pocket again and threw them into the pile of laundry. They landed with a soft *plunk*. His wallet and phone got honorary spots on the wooden crate next to his bed, and then he tried his flop once more. This time, he stuck the landing.

With a sigh, he stared up at the watermarked ceiling. His single window let in barely enough light from the streetlamps to illuminate its craggy surface.

"This place isn't you," he whispered to himself. "None of this shit is you." It was a mantra he'd taken to repeating whenever his lack of earning potential started to get him down. He'd said it so many times, it was noise to him now.

He forced himself into a sitting position, swinging his legs over the side of the bed. His laptop sat next to a pile of dusty textbooks he hadn't been able to sell after his ignominious departure from higher education. One bachelor's-degree-turned-associate's later, he had a useless piece of paper that didn't qualify him for jack. But at least he hadn't flunked out entirely.

Along with his degree, he also had the super-expensive laptop he'd shelled out for, certain that it would help him become a star student. So much for that theory. He settled it on his knees and opened it. The screen showed a loading symbol for a moment before revealing his desktop wallpaper: a headless, muscular torso dressed in tight underwear. He'd picked a black and white photo so he could claim it was artistic.

He double-clicked on his internet browser of choice, and twenty tabs popped up. He'd had them open for so long, he'd become emotionally attached to them. Job postings, Craigslist ads, and calls for him to donate a stunning variety of fluids. He could find something decent among all the crap if he were diligent enough to sift through it every day. Too bad that wasn't a word anyone would use to describe him.

His gaze wandered to the crate next to his bed. It sported a collection of cheap picture frames he'd picked up from a thrift store. His friends smiled at him from one: Ashley, Darius, and Monica. His parents waved from another. The pics were grainy and bleached of color—he'd printed them on copy paper in his school's computer lab before he'd graduated—but they never failed to cheer him up.

Come to think of it, he was pretty sure his mom had texted him earlier. She was off with husband number three, but she liked to check on him. Had he ever responded to that text? Life's little mysteries.

Just as he had every day for the past few months, he opened a new tab and typed in a search phrase: *gay porn LA*.

The first ten or so results were all links to videos. He knew better than to click on those, or else he'd get . . . distracted. He scrolled down until he found what he'd been looking for: postings from various local entertainment companies that were looking for "adult performers."

"Why can't they come out and say it?" Josh mumbled to himself. "They're looking for porn stars."

There was one company he'd had his eye on for a while now. Murmur Inc., located not twenty minutes from where Josh worked. The name had caught his attention from the get-go—it was light-years subtler than the other porn producers'—along with their expensive-looking website and the fact that they were one of the only companies that *wasn't* holding an open call. The others seemed like anyone could walk through the door and get work, but Murmur Inc.'s auditions had been closed for weeks now. It had become Josh's habit after work to check their website and see if anything had changed.

Today was no different. He clicked on the home page and spent a moment admiring its sleek design before he headed to the New Arrivals section. There, all the latest stars had head shots, biographies, and teaser videos displayed for the world to ogle. In order to see the full-length vids, he'd have to pay the subscription fee. Too rich for his blood. Instead, he contented himself with scanning the fresh faces and imagining his own head shot among them.

Not that he would, uh, ever be in porn. It was just a thought. An inkling. A fantasy, even. It must be a hell of a life, though. Getting paid to fuck hot guys, do sexy photoshoots, and have thousands of people view your face every single day . . .

Josh had twelve followers on Twitter, and he was related to one of them. His Instagram wasn't any better. What would it be like to have people notice he existed when they weren't waiting for him to finish brewing their coffee?

He dragged himself away from that train of thought before it could plow through him. He finished checking out the new arrivals—it was sparse, which made sense considering how long auditions had been closed for—and clicked on the tab for open calls. He needlessly scanned the block of text that outlined the requirements for auditioning; he'd memorized it weeks ago. His eyes moseyed down the page to where bold black letters would declare that they weren't accepting new performers, just as it had every day for the past few months.

Once, twice, three times Josh read the final sentence before it finally sank into his brain.

Murmur Inc. is now holding auditions for new talent of all ages, body types, and genders.

Josh stared at the letters until they'd burned themselves into his retinas. Auditions were finally open. This . . . this was, like, a *sign*. Right?

He tossed his laptop onto the bed and stood up, pacing the length of his bedroom. It was all of three steps and too cramped for him to move like he wanted to. He tripped over his laundry pile and sent his keys skittering under his dresser, but he paid them no mind.

Was the universe trying to tell him something? Or, with him checking Murmur Inc.'s website every day for months, was this bound to happen? If he were being realistic, he'd have to say it was the latter.

Then again, maybe the real sign was the fact that he'd never stopped checking. He could have lost interest weeks ago, but something kept drawing him back. To porn and to Murmur Inc. in particular. Why *that* company?

They were local, for one thing. Established. And they had a hell of a reputation, from what he'd seen on google. All their shit was high-quality. Like, Hollywood levels of production value. He'd read actual, academic reviews of their porn. Some might call it artistic. Not Josh, but someone. If he got the chance to star in one of their films . . . Man, he could make a name for himself. He could have fans. And *money*. Oh, how he wanted to have money.

He collapsed onto his bed again. He was getting way ahead of himself. It was one thing to be curious; it was another to go through with it. Besides, if Murmur Inc. was as quality focused as their reputation suggested, they'd want people who could act. People with movie-star good looks too. By conventional standards, Josh was a handsome young man, but he didn't have the chiseled six-pack and nine-inch cock that featured in every porn he'd seen.

Then again, maybe he was jumping to conclusions. Murmur Inc. had proven to have different standards from regular porn. Plus, Pete—the ex-coworker who'd quit to go be a big gay porn star—was above-average looking on a good day with the right Instagram filter.

Craning his neck, Josh caught sight of his reflection in the half-length mirror he'd tucked in the corner next to his lamp. Green eyes set in an angular face and ringed with light eyelashes looked back at him.

Yeah, he was confident he had the face. And his body wasn't bad. He might not be shredded, but he was tall and lean. Maybe he could scare up some abs if he started doing crunches. He was more of the cardio sort, but beauty was pain.

That just left the acting bit. A trip to the gym wouldn't be enough to help him in that department. He'd watched every teaser Murmur Inc. had on their website—or the gay ones, at least—but it was difficult to tell how much acting was required. The performers never seemed like they *were* acting, to him. Was that how good they were? Maybe he should break down and subscribe to their site.

For the low, low price of $19.99 a month.

His last bank account statement flashed through his mind. Fuck. Much as his impulsive nature was screaming at him to blow the money, he literally couldn't. Not until he got paid on Friday, and by then, the auditions could be closed again.

Opening yet another tab, he did a quick search for pirated Murmur Inc. films. Google came up with zilch. Their shit was under cyber lock and key. Jesus. If a man couldn't rely on internet pirates, who could he rely on?

So much for that. The last thing he wanted to do was sign up for an audition only to embarrass himself. Then again, his parents had always told him he was an Oscar-worthy drama queen. Maybe that was enough.

Why not give it a shot? The worst they can do is say no.

Before he could totally overthink it, he opened a blank document and drafted a résumé according to the instructions. First and foremost, they wanted to know all his "stats": age, height, weight, etc. Easy enough. Twenty-one, six foot, and . . . He scrunched his nose, trying to think of the last time he'd weighed himself. He was one-sixty? One-seventy? Would they make him get on a scale? That seemed doubtful. He plugged the numbers in.

Next, he had to list his acting experience. That was easy: none. He wrote *eager to learn and accumulate knowledge* instead. After that came any other relevant skills. He grinned. How about twenty-one years of being gay? He'd had experiences in LA's club scene alone that were hotter than any penny dreadful. He wrote a paragraph on that and moved on.

The final section prompted him to add any additional details. Hm. He had work and school history. Those couldn't hurt, right? He listed his degree and three years of gainful employment at the Globe, with some filler shit he always saw on résumés: *effective time management, good at multitasking, takes direction well.*

The familiar platitudes took on vastly different meanings in the context of a porn audition. He thought about adding *works well in groups* but decided against it.

The final instruction was to include two photos of himself: one of his face and one of his body. Nudity was preferred but not required.

His mouth puckered into a thoughtful moue. He didn't have any nudes at the moment. He'd used Snapchat to send a few to his last boyfriend, but that had been . . . God, a long, depressing time ago. He could take one right now with his phone, but he doubted a company with a rep for quality would be impressed by a selfie taken in a dark, messy room.

If nudity wasn't required, maybe he could skate by without it. He pulled up Facebook and hunted through his photos. Most of them were taken at the various gay clubs he frequented with his friends. He didn't think sending in a photo of him sweaty and drunk with smeared eyeliner would be a good idea.

After some scrolling, he came upon the photos his cousin Lacie had taken at Christmas. Jackpot. She fancied herself an amateur photographer and always had a giant camera hanging from her neck. The photos she'd tagged him in were high-res and as close to professional quality as he could get. He selected a group shot where he was flashing a cute smile and cropped it so only his face was visible from the chest up. Then he filtered through the rest of the album, looking for a suitable body shot.

Luck was on his side. They'd had Christmas at his great aunt's ranch in Oregon. She kept horses, and Lacie had snapped a photo of Josh petting one. He wasn't looking at the camera, focused as he was on the beautiful animal before him. He had a sort of dreamy expression on his face. It was the softest Josh had ever seen himself look, especially considering he was the sort to smirk or stick his tongue out for photos. Plus, he was dressed for a family dinner: a polo shirt, a nice jacket, and fitted jeans.

Yup. That was the winner. He saved both photos and the résumé onto his desktop and then composed a new email. He filled out the subject line as instructed and then wrote a brief introduction in the body detailing why he felt he'd be a great fit for Murmur Inc. Much as he wanted to enumerate his physical virtues again, he had the good sense to talk about Murmur Inc.'s impressive reputation instead.

A voice in the back of his head warned him that he should go back and write his résumé in the same serious tone that he'd used for the email, but he brushed it aside. This was a *porn* company, after all. They spent their days taking dick pics that people actually wanted to see. Even if they were high-end, how serious could they be?

When everything was attached and ready, he sent the email. Now all he had to do was wait for a response. He had a feeling he'd be hella distracted at work tomorrow, but that was a concern for Future Josh. Right now, he wanted to get some shut-eye.

He replaced his laptop on his dresser, wiggled out of his work clothes until he was lying in only boxers, and fell asleep right as his face touched a pillow.

He woke up the next morning to his phone blaring the opening song from *The Lion King*. After shutting it off, the first thing he did was grab his laptop and check his email. It was silly, he knew. There was no chance they'd get back to him that fast, and his eyes were so bleary he couldn't read, but he'd dared to dream once already . . .

He nearly pissed himself when he spotted an email in his inbox. When he saw it was from Murmur Inc., he almost made himself go to the bathroom before a tragedy occurred.

Was it one of those automated responses to say they'd received his submission? He clicked on it with trembling fingers and scanned it, eyes jumping all over the place in an effort to get the most crucial information first.

A handful of seconds later, he let out a whoop.

We are delighted to invite you to a private audition.

They wanted to meet him. He made himself read the email again in sequential order, no matter how much he wanted to toss his laptop aside and dance around his room.

They wanted him to audition later that day. If that went well, they'd book him for his first film, and they'd pay him—

Holy *shit*. Josh gaped at the screen. He'd known porn paid well, but Jesus Christ, that was more money than he made in a week.

Thoughts flitted through his mind like birds startled out of a tree. He'd expected to debate with himself about this. Hell, despite his cocky attitude, a part of him hadn't thought he'd hear back. But now that the opportunity was here, right in front of him, he wasn't as conflicted as he'd thought he would be.

Not that he didn't have doubts. There was no denying this was a porn audition, no matter how many times the email referred to it as a "performance." If he showed up, it would mean he was agreeing to have sex for money in front of a camera. For the whole world to see. And he knew from experience that the internet never forgot anything. He still had some junior prom photos from the year he'd gotten a bowl cut that his friends liked to haunt him with.

That was another con right there. What if his friends saw his videos? Or his parents? Oh God, he'd die. And there were other risks too. Rejection. STIs. Physical harm. At least he couldn't get pregnant.

A hundred valid counterarguments filled his head, but from looking at the dollar amount attached to a single video alone, all those concerns sailed right on by. One hour on his back could net him that elusive dream known as *financial security*. Hell, he could work twice a week for Murmur Inc. and make enough money to pay his bills, *and* move out of this shithole, *and* eat food that didn't say *Just add water!* on the box.

There was one other tiny, miniscule problem, though. He was working the evening shift at the Globe, and his audition was scheduled for the middle of his shift. Maybe he could email back and ask them to reschedule.

And they'd probably tell him to get lost. They clearly had no shortage of people who were clamoring to work for them, or they wouldn't need to close their auditions.

He imagined hundreds of dollar bills with little white wings soaring around his head only to fly off into the sunset, never to be seen again.

His phone was in his hand before he could process the movement. He found Sana's name in his contacts and typed a quick text.

Sana, I can't come in to work today.

He was about to set his phone down when it buzzed in his hand. It was Sana. Gulp.

Is everything okay? Are you sick?

The prospect of lying flashed through his mind for a microsecond before he discarded it. He owed Sana more than that. *No, there's something I need to do.* He didn't elaborate, largely because he had no idea how to explain.

Her response was instantaneous. *Joshua, you're on thin ice. If you miss work today without a good reason, don't bother coming back.*

Josh's fingers hesitated over the screen for only a moment. *Then I quit. I'm sorry.*

The polite thing to do would be to give two weeks' notice, or at least call her and deliver the news himself, but there was no time for that. There was so much he needed to do to get ready for his close-up.

He was going to be a *star*.

CHAPTER 2

Mike Harwood started his day as he did any other: balls-deep in another man.

A sweaty, gorgeous man who was currently moaning like Mike was trying to kill him with his dick.

"Oh God," the man groaned. He threw his dark head back in an exaggerated way. "Yes, Sean, right there. Fuck me just like that."

Mike wanted to grimace at the cheesy dialogue, but he kept his face frozen in the expression of bliss he'd had for the past twenty minutes. A camera flash went off to his left, and he had to blink away spots. Fucking photographers. It was hard enough to concentrate on what he was doing—or who, in this case—without them buzzing around. Especially when his costar brought so much ham to the scene, he wouldn't need to eat for a week.

What was the guy's name again? Dante? Damian? Something like that. Not that it mattered. The names around here were as fake as Hollywood itself. All that ecstatic mewling was starting to throw Mike off, along with the way the guy kept bucking his hips up on the offbeat.

Good thing Mike—or Sean Hardwood, as he was known to the porn world—was a seasoned vet. He'd starred in dozens of films, and the one he was making right now wouldn't be so much as a blip on the radar. Thank God. He had a reputation to think of.

But hey, money was money. Sex was sex. Though he had to admit, having men moan his fake name instead of his real one didn't have quite the same charm.

"Cut!" called a woman's voice to the left.

Mike paused mid-thrust and stilled. He yearned to pull out, and the guy beneath him was squirming with discomfort, but they'd need to pick back up in the same spot when filming resumed. "What's up, Colette?"

The blonde woman in jeans and a pink crop top eyed him from behind the main camera. "Any particular reason why you started sucking all of a sudden?"

Balancing his weight on one arm, Mike wiped his sweaty brow. "Sorry. I lost focus." He didn't bother making excuses. He'd been working with Colette long enough to know she wouldn't buy what he was selling. Normally, all he had to do was smile pretty and flex to get what he wanted, but Colette was too sharp for that. People didn't build successful empires like Murmur Inc. by being naïve, and she could smell bullshit from here to Santa Monica.

"I can't say I blame you for getting kicked out of the moment." She shifted her keen gaze to the other man. "Your costar was doing a decent impression of an overeager actor with one line. Diego, what do you have to say for yourself?"

Diego. That was it.

Diego grinned lazily and wriggled beneath Mike, making the mattress squeak. "Would you believe I was having that good of a time?"

Mike rolled his eyes and glanced at Colette in time to see her do the same. "Not with that acting, I wouldn't. Tone it down, please? We have quality standards to maintain. We're not just producing porn here." She gestured to the half-dozen crew members that were all crammed in the bedroom with them: sound and light techs, a camera operator, and of course, the photographers. "We're selling a fantasy. And for fantasies to work, they need to be *believable*. Good sex can be subtle too, okay?"

"Whatever you say, *mami*."

Colette looked like she wanted to lecture him some more, but she refrained. They were on a schedule, and time was money. Mike hadn't met the owners of the house they were filming in, but since it was in Bel Air, it couldn't have been cheap for Colette to book it. No doubt she wanted to get everyone in and out.

Nice choice of phrasing, Harwood.

"On your marks, gentlemen." She signaled to the camera operator and the photographers. When they gestured back, indicating that they were ready, she called, "Action!"

Mike resumed thrusting into Diego with the same enthusiasm as before but more concentration. He rolled and flexed his torso so every well-cut muscle in his abdomen got a chance to shine. That was, after all, what the viewers were here to see.

Diego let out another groan, but it was more controlled this time. Colette must have been satisfied, because she didn't call for them to cut again. In fact, this time, they made it all the way to the "big finish" without incident. Mike pulled out, removed the condom, and came on Diego's chest as directed. His orgasm wasn't bad, in a perfunctory sort of way, but he could have done without Diego running his fingers through the semen and moaning like it somehow gave him pleasure. He knew people who were into come play, but that was a bit much.

As flashes burst around him, capturing the big finish, his thoughts overtook him again. Why had the moaning bothered him so much? The women he performed with overdid it too, and he didn't find that irksome. Then again, they were encouraged to. Apparently straight guys couldn't tell real moaning from fake if it screamed in their ear. The gay market was different. Less forgiving, for sure. If it didn't pay so well, Mike might say to hell with it and make the switch.

But then, corny acting or not, he'd be hard-pressed to give up cock.

"Cut!" Colette clapped her hands. "Nice work, gentlemen. Let the photographers get some final shots, and then we'll wrap."

As soon as Mike was cleared, he rolled over and sank onto the bed, exhausted. The silk sheets and mountains of throw pillows might have seemed luxurious to some, but all he wanted to do was lie on a flat surface and stretch out his back. Of course, Diego chose to lounge right next to him, elbows and knees touching, though there was a whole bed. Mike wanted to shove him onto the floor. He didn't, though. He'd love to claim it was because he was too polite to be rude to a coworker, but in truth, shoving him would involve touching him, and after *hours* of skin-to-skin filming, that was the last thing Mike wanted to do.

Diego made a single attempt to strike up a conversation with him, but when Mike responded with a wordless grunt, he wandered off to find his clothes. Mike watched him go with vague interest.

As soon as he'd dressed and Colette had assured him that he'd get paid by direct deposit, Diego scuttled off. Probably to catch a happy hour or something, judging by his flashy clothes.

Mike tsked. A man without fashion sense was like a muscle car without a paint job.

Does Diego owe you money? Why are you being so harsh?

He wasn't the catty sort, under normal circumstances. Professional courtesy was an important part of the biz; he knew that better than most.

Oh well. It didn't matter. He'd never see Diego again. It was rare for two porn stars to film more than once together, and not simply because audiences were always looking for something new. Few porn stars stuck around as long as Mike had, and he'd only been at this for three years. Either the others were quitters, or they were a lot smarter than he was.

Whoa, where did that thought come from?

He let his mind wander as the crew finished packing up the equipment around him. What was up with him lately? He gave himself a little shake to dispel his sour mood, but it clung to him like stale cigarette smoke.

Maybe it was because everything from his back to his cheek muscles was sore from having to act like he was having breathtaking sex while bent like a pretzel. But he'd never been bothered by porn's artifice before. They were all here to put on a show. They all acted like they were turned on by things that looked good on camera but felt like their spines were going to crack. Mike had a bloodstream full of Viagra right now to keep him, well, at attention. It was his job, and it'd been good to him these past few years. Why, then, was he suddenly so put off by how *fake* it all was?

Because it's been a long time since you've had anything real.

He pushed that thought away. Since when was he so maudlin? He was probably being moody. He'd perk up when he got his next fat paycheck. Speaking of which.

"Hey, Colette," he called, propping himself up on his elbows. "I was wondering if you have any new projects I might be good for."

Colette, who was bent over a laptop set up on a folding table, looked up. "You just finished filming one. How can you be thinking of your next gig already?"

He shrugged, both answering her question and testing his back. He'd recovered enough to get dressed. He rolled off the bed and pulled on his boxers, which Diego had flung next to the nightstand two hours ago. "You know me. Always the workaholic."

Colette went back to reviewing the footage on her laptop. "That's true. You're one of my most dedicated performers. And one of my highest earning. Which is why I'm surprised you're fishing for all these small-time gigs. You got a gambling problem I don't know about? Gotta keep a bookie off your back?"

"Would you care if I did?"

"Of course I would. I want all my employees to be happy and healthy." Colette blinked long, synthetic eyelashes at him. "So you can make me lots and lots of money."

"That's the spirit. Got anything coming up?"

"I was actually going to ask if you mind staying late tonight. I have an audition coming in."

Mike frowned. "You mean like a new recruit? I thought you preferred to vet them on your own first before introducing them to anyone else."

"I do, but in this case, I think it'd be best to have him do a scene with a pro." She slipped a file folder off the table and flipped it open. "The guy's résumé was . . . Well, let's just say I haven't laughed that hard in a long time, and not in a good way. I expect new applicants to be green, but this guy actually wrote a paragraph about how being gay makes him a prime candidate for this. I wasn't sure whether to laugh or call the ACLU and report a hate crime."

"Sounds like a disaster waiting to happen. How do I fit in?"

"Considering your experience and delightful no-nonsense attitude, I figure you're the perfect person to put him through his paces, so to speak. I want you to see what he's got."

"I'm not going to babysit some newbie."

"All right, no need to be grouchy." Colette held a hand up, palm facing him. "This is a request, not an order. If it were that important to me, I'd have asked you earlier. But I figured since you're here and asking for work, and we have the space booked already . . ." She paused. "And you'd be compensated for your time."

Mike peaked an eyebrow. "Same rates as before?"

"Of course."

"Do I have to fuck him? Because I'm good, but even I only have so many in me per day."

"Sex is optional. In fact, I'd prefer you didn't. We're losing the light, and I have an early morning."

Mike considered it. He didn't *need* the money, per se, but that was because he worked hard to keep it that way. Colette might think these little gigs were beneath him, but they made ends meet when he was between projects and work was scarce. There was no such thing as a salaried porn star, and he had a lifestyle to maintain.

On the other hand, did he want to deal with yet another amateur today? The sound of Diego's embellished moans hung in the back of his mind like an irritating-but-catchy pop song. Plus, he hadn't been kidding when he'd said he was burned out.

He knew one way to settle this.

"You got a photo of the guy?"

Colette beamed. "Yup. I printed some out along with his résumé." She handed the file folder over.

Mike glanced at it. The résumé was on top, and Colette was right: it was a joke. The guy—whose real name had been blacked out with Sharpie; Colette was a stickler for protecting the identities of her employees, including potential ones—had listed some of the most rambling and irrelevant credentials Mike had ever read. The guy sounded like a college kid who was taking a stab at writing his first résumé. Mike peeked at the potential's stats. Twenty-one years old. That explained a lot. Mike was only twenty-five, but he knew better than anyone what a difference four years could make.

He flipped the résumé to the side, revealing the photos, and his heart twisted in his chest. He'd been expecting the typical porn fare: a greased-up shirtless guy lounging on a bed. Instead, the man in the photos was fully dressed, in normal clothing too. No booty shorts or mesh or glitter. In his head shot, he was smiling, sans dicks in the background or come on his chin. It could have been a yearbook photo had he not been wearing a goofy Christmas sweater.

The full-length shot went one step further: it looked candid. It plucked Mike's attention out of the air and held it in a firm grip. Not because the guy had an amazing body or anything—though Mike liked his whole tall, lean thing—but because his posture was so . . . open. Genuine. The angle caught his face in profile, but Mike could see that he had a relaxed, dreamy expression as he reached for a horse's muzzle with a long-fingered hand.

Of course, there was no way the shots weren't staged. Even a complete amateur wouldn't send in nonprofessional photos. Mike had to give him points for creativity, though. The horse was a nice touch.

This guy must have some serious acting verve to pull off a shot like this. Most of the male performers Mike knew relied on having washboard abs to get them work, and it showed. Maybe tonight wouldn't be such a waste of time after all. Plus, Mike had to admit, the whole blond, clean-cut look was doing it for him. He had a grittier image, and he was a sucker for taking angelic twink types and dirtying them up. It was almost enough to make him wish sex were on the table.

"Well?" Colette grinned. "Can I take that silence as approval?"

He cleared his throat, not wanting to appear overeager. "He's hot, I'll give you that."

"Hot enough to convince you to join us this evening?"

Feigning nonchalance, he closed the folder and handed it back. "I guess it can't hurt to stay. I could use the money." The lie felt heavy on his tongue.

"Wonderful." Colette's brown eyes twinkled. "I'm sure you and the money will get along famously."

She turned back to her laptop, oblivious to him now that she'd gotten her answer. He finished getting dressed. Every article of clothing he pulled on had the name of an important Italian guy on the label. It was gratuitous to wear nice clothes to a porn set—they just got stripped off anyway—but he couldn't help it. Dressing for the job helped him get into character. It was sort of a signature of his. Sean Hardwood always looked impeccable. Mike Harwood was the same way, but nobody cared about him.

Maybe the next time he was cast in a big production, he'd talk wardrobe with Colette. It had been a while since he'd landed anything decent. His last noteworthy performance had been a bit role in one of her holiday films: *The Island of Misfit Boytoys.* He'd played a horny elf who got gangbanged by a bunch of guys wearing fake antlers. He wouldn't call it a show-stealer, but he'd received favorable reviews and a lot of web traffic, especially since he was a well-known power top. No quicker way to get the fetish mill going than to switch sides.

But that had been six months ago. In porn time, it might as well have been a decade. New videos were hitting the internet every second, and customers were always chasing a new high. Staying relevant wasn't an uphill battle so much as a sheer rock climb, and his bills never stopped coming.

Jesus. The longer he dwelled, the more depressed he got. He needed to snap out of it. If the newbie performed better than him, he'd never live it down.

He sat on the bed to wait. Or brood, judging by his current mood. About twenty minutes passed, and most of the remaining crew members filed out. That left only Mike, Colette, and the camera operator, a woman named Yolanda, who was monosyllabic. Mike adored her. She never forced small talk. Which meant he had squat to do except wait. He settled into the pile of pillows on the bed and prepared to take a postcoital nap if need be.

He was beginning to nod off when Colette's phone dinged. She pulled it out of her pocket. "He's here. Yolanda, you mind fetching him?"

Yolanda nodded once and disappeared down the hallway. Mike sat up in anticipation. He ran a hand through his hair and noted with dismay that it was still damp with sweat.

"You look fine." Colette was watching him with a knowing smile.

"Like I care," he grumbled, disturbed to discover that he did.

A few minutes later Yolanda returned with a tall blond man trailing behind her. He had a wide smile on his handsome face—like he couldn't be happier to be there—but there was something off about it. Something saccharine. Mike found it disconcerting.

"Welcome." Colette held her hand out to the man. "I'm Colette. We spoke on the phone."

The man took her hand and, to Mike's abject horror, kissed her knuckles. "Nice to meet you."

Colette blinked at him. "Pro tip, pal: professionals shake hands when greeting each other. Unless that doorway you stepped through led to the fifties."

"Right. Sorry." He took her hand and shook it this time. His smile was still in place, but now it looked like a grimace. "I'm Joshua Clemmons."

Colette yanked her hand back. "We talked about this." She'd hissed it under her breath, but Mike heard her anyway. "Remember?"

For a second, Joshua's expression flickered. Then his smile fell off like an anchor dropping into the sea. "Oops. I forgot. I'm, uh, Dick Reams."

A light bulb went off over Mike's head.

Did he just give his real name? Mike sat straight up and stared at him. Holy shit, this guy had *no clue* what he was doing. Good thing the other crew members had left. Not that they would say anything, but the fewer people who'd heard that colossal blunder, the better.

Now that Mike knew his real name, he couldn't disassociate it with the man in front of him. He'd have to be careful not to call him Joshua out loud. *I wonder if he goes by Josh.*

Colette pinched the bridge of her nose. "Will you please pick a less ridiculous stage name?"

"But aren't cheesy names expected?"

The look Colette gave him could wither a whole orchard. "Maybe for the other dollar-bin entertainment companies out there, but Murmur Inc. is different. We have these funny things called *standards*."

Mike snorted. It'd been far too long since he'd gotten to watch Colette eviscerate a new kid. Or *ream* one, as he might prefer.

The sound of his laughter caught Joshua's attention. He looked over, and Mike met his gaze without hesitation. Even from a few feet away, the delicate seafoam color of his eyes was apparent. Mike's laughter caught in his throat.

"Who's that?" Joshua asked in what had to be the loudest stage whisper of all time.

"That's Sean Hardwood, one of my top performers."

"He gets to use the name *Hardwood*, but I can't be Dick Reams?"

The groan that issued from Colette was reminiscent of a dying sea mammal. "Please stop talking. You're so much more handsome when you don't talk."

Joshua ignored her. "Am I auditioning with him? You didn't tell me I was going to have sex with anyone today."

"That's because you're not. Sean is here to help you test the waters. We need to see how well you play with others."

"No offense, but he's not my type." Joshua glanced at him, his gaze roving over his hair. "I'm not into gingers."

Mike probably should have been offended. He'd been teased for having red hair his whole life, though his auburn locks were now a part of his brand. But instead of getting angry, he found himself studying his bewildering new costar. Joshua's mouth probably got him in a lot of trouble, but Mike found it sort of . . . refreshing. Charming, even. It was a far cry from the phony flirting he was used to getting from costars.

Colette, however, seemed unamused. "Let's get one thing straight: Whatever preconceived ideas you have about porn, toss them all out right now. All of them. Porn isn't just getting paid to get laid. It's hard work. Uncomfortable, grueling, and exhausting work. Your personal preferences are inconsequential, and if you *ever* insult one of my employees again, that'll be your last day with this company. If I book you for a gig and you accept it, then you will do your damn job. If you don't like it, you can quit. Is that clear?"

Joshua swallowed so hard Mike heard it. "Crystal."

Mike's whole face had been consumed by a grin. There was nothing more validating than having Colette disembowel a man for him. He hoped he was never on the receiving end of her ire.

"Much better. Now, meet your new costar, if you should be so lucky." Colette gestured for Mike to join them.

As instructed, he slid off the bed. He only had a few feet to work with, but he managed to put some sway into his hips as he approached. He stood next to Colette and ran a hand through the hair Joshua found so offensive, flexing his arm muscles. A professional would be able to spot his seduction techniques right away, but he was willing to bet Joshua would fall for them like a cheap card trick.

Right on cue, Joshua's bravado slipped, revealing clear interest as he looked Mike up and down.

Might as well give him something to look at.

When Mike finished tousling his hair, he folded his arms behind his head, stretching his shirt up over his toned torso. Joshua's eyes latched on to the V-shaped cut of muscle visible above his jeans and followed them down to—

"So, Dick, huh?" Mike asked. "Or did you want to be called something else?"

Colette shot him a warning look, but he ignored it. If the newbie was dumb enough to shout his name from the rooftops, he deserved a little good-natured ribbing.

Joshua shrugged. "You can call me Josh, I guess."

Colette shook her head. "I advise against letting anyone call you by your real name on set. Unless you want it spread around. We have office gossip, same as any other job."

He chewed on his lip. "Dick, then. I go by Dick."

"I'm Sean. It's a pleasure." He gave Josh one of his finest sultry once-overs. "Or at least, it will be soon."

It was amazing what one look could do. In a breath, the vestiges of Josh's fake confidence vanished and were replaced by a mixture of arousal and nerves. His Adam's apple bobbed, and he shifted his weight in a way Mike recognized all too well. He would have bet money that Josh was starting to get hard.

"It's, um, nice to meet you." The flush that spread over his fair cheeks was beautiful. For the first time, he looked like the wholesome, American Dream type Mike had first seen in his photos. The one he wanted to pin down and dirty up, in every sense.

A predatory emotion within Mike lifted its head and sniffed the air. He shouldn't be turned on by Josh's naïveté. Colette was taking valuable time out of his day to have him train a newbie so green, he was like a sapling trembling in the breeze. Josh couldn't even pull off a decent fake-it-till-you-make-it. And yet, Josh was pushing buttons for him that were coated in dust, it'd been so long since someone touched them.

Mike knew better than to mix business with pleasure—beyond the literal—but the idea of performing with someone he had actual chemistry with was tempting. "I get the feeling that by the time we're finished, you're going to develop a taste for ginger."

Josh's mouth flapped like a fish, speechless. Mike's grin grew. *He must not know that it's customary for porn stars to flirt with each other before a shoot. He thinks I'm being serious. Which, to be fair, I am a little bit.*

"Sean. A word, please?" Colette stepped out into the hallway without looking to see if he was going to follow.

He did, shutting the bedroom door behind him. "What's up?"

Colette faced him and crossed her arms over her chest. "I'm having doubts about our latest addition. I intended to film a teaser for the website with him today, but now that I've met him . . ." She clicked her tongue. "I'm not sure he's worth the money."

To Mike's surprise, defensiveness rose up in him. "That seems harsh. Give the guy a chance. Teasers are only three to five minutes long, which means they can't take more than an hour to film. How much can that cost?"

"Fifteen hundred dollars."

Mike whistled. "Shit. I always knew it was a lot, but that's outrageous."

Colette started ticking off on her fingers. "There's the cost of renting this location. Production expenses. Video editing. Yolanda's compensation. Your compensation—"

Mike's tongue acted without his volition. "I'll do it for free."

Colette's eyebrows shot up to her heart-shaped hairline. "You'll *what*?"

Her shock was justifiable. Mike hadn't done a freebie in . . . ever.

Despite questions racing through his head, he stood his ground. "You're a sucker for natural light, right? That's why you scheduled him for right before sunset?"

"That was the plan, yes. But if he fucks up and takes too long—which I suspect he will—we'll have to shoot with overhead lights. Or cut our losses right now. I could pay to rent this place for another hour, but somehow I doubt he'll be worth it."

"Just give him until the sun sets. That's less than an hour of filming, and since we're not having sex, I don't think it would be fair for you to pay me for that. You can cut some costs, and I'll consider it a favor."

Colette looked at him askance. "That's generous of you. Should I be concerned?"

"Why, because I want to watch the new kid flounder some more? This is pure Schadenfreude on my part." Mike shrugged. "Well, that and he's hot. Besides, don't think for a second I won't call in my favor the next time you're holding auditions for one of your big films."

That's not the whole truth, and you know it.

Mike slapped a muzzle on his mental voice. "Murmur Inc. has done a lot for me, so I don't mind giving back. Especially if it keeps me in the forefront of your mind come casting time."

She tapped a manicured finger against her chin, considered him, and then her expression gave way. "All right. You're on. Dick seems to respond to you anyway. Maybe you can coax some star quality out of that lifeless rock." She opened the bedroom door and marched inside without another word.

Mike followed after her. She made a beeline for Yolanda and started discussing lighting. Thanks to a large west-facing window, the room was suffused in warm, golden light. It was perfect for filming right now, but it wouldn't last. They needed to hustle, loath as he was to rush. If they produced a sub-par piece, Sean Hardwood would look terrible right along with everyone else. He'd have to hope Josh could produce.

Josh had taken a seat on the edge of the bed. When Mike entered, Josh caught his eye and smirked like he was trying to pull his confident mask back on. As Mike approached, it slipped off his face as if it had been oiled.

"Mind if I join you?" Mike gestured to the space next to Josh.

Josh opened his mouth as if to speak, but nothing came out, and his bottom lip trembled. Mike was overwhelmed by the desire to take it between his teeth and bite. Josh must've been at a loss for words, because he ended up just nodding and scooting over a little. Mike took the seat, struggling to keep his face neutral. If he acted too wolfish, Josh might spook. He'd never be able to explain to Colette why her new recruit had run screaming from the room.

"So, Colette says this is your first time." Mike smiled. "Nervous?"

"No." Josh sounded defensive. "I'm not a virgin."

Mike suppressed a laugh. "Good to know, but you're still a porn virgin, which is a whole 'nother ball game. You're about to learn that having sex and filming porn are different things."

Josh bit his lip, and Mike was hit by that urge again. "I don't understand."

"You will when we get started."

"All right, gents." Colette directed her attention at them. "We have to move fast. We've got about forty minutes to get this done. Anybody need to hydrate or stretch or anything?"

"I'm good," Mike said.

Josh glanced at him and then back at Colette. "Me too." His tone sounded like a challenge, or maybe like he was trying to prove something.

Mike's mouth twitched. *If he wants to get competitive with me, I can think of all sorts of ways to make that fun.*

He was somewhat alarmed to realize how much he was looking forward to this. Man, he needed to get out more.

"I want you both to sit back against the headboard like you're two buddies having a normal conversation."

"In bed," Josh quipped. "Like you do."

Mike snorted before he could stop himself.

Colette glared at them both. "We're on a time crunch, remember? As I was saying, I don't have a script prepared for you, so you can talk about whatever comes to mind. This is informal, and it isn't about dialogue so much as chemistry, which you two seem to have plenty of."

Mike snuck a look at Josh. He was blushing again.

"Dick, bear in mind," Colette continued, "this is your first introduction to Murmur Inc. and our clientele. Make an impression and you may start off with a strong fan base. That'll drive demand for you, and hopefully it'll give some new people a reason to hit that subscribe button." She winked and looked to Yolanda. "Ready?"

Yolanda gave a thumbs-up from behind the tripod.

"Get into position, gentlemen."

Mike and Josh both scooted back so they were sitting against the pillows with a couple of inches between their bodies.

"Perfect. Action!"

Yolanda flipped a switch, and the red recording light flashed on.

Mike turned to Josh, ready to strike up a conversation, but stopped short. Josh was staring at the camera like it was going to bite him: eyes wide, mouth open. His face was so comical, Mike burst out laughing.

"Cut!" Colette massaged her temples. "Dick, I didn't think I had to mention this, but you're not supposed to look directly at the camera."

"Oh, right. Sorry." Josh's expression was sheepish. "Where should I look, then?"

". . . At your partner."

"Ah! Of course. Got it. I'm ready now." Josh peeked at Mike and sent him a small smile. Mike had to fight the urge to giggle. Josh was like a rubber ball. With the slightest touch, he went ricocheting between bravado and uncertainty, leaving utter calamity in his wake.

Colette signaled to Yolanda again. "Action!"

This time, Josh kept his focus on Mike. It was an improvement, though there was still something unnatural to the stiff set of his shoulders and the way his gaze never wavered.

Mike didn't know what it was about Josh that put him in such a charitable mood, but he resolved to loosen the kid up before Colette nixed the whole project as a lost cause. "So, Dick, you said this is your first time filming porn?"

In lieu of an answer, Josh glanced at Colette.

Mike chuckled. "Don't worry. We're allowed to break the fourth wall. You can answer."

He looked back. "Uh, yeah, it is."

"How do you feel about it so far?"

"Fine, I guess. I honestly didn't know what to expect." His eyes wandered once down Mike's body before they met his again. "But I have a good feeling about it."

Shit. Maybe he's got a knack for this after all.

"I like your confidence. Let's see if you can back it up." Mike leaned forward, reached behind himself to grab hold of his shirt, and slipped it off in one fluid motion. He tossed it to the side before flicking his hair away from his eyes and grinning at Josh. "Your turn."

Josh didn't move. Instead, he stared at Mike's defined chest with a distinct awed expression. It was immensely satisfying.

"What's wrong?" Mike edged closer. "Never seen a shirtless man before?"

"Yes. I mean, no, I have." His bratty, defensive tone was back. "You just . . . surprised me." He pulled his shirt off too, tossing it onto the floor like Mike had.

Mike whistled, studying his torso without bothering to be subtle about it. Josh wasn't as cut as Mike was, but he was so damn *lean*.

He probably did cardio, like jogging or something. And he was tall. Mike had no complaints—at least, with what he'd seen so far.

"Are you a top or a bottom?" Mike asked.

It was a standard question in the biz, but Josh seemed put off by it. "That's a little personal, don't you think?"

"Dude, this is porn. You're gonna fuck on camera at some point."

"Oh, right." Josh ran a shaky hand through his hair, and the light strands fanned over his brow. "I'm a top."

Mike smirked. "Not with me, you're not."

Josh pouted. "You can't—"

Mike reached over and trailed a finger down his bare chest. "Look at all that fair skin. I bet you bruise like a peach."

It was impossible to tell if the flush that swept over Josh's body was from embarrassment or arousal, but judging by his quickened breathing, Mike would have put money on the latter.

Before Josh could respond, Colette interjected with some direction. "Not bad, newbie. You're a little stiff, but your reactions almost seem genuine." She glanced at her laptop, which was streaming the live feed. "And the camera loves you. That's always a plus. We've got about twenty-five minutes left. That's enough time for us to film a kiss."

Mike nodded, excitement bubbling up in him. He'd have to examine why that was later, but for now he was prepared to give the whole world a show. Except, when he looked at Josh, he was frowning.

"A kiss?" Josh's eyebrows knit together.

"Yes. Please tell me you've heard of it."

"Of course I have. It's just . . ."

Colette signaled for Yolanda to cut. "Is there a problem? Again?"

"Isn't kissing supposed to be off-limits, or something? Like, too intimate for porn?"

Colette blew out an exasperated breath. "Where did people get the ridiculous idea that kissing is more intimate than sex? I blame *Pretty Woman* for this. No, kissing isn't too *intimate* for porn. Or maybe it is for some companies, but we're not peddling emotionless titillation here. Our porn has romance. Storylines. Production value. Didn't you do your research before applying to work for us?"

"I did, I swear. I guess I thought . . ." He glanced at Mike as if looking for help. Mike shook his head. "Never mind. I dunno what I thought."

"Less thinking. More doing. We're burning daylight. Action!"

Mike eyed Josh, wondering what sort of kisser he was. Every guy was different. Some liked to ease into it while others went in guns blazing. Or tongues blazing, as was often the case. Mike sincerely hoped that wasn't Josh's style. If one more porn star decided it was sexy to shove his tongue down Mike's throat, he'd gag. Or at least, he would if he hadn't trained away that reflex a long time ago.

As it turned out, Josh's style was to do nothing. He looked at Mike with wide eyes that said one thing: *I'm at a loss.* His trembling had returned. Mike couldn't tell if it was stage fright or genuine fear, but Josh seemed like he was one loud noise away from a meltdown. This was the most transparent his inexperience had been thus far.

Impatience flashed through Mike—they had a job to do, after all—but there was a tinge of something else. Like sympathy, only . . . deeper.

Throw him a bone, said a voice in the back of his head. *He's scared. You were a scared newbie once too.*

"Hey." He made his voice soft and gentle, like the brush of a hand. "You all right?"

"Yeah." Josh's eyes twitched like he wanted to look at the camera.

"Relax. I'll only bite if you like that sort of thing."

That earned him a laugh. Before his eyes, Josh relaxed a little bit. "I only like biting sometimes."

"Let me guess." Moving slowly, Mike thumbed the hollow of Josh's throat. "Your neck."

"Yeah." Josh's voice was breathy. For the first time since they'd started filming, his full attention seemed to be on Mike. There was a sliver of a chance he'd managed to do what every porn star had to learn to do: forget the camera, forget the other people in the room, and *relax.*

Mike wondered if he could claim this act of charity on his taxes. But then, if he was just being nice, why was his heart beating so fast?

You're probably picking up on the newbie's nerves. Stay in character.

He leaned closer, twisting his torso until their faces were inches apart. "Can I kiss you?" He wet his lips and dropped his eyes to Josh's mouth. "I want to."

"Um." Josh's chest was visibly rising and falling with his quickened breaths. The air between them had a notable charge, but even with all the sexual tension crackling around them, Josh was still shaking.

Mike lowered his voice, too low for Colette or the camera to pick up. "You're just a scared kid, aren't you?"

"I'm not a kid." Josh managed to sound defiant, though his voice cracked.

Why is that so endearing?

"You didn't answer my question."

"I, um. I . . ."

"Something on your mind?" Mike cocked his head to the side. "Whatever it is, you can tell me."

It was like Mike had punched a hole in a dam. The words seem to burst from Josh. "Your cologne. You smell like citrus. Like oranges or something. It smells so good, I can't think straight." As soon as his outburst was over, a full-body flush swept over him.

Mike was shocked by his own reaction. Coming from anyone else, he would have thought that was a line, but from Josh it came across as genuine. Real and raw and honest. Mike found himself closing the distance between them before he could think about it. "Let me kiss you. I need to."

Josh whimpered. "*Please.*"

The last thing Mike noticed before he closed his eyes was the hot brush of Josh's panted breaths against his lips, and then they were kissing.

It was artless, if Mike were being honest. Frantic and messy and probably the least-skillful kiss he'd ever experienced, but *fuck*. It felt amazing.

The room melted away. Mike forgot about Colette and the camera and everything but the man next to him. Mike hadn't kissed someone for the sheer pleasure of it in . . . Nothing came to mind, which meant it had been far too long.

Josh's mouth was soft and just the right amount of pliant. He opened easily beneath Mike's firmer touch, allowing him to take charge of the kiss. Precisely how Mike liked it.

He leaned into Josh's body, guiding him back, and noted with heady delight that Josh moved with him without resistance. They fell against the sheets together, chest to chest, and everything from their mouths to their bodies slotted into place like puzzle pieces. Mike was hard within seconds, and this time, he wasn't relying on Viagra.

For a dizzying moment, Mike thought, *I could get totally lost in him.*

"Cut!"

Damn.

Mike jerked his head up and wondered if his eyes were still closed. The room was much darker than it had been before, illuminated by the final few rays of a fading sun. He blinked, disoriented. A small noise drew his attention beneath him. Josh was staring up at him, red-lipped and disheveled in a way that screamed sex. Jesus, Mike wanted to kiss him again.

But Colette had other ideas. "That's a wrap, gentlemen. You can stop now."

"Really?" Mike asked. "You don't want us to do an outro?"

"No, the point of a teaser is to leave them wanting more, as you well know. If the video cuts off, people will think there's a full-length one out there, and they'll subscribe to the site."

"Oh. Right. I knew that." Mike couldn't keep the disappointment from his tone. He looked down at Josh again, only to find him squirming. Oops. Mike was still on top of him, and his weight must be getting uncomfortable. He rolled off him and ordered his pulse to get back under control.

Colette tucked a fist under her chin and considered them. "Good work, Sean. Dick, you weren't a total disaster. Shocked as I am to admit it, I'm impressed."

Josh gave her a baleful look.

Mike laughed. "Don't pout. From her, that's a compliment."

But Josh's attention was on Colette. "So, am I in, or what?"

Easy, newbie. Don't poke the bear.

Colette was already bent over her laptop, but she spared him a glance. "I think it's safe to say you've earned another shot. Congrats, Dick. I'll send you an email with some scheduling options, and then next time, we'll film for real."

"Looking forward to it." Josh hopped to his feet and scooped his shirt off the floor in seconds.

Mike watched him with a combination of bewilderment and amusement. Either Josh didn't like being shirtless in front of strangers, or he'd realized he'd left his stove on. "Where's the fire?"

"There's no fire." Josh directed his response at the carpeted floor. "If we're finished filming, I can go, right?"

Colette answered. "Yup. We're all set here."

"Great." Josh pulled his shirt on like he was being timed.

It was silly, but Mike almost felt insulted. He'd stuck his neck out for Josh, and yet Josh hadn't even said thank you. Of course, Josh didn't *know* what Mike had done for him, but still. He could at least extend the usual after-performance courtesies. A simple *Hey, it was nice working with you* would have sufficed.

If this seems familiar, it's because this is how you treated Diego not two hours ago. Karma's a bitch.

Damn. He couldn't argue with that. Nevertheless, maybe Josh didn't know what the protocol was. He was new after all.

Mike reached out and caught his arm. "Hey."

Josh froze with his face turned away. "What?"

"You don't have to rush out of here. You can stay behind and review the film if you want. It needs to be edited, but you'll get a kick out of seeing yourself on camera. Also, just so you know, I thought you did great. It was nice working with you." There. He'd led by example, and Josh seemed like the sort of person who needed praise. Three good deeds in one night.

To his surprise, Josh tugged his arm out of Mike's grip. "I have to get going. I have places to be. It was, um, nice working with you too."

With that, he headed out the door and disappeared down the hall. Mike heard the front door slam a moment later. Hard.

Colette looked up at the sound, frowning. "What was that all about?"

Mike stared at the spot Josh had just vacated, stomach churning. "I have no idea."

CHAPTER 3

His first mistake, Josh realized later, was quitting his day job. Looking back, he had no idea why he'd thought that was the right move, especially *before* he'd auditioned. Thank God Colette was giving him another chance, or his "brilliant" plan to become a porn star would have been over before it began. Not to mention, he'd have no way to pay his bills.

Although, according to her email, they weren't filming again until the weekend, which meant he had four whole paycheck-free days to kill before he got his second shot. And thanks to his lack of steady employment, he had no way to fill those hours.

Not that he wasn't a pro at wasting time. He binge watched nine seasons of some screwball sitcom on Netflix—worst ending *ever*—and played Halo with A.J. until he thought his thumbs would fall off. He talked his friends into going clubbing with him on a Tuesday—which was almost as boring as staying in—and again on Wednesday. By Thursday, Monica stopped answering his calls, Darius claimed his hangovers were accumulating like rollover minutes, and even Ashley, their resident party queen, said she was tapped out.

That left Josh with plenty of time to think about what had transpired at that house in Bel Air. He couldn't seem to *stop* thinking about it. Which brought him to his second mistake: he'd been utterly unprepared for what filming porn was actually going to be like. And nothing could have prepared him for Sean Hardwood.

Josh couldn't say what he'd expected, but he hadn't gotten it. He'd known that there would be cameras and crew members and strangers he was expected to have sex with, but he hadn't grasped the reality of it. The awkwardness. The stage fright. Schedules and lighting and editing, oh my.

Then, at the height of his discomfort, Sean had broken through all of that. Josh was embarrassed to admit how into their kiss he'd gotten. If Colette hadn't called cut, he was positive he would have let Sean do whatever he wanted to him. Sean kissed like a fucking pro, which made sense, considering he was one. But it wasn't merely skill. It was *heat*. His touch smoldered in a way that felt too real to be feigned.

And yet it was. It had to have been. Afterward, Sean had been all business. Talking about reviewing the footage and saying, *"It was nice working with you,"* like they'd just finished a business meeting. He was every inch the consummate professional—no more flirting or flexing or making bad ginger puns—and there Josh had been, breathless and turned on like crazy. He hadn't meant to leave so abruptly, but he'd known that if he didn't put some space between them, he was going to say something he'd regret. He had a big enough mouth when he wasn't lust addled.

He wasn't claiming to be an expert, but it didn't take one to know porn stars weren't supposed to develop feelings for each other. Well, not feelings. That was going a bit far. But he'd definitely felt a spark of something the moment Sean's lips had touched his, and in the four days since they'd filmed together, his interest hadn't waned.

Which was *ridiculous*. He didn't know Sean. Sean Hardwood wasn't even the guy's real name. Josh had told "Sean" to his face that he wasn't Josh's type, and now he had a crush on him. God, his life was a dumpster fire.

The night before he was scheduled to shoot his first porno, he lay awake in bed, staring at his ceiling and willing himself to sleep to no avail. Sean was at the forefront of his mind, like always. He wondered if Sean would be at Murmur Inc. tomorrow. Or would he be off at some other house, having sex with some other guy?

That was a depressing thought.

How did porn stars do it? Maybe that was the root of his problem. Among all the other things he hadn't been prepared for, he didn't know how to kiss someone and *not* feel something. He needed to remind himself that it was all acting. Considering the sheer volume of porn that existed, there was no way all those people were as into their costars as they seemed. It wasn't possible. It was all fake. Like movies and TV.

That was the lesson he needed to learn, and he needed to do it *fast*. It wasn't just thoughts of Sean that were keeping him awake. He was going to film again tomorrow, and not some short teaser. A real porn video—the intimacy might be fake, but the sex wouldn't be. He'd never had nerves like this before. His skin prickled like his blood was carrying an electric charge throughout his whole body. He could feel his stomach acid gnawing at the instant rice he'd eaten for dinner.

No matter how nervous he was, he had to go through with it. He needed the money. Josh had no idea what financial security felt like. His parents were working class. He'd gotten his first job at sixteen. Minimum wage was all he knew, and getting a college degree hadn't changed that. Porn seemed like his one chance to bust out of the tax bracket he'd been born into. He had to try, didn't he?

God, he hoped he didn't choke again. He'd been told his whole life that he was so dramatic, he should be in theater. But that hadn't translated when a real camera had been on him. Colette had told him he wasn't a total loss, but was that because of Sean's help?

Much as Sean threw him off, Josh almost wished he would be there. Maybe he could coax out the same morsel of talent he'd gotten Josh to show before. And maybe he'd be shirtless again. With his perfect, taut stomach, and all those freckles. They seemed to swarm at his shoulders and then trickle down his chest, like they were leaving a trail of bread crumbs that led to his—

Josh shook his head, his pillow rustling beneath him. Even if Sean was good for his acting, he wasn't good for his professionalism. It would be better if he wasn't there. Right?

Who knew porn was so complicated?

Maybe I got a little ahead of myself.

He must have dozed off at some point—probably exhausted from his mental back and forth—because the next thing he knew, his phone was blaring the hip-hop song he'd set as his alarm.

Before he could reach for it, he heard swearing through his wall.

"What the fuck, Josh?" came Will's muffled voice. "Turn that off!"

"I am. I am." Josh snatched his phone off his nightstand and blearily tapped at the screen until Nicki Minaj's voice cut off. "Sorry!"

"It's six in the fucking morning."

Chris's voice joined in, "You're making more noise than his fucking alarm, Will!"

That launched a shouting match through the walls that Josh was happy to excuse himself from. Colette had sent him an intro email stating everything he needed to bring with him: two forms of ID—same as he'd had to show before his audition—a void check so they could set up direct deposit, and any medications he needed to "perform healthily." He had no idea what that meant, but he didn't have any prescriptions, so he figured it didn't apply to him.

There had also been an intimidating list of suggested hygiene practices, which included some obvious things, like wearing mild cologne, and some not-so-obvious things, like cleaning out his ass. And there were some things that were *required*, like showering, teeth brushing, and using deodorant before every shoot. Josh wondered if someone was going to sniff his armpits at the door.

He got ready at lightning speed. Colette had instructed him to wear street clothes, so he threw on jeans and his lucky Jameson shirt before zipping out of the room. His belongings found their ways into his pockets, and after that, it was just a matter of getting to central LA. Which meant taking the bus. Joy.

Josh wasn't hating on public transportation. He was grateful for it and all its sweaty, smelly, uncomfortable glory. It wasn't the glamorous entrance he wanted to make, and wedging himself between a woman with a screaming baby and a man who was muttering to himself didn't put him in a sexy mood.

Maybe if all this worked out, and he made as much money as he thought he was going to, he could buy a car. The thought was almost enough to block out the smell of exhaust with a hint of urine.

One bumpy hour later, he found himself standing outside of a nondescript, three-story office building. It might have been the same as any other, except there were no identifying marks of any kind. No sign out front. No name plastered on the face. Nothing. Colette had told him it was to keep protestors away. Apparently, the address was unlisted as well. The only way to get to Murmur Inc. was to pass an audition, like he had. The way Colette told it, very few of the Bible-thumping jerks they dealt with were willing to go that far.

Josh spotted a plain metal door on the side of the building, right where Colette had said it'd be. As he approached, his anxiety swelled up again like a rising tide. He distracted himself by thinking about Colette. He still couldn't quite make her out. She was ruthless when it came to her business, of course, and intimidating as fuck, but little things made him think she cared about her employees a lot. Like how hard she tried to keep protestors away, and the way she'd threatened him for insulting Sean.

Well, if this whole thing worked out, he supposed he'd have plenty of time to get to know his new boss. Though come to think of it, she reminded him a bit of Sana.

Josh took hold of the doorknob at the same time as he took a deep breath. Here went everything. Josh opened the door and saw . . . nothing. An empty stairwell. He didn't know what else there would be—an office, a boudoir, or maybe some sort of sex dungeon—but this was anticlimactic.

The wall lights lit up the staircase just enough to make it creepy. He glanced around and spotted a sign with an arrow pointing up. *New Arrivals proceed to Second Floor.*

Josh bounded up the first flight of stairs. There was another metal door at the top of the landing. He didn't pause before he pushed this one open. If he had, he wouldn't have been any more prepared for what awaited him on the other side.

It looked . . . sort of like a hotel lobby. What might have once been an office space had been cleared of cubicles and desks and had instead been filled with couches and chairs. There was a large wraparound desk along the far wall, like a reception area. And most notably, there were a *lot* of people.

Including Sean. Oh boy.

He was standing up front with Colette and a handful of others, while everyone else draped themselves over the couches and chairs. And Josh meant *draped*. Half of them looked like they were posing for a magazine ad. They were all beautiful too. He'd never seen such a collection of attractive people, in all colors, shapes, and sizes. One of the women nearest him was so pretty, with her high cheekbones, ink-black skin, and limpid green eyes, that Josh spent a moment calculating how gay he really was.

These must be the other new arrivals the sign had mentioned. Josh had expected to meet with Colette individually, but now he wondered if this wasn't going to be some sort of group event.

Oh God, am I going to have to have sex in front of all these people? Is this like a focus group kind of thing? Are they going to critique me?

When he'd opened the door, no one had spared him a look, but now that he was standing there staring, people were starting to stare back. Colette was among their number.

Even from across the room, her gaze was sharp. "In or out, Dick?"

"Um." He glanced at Sean, who wasn't paying him the slightest attention. "In."

"Then by all means, take a load off."

He scuttled to an empty seat in the back, seemingly in the nick of time. Colette cleared her throat a moment later.

"Welcome to Murmur Inc., newbies. We're always delighted to have fresh meat." She flashed a bright smile that had a hint of fang. "Congratulations on passing your auditions. You're our newest stars."

The room broke out into applause. Josh didn't join in. He was piecing together what was happening. This seemed to be some sort of welcoming committee. It made sense. He couldn't have been the only person to audition. There must have been hundreds of applicants. That meant all these beautiful people around him had also survived the Hunger Games.

Colette silenced their clapping with a look, and Josh thought, *Confidence goals.* "Consider this your new-employee orientation. Today you're going to learn some of what you need to know to be successful in this industry. Though of course, your work is never finished. We'll also go over company policies, safety procedures, and have a brief Q&A. At the end, if you still want to be here, you'll proceed upstairs to the filming booths, and you'll make your debut."

Another round of applause. Josh kept his sweaty palms in his lap. He glanced at Sean and immediately regretted it. Sean was looking right back at him, a smug smile on his face. The challenge was as clear as if he'd spoken words. *Are you gonna make it that far?*

I guess we'll find out. Josh refocused on Colette.

"If you decide to stay, take one of our company handbooks." She indicated a pile of small blue books on the desk behind her. "These will explain the intricacies of working here better than I can in the brief time we have. I'm going to give you a quick rundown of the highlights now, but it's required that you read this handbook before your first week is up."

She opened her mouth to say more, but acting on impulse, Josh raised his hand.

Colette blinked at him like she had no idea what nuclear power plant he'd crawled out from under. There was a rustle as everyone turned in their seats to stare at him.

Gulp.

"Yes, Mr. Reams?"

Josh willed himself not to blush. "Will there be a test?"

The staring intensified. Out of the corner of his eye, he saw Sean lower his head. To hide his face? His shoulders were shaking. Was he . . . laughing?

"No," Colette answered slowly. "There won't be a test."

"Then how will you know if we read the book?"

If looks could kill. Josh almost swallowed his tongue.

"I'll know because if you *don't* read the book, you will likely put yourself or someone else in harm's way. The handbook has detailed instructions for how to keep all of you safe—from overzealous fans, physical injury, stalkers, bigots, and more. If you fail at any point to follow these instructions, I'll kick you out so fast, Murmur Inc. will win the next World Cup."

A titter wafted through the crowd, but Josh could tell she wasn't joking.

Colette leveled him with a crisp glare. "Is that understood?"

"Yes, ma'am."

"Good. Rule number one: never call me ma'am."

That time Josh laughed along with everyone else. Some of the tension in the room melted, and Josh dared to sneak another peek at Sean. He had a wide grin on his face, which confirmed what Josh had suspected: he'd been laughing before.

"Rule number two," Colette continued, "is to keep your safety and the safety of your fellow performers in the back of your mind at all times. This means following our hygiene standards, never revealing anyone else's real name in public or in private unless you have permission to do so, minding what you say during interviews and at conventions, and most importantly, getting tested for STIs, using condoms, or both, depending. We'll talk about that more later."

Colette went on to outline everything from their drug policy to how to deal with hostile fans. Murmur Inc. apparently had private security that dealt with protestors and any suspicious figures that showed up at the building, but when employees were at home, they were encouraged to contact the police and start paper trails on any potential aggressors.

Josh fluctuated between zoning out and freaking out. It was becoming clearer by the minute that he knew *nothing* about this industry. The politics were boring as fuck, but some of the stories Colette told were downright terrifying. Apparently one of "us"— as she now referred to them all—had shown up at an unauthorized shoot once at a house and had the director tell her there had been a change of plans. He would be acting as the male performer, and the condom he'd said would be used had been nixed. Oh, and she'd be compensated in exposure instead of money.

According to Colette, scams like that were common. It made Josh feel grateful to be associated with a company like Murmur Inc. instead of out there on his own. He was certain the stories were intended to make him feel that way.

Colette explained their hours of operation (boring), how performers were expected to market themselves (really boring), and pay scales (*cha-ching*). Josh could not, as he'd thought before, make an unlimited amount of money. Market demand had a lot to do with what he'd be paid and how often he'd be scheduled. Since they were all new faces, Colette assured them that viewers would clamor to see them, but porn moved fast. People were always looking for the next new extreme. If they wanted to stay on top, they would have to accrue a loyal fan base, find a niche, and/or perform increasingly extreme sexual acts.

"That's why," Colette explained, "most porn stars have a short shelf life."

Josh didn't bother raising his hand this time. "How short?"

Colette answered, though she looked peeved about it. "Some of you will star in one film and never do it again. In the biz, we call you shooting stars. A brief, bright streak across the sky, and then you flame out. Realistically, most of you will work for three to six months."

There was a grumble from the crowd. Josh was too surprised to add his own murmurings to the mix. *Six months max? That's all?*

Colette waited for them to quiet before continuing. "I'm not going to lie to you. That's a promise you can hold me to. Most of you are not going to be the next Linda Lovelace. You'll never be a household name. The people who make a career out of porn are one in a million. However, in three months, my average porn star makes the same money that most people make in a year. And that's *average*. My top earners make enough money to make CEOs jealous."

Josh let out a low whistle. *If I can become a top earner and not burn out, I can make one hell of a life for myself . . .*

"But don't take my word for it." Colette turned to the people next to her. There were five of them, Sean included. "Talk to them yourself. I've gathered a few of my best and brightest stars. They're here to answer questions, tell you about the harsh realities of the biz, relate some of their personal experiences, and, in a sense, mentor you. Their time is *extremely* valuable—I know; I sign their checks—so use it wisely."

Colette turned the floor over. There were two men, two women, and one person who was the definition of androgynous. But Josh only had eyes for Sean. He looked ultra-sexy in a white dress shirt, a black suit vest, and tight, dark jeans. Something about the mix of business and casual made Josh want to mix some business with pleasure.

Focus, dude. You gotta prove him wrong.

One of the women asked if anyone had any questions, and hands shot up into the air. Josh realized that he should have saved his questions for the Q&A session.

Oops.

He tried to pay attention to what everyone was asking, but his eyes kept drifting over to Sean, and with them, his focus. Sean was standing with his chin up, legs apart, and his arms folded over his chest. It was a classic confident stance, and it suited him. In fact, as he fielded a question about the use of condoms in gay porn, he looked as natural as a teacher standing in front of a class. A sexy teacher, whom Josh wouldn't mind staying after school with . . .

"I'm what's known as a crossover," Sean said in reference to some question.

The unfamiliar term brought Josh's attention screeching back to the present.

"That means I work with people of all genders."

"Does that give you more opportunities?" asked a young and devastatingly handsome blond man.

Sean's eyes moved to the beautiful blond. "Yes and no. While you would think working with more than one gender would multiply your opportunities, some performers won't work with me at all because of it. It has to do with STI testing and some complicated politics."

The blond cocked his head to the side in a way that was infuriatingly coy. "Why not just do straight gigs, then?"

"Because traditional gay porn pays better." Sean flashed a wicked smile that went straight between Josh's legs. "And because I love dick."

The crowd laughed, but Josh was too busy being jealous and turned on to join them. The effect Sean had on him didn't make any sense. But he knew one thing: he did *not* like the way Sean was eyeing that blond.

Once again, Josh's hand flew into the air.

Sean's gaze snapped to him. His smile turned from wicked to downright evil. "Ah, Dick. Good to see you again."

There were some titters from the crowd. More than one person turned to get a glimpse of the man who knew one of Colette's stars.

"You too." It wasn't a lie.

"What's your question?"

"My question is actually for Colette." Even as he said that, Josh's gaze never wavered from Sean. The same strange charge that had sprung up between them at the audition rose again, like a trail of fire.

"Yes?" It was Colette's voice.

"You said if we don't quit, then we're going to film our first video after this, right?"

"Right. Was that your question, or did you think the room was missing a parrot?"

More laughter. Josh ignored it.

He delivered his next question still without taking his eyes off Sean. "Do we get to pick our first partners?"

A hush fell over the assembly. Something in Sean's face changed. It was subtle, but Josh saw every minute twitch. The heat between them lowered, but became more focused, like an ember still burning long after the log had collapsed into ash. Sean looked much more serious than a moment before, but also curious. It was as if this were his first time seeing Josh.

"No," Colette answered. "Your partners will be chosen by me."

Josh's disappointment cleaved him in two.

But Colette wasn't finished yet. "I do, however, take preferences into account when I make my selections, and I try to pair up people who work well together. If you don't like what you get, no one is forcing you to be here. You can always back out of any performance at any time. But this is a business, first and foremost, and we have to give the clients what they want. Keep in mind, the more money the company makes, the more money you make. We're in this together. Understood?"

Josh finally looked away from Sean. "Yes."

"Good." Colette considered him. "In your case, I think I have your partner in mind already, should you make it that far."

His pulse doubled. *Does she mean* . . . He hadn't dared to think he'd get to work with Sean again. And yet, every time he'd imagined filming, he'd imagined Sean.

Colette shifted her focus back to the crowd. "Are there any more questions?"

No one raised their hand.

"All right, then. It's showtime. Those of you who've decided to stay can follow me up to the third floor. The rest of you can go out the way you came." She strode to the door without looking back. Her stars fell into step behind her like ducklings following their mother.

Right before Sean ducked through the doorway, he glanced back. Josh had no idea if it was intentional or a coincidence, but his eyes locked right onto Josh. Fuck, it was ridiculous how much that one look excited him.

Sean was gone before Josh had a chance to react. As soon as the door shut behind them, the newbies broke into whispers. One guy made a beeline for the exit, heading down. A handful of others meandered over to the desk and picked up a handbook. And a few others, including the handsome blond, grabbed handbooks and then went for the door, except they went up toward the third floor.

Josh didn't need to deliberate. He knew what he was going to do. What he had to do, not simply for financial reasons, but because he had something to prove. To Sean. To Colette. To himself.

After taking a book, Josh made his way to the stairs and climbed up.

CHAPTER ◉ 4

"**Y**ou know you're the perfect man for the job."

Mike struggled with both his desire to argue and his knowledge that arguing with Colette was fruitless. "I don't think it's a good idea."

"Why not?" Colette was perched on the edge of a desk, a stiletto-clad foot swinging in the air. They'd excused themselves to one of the empty cubicles that populated the third floor of Murmur Inc., where the phone sex operators were busy making calls all around them. "You saw the way he was looking at you during the Q&A. You don't think you two have chemistry?"

That's exactly the problem. I think we do.

"Yeah, but *you* saw how abruptly he left after we finished filming in Bel Air. He couldn't get away from me fast enough."

"That doesn't mean anything. He probably had somewhere to be, or he was embarrassed. He'd recently finished filming his first scene, after all. I was there, babe. I saw for myself how well you two got along. I think you can do it again."

"It's not a good fit. He's too green." Mike prayed she couldn't read his true feelings in his body language. He had a decent poker face, but Colette had a knack for seeing through it. Then again, he couldn't consciously hide feelings he didn't fully understand himself. All he knew was he was resistant to working with Josh. Or Dick, as he'd have to call him on camera.

He'd come up with a number of great excuses—like the newbie thing, or the fact that Josh seemed to have imprinted on him like a fucking gosling—but that was all they were: excuses.

The truth went deeper than that, though he didn't know how far. His gut told him that working with Josh would change things, and for some reason, it scared the hell out of him.

Colette shrugged. "It seemed like a good fit the other night. I think you bring something out in Dick."

"He could be like that with everyone for all you know. Pick someone else." Mike gestured to the busy room around them. There were two dozen or so performers on standby, waiting to see how many of the new recruits showed up. "You have no shortage of people who'd love to work."

"I will, if you insist. You've paid your dues, so if you object to the pairing that much, I'll respect your wishes."

Mike breathed a sigh of relief.

"But—"

The sigh caught in his throat like a shard of glass.

"—first you have to look me in the eye and tell me that you have no desire whatsoever to work with Dick. If that's the case, I'll never assign you two to the same project. Ever."

Fuck. She knew exactly how to manipulate him. Mike didn't think he could tell a lie that egregious to her face. He wanted to work with Josh. *Really* wanted to. He couldn't explain why. Josh had a mouth the size of the Midwest, and he was clueless to the point of his own detriment, but Mike *liked* that about him. Somehow.

It didn't hurt that Mike found him ridiculously attractive, either. Since their first meeting, he'd had dreams about kissing bruises into that long neck of his. Just thinking about it made him want to—

No. He was a professional. This was another gig, like any other. He'd do his damn job, as he always did. He'd show Colette he could handle whatever she threw at him.

"All right, I'll do it," Mike said. "But only because I can't blacklist a new porn star before I know what sort of career they're going to have. For all I know, Dick's gonna be the next Brent Corrigan." It wasn't a total lie, and so he was able to deliver it without flinching.

"Then it's settled." Colette climbed to her feet with a *click*. "Assuming Dick shows up—which I'm quite certain he will—he's all yours." Her gaze flickered over his shoulder. "Speak of the devil, there he is now. I've reserved Booth Seven for you. I'll meet you in there."

Mike blanched. "You're gonna direct us? Don't you have bigger projects you could be overseeing?"

"And miss Dick's debut with one of my brightest stars? Never. I'm expecting big things. Nothing short of a mouth-watering performance will satisfy me, so you'd best give it your all." She winked and sashayed off in the direction of Booth Seven, dragging Mike's dropped jaw after her.

His attention didn't stay on her for long, though. Movement out of the corner of his eye drew his gaze to the doorway, where Josh had, in fact, walked in. As Mike watched, Josh took in the room in a sweep. His gaze lingered on the wide windows on the far wall before skipping across the sea of people hard at work. Mike thought maybe he wouldn't notice him, tucked away in a cubicle like the other buzzing bees, but unerringly, Josh's beautiful eyes rested on him.

When did I start describing his eyes that way?

Before he could think of an answer, Josh approached him. "Hi."

"Hi." Mike gave him a once-over. "You look well."

"Good, because I feel like I'm going to be sick."

"Nervous?"

"Oh yeah." He smiled. "But excited too."

"Glad to hear it." Mike studied him. Beneath the steady fluorescent lights, he was able to pick out details about Josh's appearance that he hadn't noticed before, like the couple of whiskers he'd missed when shaving, or how his eyelashes were a shade darker than his hair. "Welcome to the third floor. That means you made it, more or less."

"Thanks. Though I gotta admit, this isn't what I was expecting." Josh looked around. "Doesn't look like a porn set to me."

"This building used to be a recording studio, but Colette scooped it up decades ago and turned it into Murmur Inc. The office area, as you can see, is where the phone sex operators work." He pointed at the booths that lined the walls, all of which had opaque glass and red "live" lights outside the doors. "Filming takes place in those booths when it's not on location. They've been cleared out and made into individual sets. They're bigger inside than they look."

"Wow. I'd love to see one."

Mike shifted his weight from one foot to the other. "You're in luck. We're about to head into one right now."

Josh jerked his head toward him. "'We'?"

"Yeah." He swallowed. "Colette assigned me to work with you."

There was a pregnant pause.

"So, you're gonna be my first?"

Mike winced. "Don't say it like that. It sounds all—" He waved a hand. *Sexy.*

"Oh, sorry." Josh looked anything but. Mike swore his eyes were actually sparkling with mischief. "Let's go, then." He turned away.

"Wait." Mike grabbed his shoulder, which was a huge mistake. Josh was warm and firm beneath his fingers. He snatched his hand back like he'd been burned. "We should go over some things first. I'm supposed to be mentoring you, right?"

"Right." Josh licked his lips. "Teach me."

Oh, that's just unfair.

Mike cleared his throat. "When you get in there, you have to be professional at all times. No fucking around, no bad jokes, and most of all, remember what we're here to do." His mouth was dry as he said the next part. "We're going to have sex, yeah, but this is a job. You're at work, and you need to act like it."

"Does that mean I'm not allowed to enjoy it?"

Heat rushed through Mike's body before he could rein it in. He managed to keep his facial features from so much as twitching. "You can, and if I have anything to say about it, you will. But that's a by-product of the industry, okay?"

Are you talking to him or yourself?

"Right. Good advice." Josh smiled. "Thanks, Sean."

Mike's stomach lurched. That didn't sound right at all. He took a quick peek around. No one was paying the slightest attention to them. He blurted out, "It's Mike."

Josh blinked. "What's Mike?"

"Me, smart-ass. My name's Mike." *Christ, why am I telling him this? The newbie probably won't understand the significance.*

"Oh." Josh's eyebrows pinched together, which suggested he had an inkling after all. "Wow. Okay. Hi, um, Mike." He looked like he was struggling with words. "Downstairs, Colette said porn stars have to be careful with their real names. Why'd you tell me yours?"

I'd love to know that as well. He shrugged. "It . . . seemed like the right thing to do."

"Because you know my real name?"

Mike seized onto that like a lifeboat bobbing next to the *Titanic.* "Yeah, that's it. Now we're even." He glared at him. "But don't you dare tell anyone. Not your priest. Not your mother. Not *anyone.* Capiche?"

Josh nodded, eyes grave. He seemed sincere enough. Mike expected a wave of panic to hit him any second now, but for some reason, he believed Josh would keep his secret.

"C'mon. We can't keep Colette waiting." He headed for Booth Seven.

Josh fell into step next to him. "Colette's going to be there?"

"Yup. Lucky you. She wants to oversee your debut personally."

"How is that lucky? She's terrifying."

"Do you have any idea how many porn stars would kill to be directed by her? She's a living legend, and she's got the awards to prove it. For her to take time out of her day to coach a newbie . . . I can't imagine what her motivation is." Mike wove through the maze of cubicles to the correct door. The red light next to it was on. The crew must already be in there, setting up.

As he reached for the door handle, Josh said, "Colette doesn't believe in me, does she?"

Mike paused, swilling words around in his mouth. "Honestly? No. But why would she? She's only seen you once, and you were a nervous wreck. I've been working with her for a long time, and she still gives me shit when I don't deliver a stellar performance. It's like I said: this is a job like any other, and she's your boss. You gotta make her happy."

"I'll try."

"If it's any consolation, I think you have it in you."

"Why?"

Mike should lie. For both their sakes. But Josh looked so torn, he couldn't help but encourage him. "Because that kiss we shared was one of the best I've ever had."

Mike opened the door without waiting for a response and strode into the room. It was crammed with filming equipment and the people who operated it, but the set was clear: a simple faux leather couch set on a white rug in the center of the room. Box lights and boom microphones hung above it, ready to highlight every curve and capture every moan. Off to the side, Colette was setting up monitors hooked up to the cameras, on which they could review the footage in real time.

She caught Mike's eye and raised a brow, asking a question: *You ready?* He nodded. She flicked a hand toward the sofa. That was one upside to working with Colette for so long. Mike could follow her vaguest instructions.

But first, Mike stopped off at a table that had been set up on the right side. Half of it was covered in bottles of water and snacks, and the other half acted as a mini wardrobe station. Mike removed his shoes and socks and tucked them out of sight before depositing everything in his pockets onto the table: phone, keys, wallet, gum, all of it. He couldn't very well have it falling out of his pockets or jabbing anyone in any unfortunate places.

To his delight, Josh followed suit without needing to be instructed. He dumped a similar assortment of personal belongings onto the table, removed his shoes, and pulled off his socks. As he bent over, his shirt rode up in the back, making it apparent once again how tight and compact his body was. Mike was looking forward to seeing all the parts he hadn't gotten to yet.

He caught himself staring a second too late and looked up to find a full-blown smirk on Josh's face.

He glowered. "Shut up."

"I didn't say anything."

"Brat."

They made their way over to the couch. Mike sat down first while Josh hovered like he wasn't sure what he should do. Mike sighed. There was still plenty his new mentee didn't know. He patted the seat next to him, and Josh took that as permission to flop onto it. A photographer appeared as if from nowhere, snapped some shots of them sitting together, and then disappeared only to be replaced by a light tech with an umbrella lamp. Mike blinked spots out of his eyes. Fucking lighting, always blinding him.

Josh was sitting on the edge of his seat like they were watching an action film together. "What now?"

"Colette will let us know. I'm sure we're not going to do anything too complicated today. There aren't any scripts, since we never know who's going to make it past orientation. She'll keep it short and sweet."

Josh squirmed. "Do you think she'll have us . . . go all the way?"

Mike raised a brow at him. "I'm sorry, I don't speak high school. Are you asking if we're gonna fuck?"

"Uh, yeah." His flush was back, creeping up his neck.

"Maybe, but I doubt it. Colette likes to ease the newbs in. Last time I did one of these, we had oral."

"One of these? You've mentored a newbie before?" Josh shook his head. "I dunno why I'm surprised. You've probably done this hundreds of times."

"I wouldn't say *hundreds*." Mike did some quick math in his head. "Dozens."

Josh was looking down at his hands, which were hanging between his legs. His expression was caught somewhere between resignation and uncertainty. There wasn't a trace of the bravado he'd plastered on before.

"Hey. Look at me." Mike waited until he did before asking, "What is it?"

"Do you wish Colette had paired you with someone else? Someone better?"

Mike blinked. "What?"

"You have all this experience, and here you are, stuck here with me."

Mike stared at him. "This isn't like you. Where's the annoying cockiness?"

Josh laughed, but there was no mirth behind it. "I'm not feeling like myself. Problem is, I'm not feeling like Dick Reams either. I'm about to have sex in front of a room full of people, and I can't stop thinking about that mole I never got removed, or how my bare ass is going to be plastered on the internet forever."

"If it's any consolation, I'm sure it's a great ass."

Josh snorted but didn't look any less panicked. Mike's heart throbbed. So much for keeping things professional. But he was the mentor here. It was his job to be responsible.

"You can still leave, you know. It's not too late."

Josh startled. "Huh?"

"You don't have to go through with this. If porn isn't the right job for you, there's no shame in that. Plenty of people try it and don't like it."

"Shooting stars, right? I'd hate for Colette to think I was one of those after she gave me another chance."

"Fuck what Colette thinks. And hey, you're only a shooting star if you quit *after* we film this scene. That kissing scene didn't count. You can quit now, and it's like it never happened."

That was supposed to be comforting, but Josh's brow furrowed. "I think I'm uncertain. There are things about this that I don't get. I don't want to sound judgmental, but I don't understand how you . . . detach. Like, how do you have sex with all those people and not— you know?" He gestured at empty space as if the rest of his words could be found there.

Mike thought he understood what Josh was going for. "You just do. We all perform with whoever we're told to perform with that day, and you can't get invested in your costars." *Including me.* "Can you handle that?"

"I think so." He chewed his lip. "I knew what I was getting into when I signed up for this, but I guess I'm still figuring things out."

"Well, it's not going to make any more sense after, trust me. I'll get Colette, and we'll call this whole thing off."

Mike climbed to his feet, but Josh grabbed his arm. "No, wait. I want to do this." He hesitated. "I want *you.*"

Mike's whole body flashed hot. "I'm flattered, but you don't know me."

"I know." Josh wet his lips. "But I'm still glad it's you." He didn't elaborate; he didn't need to.

Had Mike been a stronger man, he would have reminded Josh what he'd said about not getting invested. Wanting him could only complicate things. Then again, it was good for costars to have chemistry. Wasn't that why Colette had paired them together?

A smile curved Mike's lips. "I thought you weren't into gingers."

Josh burst out laughing, and the uncertainty between them shattered like thin glass. Mike took his seat again and threw an arm over the back of the sofa. When Josh leaned into it, Mike pretended not to notice.

Colette walked over then, heels clicking on the tile floor, and stood next to the main camera with her hands on her hips. "We're almost finished setting up. Do either of you need anything before we get started? Water? Food?" She looked at Mike. "Medications?"

It was no secret that Mike usually took Viagra before a performance. This time, though, he was certain he'd be able to perform without it.

"We're all set," Mike said.

Colette nodded and turned away to check something.

It took him a moment to realize Josh was staring at him. "What?"

"Way to answer for me." His ridiculous pout was back. The urge to bite it was getting harder and harder to resist. "Gonna order for me at restaurants too?"

"Of course not." He grinned. "I would never take you to a restaurant."

"Good point. I can't see you picking such a boring first date."

This time, it was Mike who flushed. "Date? Getting a little ahead of yourself, don't you think?"

"*Ooh,* am I embarrassing you, Mikey?"

Mike whipped his head around to see if anyone was close enough to hear them. No one was. "Dude, shut up."

"What? That's not technically your name, so I'm not breaking the rules."

"You still can't call me that when we're on set."

"Then when can I?" He batted his eyelashes. "When we're alone?"

Is he trying to flirt with me or annoy me? Mike honestly couldn't tell. "Stop that."

"Make me." He leaned closer and mouthed, *Mikey.*

God, he's such a brat. Mike got a wicked idea. "You know what? I've changed my mind. You're welcome to call me Mikey."

"I am?"

"Sure. And I'll call you Joshie."

The horror that crept over Josh's face made Mike's entire day. "I'll never call you that again."

"Good boy."

Mike wasn't sure if he imagined it or not, but he thought he saw Josh shiver at that.

Colette reappeared, laptop in hand. "All right, gentlemen, I think we're all set. How's everyone feeling?"

"Fine," Mike said.

"Nervous," Josh admitted.

"Relax. This is an informal shoot. All you have to do is look pretty and follow directions, one of which you already have down."

Josh preened at the compliment. Mike took note. He'd wondered before if praise was the way to coax a good performance out of Josh. He might need to put it to the test.

"What are we going to be doing?" Mike asked. "Something ending in 'job,' I'm guessing."

Colette was looking down, cradling her laptop with one arm and pressing keys with the other. "Nope. Anal."

Mike tensed. "What?"

"Can you not hear me?" Colette snapped her fingers at one of the sound techs. "Are the microphones giving off feedback on your end?"

"No, I heard you. I'm, um, surprised." Mike snuck a peek at Josh. He was staring at him with a lost look on his face, like he was waiting to see what Mike did before he reacted. "You don't usually have the newbs do penetrative sex on their first run."

"Well, I think Dick here can take it, no pun intended. Besides, if I'm going to take time out of my day to coach a newb, I might as well be thorough about it."

"Does that mean I'm going to have to bottom?" Josh asked.

"'Fraid so. Sean is known for being a power top, and since you have no reputation to defend, you'll have to fall on that sword. Forgive my word choice."

Damn. As much as Mike's cock was already swelling at the idea of getting to top Josh, he felt bad for him. Josh's first porn experience was not only going to be a bang instead of a whimper, but he'd have to switch sides too. This could go all sorts of wrong.

Josh leaned closer to him, lowering his voice. "Should I be worried?"

"No." Mike swallowed. "Why?"

"Because you look as nervous as I feel."

Fuck. His face must have slipped. He affixed it back into place and wondered why he was feeling what he was. There were a few obvious answers: Josh was showing all the classic signs of confusing fantasy with reality. If Mike were smart, he'd nip that particular bud before it got messy. But it wasn't his job to protect Josh, no matter how much he wanted to. And if he were being honest with himself, the chemistry between them was real. No wonder Josh was confused.

Josh hadn't listened to any of the advice Mike had given him thus far. If Josh insisted on going through with this, what more could Mike do?

You can leave. You can do exactly what you told Josh to do and call this whole thing off.

But that wasn't the way professionals acted. He'd be setting a bad example in front of one of the new recruits. If he did that, Colette would remember it the next time she was picking leading men. And she'd never cast Mike with Josh again. For some reason, the thought of *never* getting to work with Josh was painful, and not just to his bank account. God, he hoped he wasn't starting to feel something for the newbie. Who was he to lecture Josh on staying unattached when he couldn't manage it himself?

The clock was ticking. He needed to make a decision.

Should he take a more hands-off approach? Stop meddling and let Josh learn for himself what this industry was really like? Mike wasn't his babysitter, plain and simple.

He looked over at Josh, as if he were hoping to find the answers written on his face. Josh met his gaze, and in his light eyes, Mike saw the memory of what he'd said to him moments before. *"I want to do this. I want* you.*"* So much for hands-off.

"Sean?" Colette gave him a curious look. "Everything all right?"

Mike swallowed hard. "Yeah. Let's begin."

CHAPTER ⊚ 5

During the days since his audition, Josh had often thought about what Mike had told him: having sex and filming porn were different things. At the time, he'd assumed Mike was referring to the surface differences: the other people in the room, the lack of intimacy, and the safety procedures they were expected to follow.

He'd never expected, however, that the act itself would be different. Within the first hour of filming, however, he discovered exactly what Mike had meant.

Porn was, without a doubt, the least sexy and most uncomfortable thing he'd ever done.

It'd started when he had to strip down to his underwear in front of the entire crew. He'd known he was going to have to do that, but he'd thought they'd avert their eyes or something. But no, they all watched him with the attention of a dozen hawks. No one was leering or anything, but he still felt every eye on him like a damp touch.

And sooner or later, he was going to be naked. He could imagine how much more vulnerable he'd feel without his boxers acting as a thin cloth barrier.

It didn't help that Mike showed not the slightest shred of self-consciousness. He'd thrown off his clothes and lounged on the couch like he did this every day. Which, now that Josh thought about it, he might.

Josh tried to mirror his relaxation, but there was no faking that kind of experience. Where Mike was relaxed and confident, Josh was stiff and weird.

Things had only gotten more awkward when they'd started fooling around. Josh had been instructed to lie on the couch with

Sean on top of him—which was the most pleasant part of the whole thing—while bright lights blinded him and Colette shouted endless directions at him.

According to her, he couldn't do anything right. His angles were off, his limbs needed rearranging, and his facial expression showed every shade of his discomfort. Within minutes, his head was spinning from trying to remember everything he was supposed to be doing.

Then there was the sex itself. Or the distinct lack thereof. They'd been at this for *hours*, and they still hadn't gotten to the main event. Josh was beginning to think he and Mike were never going to fuck. Every time they got going, Colette would call cut because Josh had made yet another mistake.

By their sixteenth take, irritation was radiating throughout the room. It came from Colette, the crew, and even from Mike, who was whispering almost as many instructions to him as Colette. Josh knew he was trying to be helpful, but if anything, the added commentary was making him more confused.

"You know what?" Colette announced after bad take number seventeen. "We're gonna roll with it. We've wasted enough studio time as it is."

Josh was almost too afraid to ask. "What does that mean?"

"It means I'm not directing you anymore. It doesn't seem to be helping, so do whatever feels right, and we'll piece something together postproduction. Right now, we're burning money. Sean, keep doing what you're doing. Dick, please try to follow Sean's lead."

She took a seat at a table with her laptop and zeroed in on it instead of them.

"Um, Colette?" Mike said.

She didn't glance up. "Oh, right. Action, or whatever."

Josh bit his lip. That stung more than he'd thought it would. He was doing such a bad job, Colette didn't want to look at him anymore.

Mike's weight shifted on top of him. "Hey. You doing okay?"

Josh glanced at him. From this close, it was easy to pick out the natural brunet lowlights in his red hair. "I'm sorry."

"What for?"

"For fucking this up."

Mike bent down and shushed him with his mouth. It would have been a romantic gesture under other circumstances, but they'd done so much kissing in the past hour, Josh's lips were starting to hurt. "Don't worry about what happened before. Think about what we're about to do. You don't need Colette's direction. You need to relax."

"You think so?"

Mike brushed his lips along Josh's cheekbone. "When we performed together before, you got the hang of it when you stopped thinking and started doing."

Josh smiled. "No, it was when you kissed the thinking out of me."

"I can do that again." Mike moved down to his neck, and the feel of his hot breath made Josh dizzy. "Pretend it's just us. What would you like for me to do to you?"

Well, that got Josh's attention. Between the small touches Mike was delivering to all the right places and his sexy, deep voice, Josh's cock perked up. The last hour had been as confusing for his cock as it'd been for Josh. One minute, he and Mike were going at it. The next, Colette had been killing his buzz. With her warming the bench, he might be able to get going again.

"Well, you're the expert." Josh did his best to mimic Mike's seductive tone. "Tell me what you want to do to me."

Mike smirked. "We don't have time for all that, trust me. I think I know a fun way I can learn what turns you on." He spoke between kisses down Josh's neck. "I'm going to touch you, and if you like it, tell me I'm getting warmer. If not, say colder. Got it?"

"Yeah, even I can follow those directions." He stretched his head back to expose more of his throat. "Warmer, by the way."

"I was hoping you'd say that." Mike latched on to a tender section and bit down.

Josh gasped and arched his back. "Fuck, warmer."

"Good. I've been wanting to leave marks here ever since I met you."

"Did you guess I'd like that, or—"

"No, I remember. You said you like having your neck bitten." Mike lowered his voice to a whisper. "During your audition."

Josh almost asked why he'd whispered, but then remembered the microphones all around them. They probably couldn't allude to other performances on camera without confusing the audience.

"You're thinking again. Let me fix that." Mike had insinuated one of his legs between Josh's, and now he rolled their hips together.

Josh whimpered. The motion gave his cock just enough stimulation to make his pulse jump but not enough to give him any real satisfaction. "Warmer."

"Me too." One of Mike's hands was propping him up, but the other had been stroking Josh's side. Now, it moved to his chest, trailing up until it found one of Josh's nipples. He thumbed it.

"Colder," Josh said. He'd never been a nipple guy.

Mike's hand slipped down again, this time skimming along Josh's stomach to the waistband of his underwear. All Mike did was finger it, threatening to slip his hand underneath, and need crackled through Josh's veins.

"Oh, warmer. Much warmer." Mike hadn't even touched him yet, and Josh was getting hard again. He could feel Mike's answering erection against his thigh. Mike had been unflaggingly hard this whole time, and it was a huge turn-on. Emphasis on *huge*, from what Josh could feel.

Josh canted his hips up, trying to encourage Mike to keep going. Mike took the hint and slid his fingers under the waistband . . . only to stop just shy of Josh's dick. Josh was taut beneath him, trembling with the effort of not thrusting up into the touch.

"Want these off?" Mike's tone was teasing as he toyed with Josh's underwear.

"Burn them, for all I care." Josh sucked in a breath. "Please— Will you—"

Mike mouthed his neck again. "You're sexy when you beg. I think you deserve a reward."

Mike suddenly kissed him, hard and deliberate. Fuck, but Mike could kiss. He was passionate without being overbearing. He teased Josh with nips and flashes of tongue, keeping him wanting more until Josh was so hungry for it, he was the one who deepened the kiss.

While he was distracted, Mike wrapped his hand around Josh's cock, and the mixture of pleasure and relief that washed through Josh was too profound for words. He tore his mouth away and threw his head back, giving a long, luxurious moan.

"Not bad," Colette commented. Josh's head snapped up. She'd resumed her post by the main camera and was watching them with renewed interest. "That was convincing, for once. Nice acting, Dick."

Finally did something right, did I?

"It wasn't acting," he muttered under his breath.

Mike nipped at his jaw, drawing his attention back to him. He had a smug look on his face. "Liked that, huh?"

Josh was hit by a sudden wave of shyness. He was achingly aware of Mike's loose hold on his cock, and not only because it felt incredible. His enjoyment of it was matched only by his awareness of all the people around them. Embarrassed, he bit back the little moans that wanted to come pouring out of him with every stroke.

"Don't hold back. Let it all out." At first, Mike spoke at a normal volume, probably for the benefit of the mics, but then he lowered his voice again so only Josh could hear. "Forget about them, okay? Focus on me."

"Okay." Josh relaxed, and to his surprise, it was easier this time. Maybe it was because he had some real stimulation to distract him, but soon he was back to full hardness in Mike's grip. Pre-come had started to slick Mike's hand, which made the whole thing feel a thousand times more intense.

"Feel good?" Mike asked needlessly.

Josh nodded, eyes closed and hips bucking up into his fist. "Incredible."

"I love the noises you make. Every time I get to the head of your cock, you whimper, and it's so hot. So much hotter than all the loud moaning you normally hear. Though I didn't mind that moan you let out before. You sounded like you couldn't get enough of me." He kissed Josh again, gentler but with no less heat. "I could listen to you falling apart all day."

Fuck. Josh realized with a jolt that he was right on the edge. He couldn't come before they got to the main event. He jerked away. "Shit. Stop. Stop touching me."

"What?" Mike sounded startled but immediately yanked his hand out of Josh's underwear.

Josh gasped and tensed up. "I'm gonna—" He shuddered, eyes clenched shut, but managed to fight off his body's desire for orgasm.

His instincts were all snarling at him to grab Mike's hand and put it back where it was, but after some deep breaths, they slunk off to lick their wounds.

When Josh opened his eyes, Mike was staring at him. "Were you about to . . .?"

Heat rose up in Josh's face like magma. Too embarrassed for words, he nodded.

Mike eyes *blazed*. "Holy fuck, that's hot."

"For once, I'm in agreement." Colette had a thoughtful hand tucked under her chin. "Nice job, Dick. I owe you an apology; I was going about this all wrong. I should have let you do your thing from the start. Though keep in mind, if you come, we have to keep going. There's no waiting around for refractory periods in these parts."

Josh nodded again, caught between her apology and her admonishment.

Colette clapped her hands. "All right, gentlemen, let's get this show on the road before Dick erupts. Underwear off, and take your positions. Sean, I want you on your knees between Dick's legs. Dick, I hope your flexibility is up to snuff, because you're gonna need it." She waved at one of the crew. "Get the supplies."

Mike wriggled out of his underwear and kneeled naked before Josh like it was the most natural thing in the world. Someone came over and handed him lube and a condom, which he took with a wink. There wasn't a single crack in his confidence.

Josh knew he was supposed to be getting naked too, but he was too busy staring at Mike's dick. It was *big*. Like . . . well, porn-star big. Josh wasn't sure why this surprised him so much—he'd thought it felt larger than average when Mike had thrust it against him—but that still hadn't prepared him for this. He spent a moment wrapping his brain around it.

In truth, he was being dramatic. While it was the biggest one he'd ever seen in person, it wasn't like Tommy Lee huge or anything. It probably seemed way bigger than it was because of where it was going to end up. Yikes.

Mike caught him staring and grinned. "See something you like?"

"You're, um, bigger than I'm used to." He swallowed. "But then, I'm used to topping."

"Don't worry. I know how to use it." He reached for Josh's underwear. "Let me help you with these."

Josh lifted his hips. Thank fuck for Mike's initiative. He might not have been able to strip in front of all these people, but Mike pulling the fabric down, staring at every new inch of exposed skin like he wanted to devour Josh, made it sexy.

When his cock was freed, he tried not to think about how he sized up, no pun intended. He wasn't small, and he'd never been self-conscious about his size before, but then he'd never had it out for the world to see. And next to a bigger dick. The comparison didn't work in his favor.

Mike seemed pleased, however. "It's exactly as I thought. You're the perfect size. I thought as much when I was touching you before."

"You want to bottom, then?" Josh was only half-joking. He'd resigned himself to the fact that he'd have to bottom, but that was before he'd seen the tree trunk Mike was sporting.

Mike laughed. "No way. I've been thinking about your ass for days." He hooked one hand under each of Josh's knees and eased them up to his chest. Josh fought the instinct to cover himself as he was exposed.

Mike was shameless about looking him over. "Yup. Every bit as good as I thought it'd be." With one hand, he rubbed Josh's thigh. With the other, he swiped a thumb over his hole. His eyebrows shot up. "You didn't prepare yourself ahead of time?"

Josh was having trouble focusing on Mike's question with his fingers on Josh's ass. "Was I supposed to? I'd think that'd be something they'd want to film."

"They do, and they will, but the on-screen preparation is for show. Most bottoms do it to their own specifications before filming. Now you know for next time."

Next time in general, or next time we fuck?

Josh didn't have long to think about it, because Mike held up the lube bottle. "May I?"

Oh, yes. "Of course."

Mike looked to Colette. "Are we still rolling?"

She'd moved over to the monitors and was watching the feed. "Yes, and that bit of back and forth was great. With some editing, it could make the final cut."

"Do I have time to prepare him?"

"Yeah, but we've shot enough foreplay already. Don't do anything fancy."

Josh almost rolled his eyes. *That's what every man wants to hear.*

Mike snapped the lid of the lube bottle open, poured some onto his hand, and smiled. "You said you're usually a top, right?"

"Yeah."

"Ever had a guy fuck you open with his fingers?"

Josh's cock twitched, and Mike's smile grew. "No. But I've done it to myself before, once or twice."

"Tell me about it. What did you do?" As Mike spoke, he slipped his hand between Josh's legs, brushing his inner thigh.

Josh made a soft sound. "I started slow."

"Like this?" Mike sunk one finger into him. Josh didn't know how far in he went, but the amount of sensation that came from that single touch was incredible. When Mike repeated the motion, Josh's toes curled of their own accord.

"Yeah, like that." Josh shuddered. "I was just trying it out. I thought it felt sort of weird."

"Well, let's see if I can make it feel good." Mike added more lube and another finger. He was careful, but quick.

Josh was caught between uncomfortable stretching and a myriad of new feelings he couldn't begin to categorize. "I dunno if it's my thing. I've never— Oh."

Mike curled his fingers and found Josh's prostate with stunning accuracy. "Feel good?"

"Y-yeah." Josh huffed a breath. "Do that again."

Mike complied, and Josh's vision blurred. Maybe he could get used to this after all.

"Would you mind hurrying it up, Sean?" Colette called. "This is all very hot, and of course I want Dick to be comfortable, but we need to get going."

Mike swore under his breath and gave Josh an apologetic smile. "I would do this right if we had time. I'd spread you out and fuck you open until you were begging for my cock."

Josh groaned. "Keep talking like that, and I might anyway."

"Need another minute, or can we get to it?" Mike said.

Josh didn't feel in any way prepared to take a dick, let alone Mike's literal porn-star dick, but he was plenty eager to get to the sex part at long last. "Yeah, I'll be fine."

Mike pulled his fingers out. "Excellent."

Josh looked to Colette for direction, but with the lube-free hand, Mike turned his face back. "Keep your focus on me. I'm the one who's about to fuck you."

"Yes, sir." Josh had meant it as a joke, but Mike got a wicked gleam in his eye.

It took him all of five seconds to roll the condom on, get into position, and press the head of his dick against Josh's hole. "You ready to take my cock?" The dialogue seemed in part for the cameras and in part to give Josh one final chance to protest.

Josh played along. "Oh, yeah. I want it. Fuck me with your big cock."

Mike eased in to him, and Josh grabbed his shoulders for dear life. As big as Mike looked, it didn't compare to how he felt. Josh had already never been so stretched, and Mike wasn't close to being done.

About halfway in, Mike paused, panting, and leaned down to kiss Josh. "Okay so far?"

Josh made a strained sound. When Mike had bent over, his cock had moved with him, and even that was almost too much sensation. "I dunno. It doesn't hurt, but it's kinda uncomfortable."

"It'll get better, I promise." Mike kissed him again, soothing him with his lips. "If it's any consolation, you feel incredible. Let me know when you're ready for more."

Josh forced himself to breathe. If he didn't relax into this, he was going to make it harder on himself. He wriggled beneath Sean as best he could, trying to get comfortable. Easier said than done when there was a big solid rod bisecting your body.

After some adjusting, he found an angle that didn't make his ass burn. The discomfort started to fade. He gave an experimental half thrust and found that while the somewhat unsettling fullness was still there, he wasn't in pain. Mike took the cues Josh's body was giving him and thrust in another inch. Josh breathed out in time with the movement, and Mike sunk in easily.

Mike nuzzled his cheek. "You're doing so good. So good. You're gorgeous like this, all sweaty and flushed."

Josh whimpered as his cock twitched between them. He wasn't sure what it was, but the shift in Mike's dirty talk had a strange effect on him. It'd been hot before, but now it stroked something deep inside of him.

A few more breaths, and Mike sunk the rest of the way in. He switched his position so he wasn't kneeling anymore but was instead lying on top of Josh, chest to chest. Somehow, with their bodies pressed together, the fullness felt . . . right.

Mike brushed his mouth against the shell of Josh's ear. "Still doing okay?"

"Yeah. I think it's starting to feel good."

Mike shuddered, and Josh felt it inside him. "Perfect, because holding back has never been this hard. I want to fuck you so badly."

Arousal thrummed through Josh. This was the first time this experience had resembled actual sex to him. He hoped it would stay like this.

"I'm going to take it slow," Mike murmured. "Stay relaxed."

True to his word, Mike's rhythm was gentle. He pulled out almost all the way only to slide back in at a measured pace. Josh breathed with his thrusts, and before long, he felt comfortable enough to move with him. Not quickly or well, but enough to wring some moans from Mike that shot straight between his legs.

When Josh tilted his hips up and rolled his body to meet Mike's next thrust, Mike cursed under his breath. "Jesus. Now I'm trying not to come."

"You can if you want to," Colette called to him. "I think we have enough to edit together a decent debut for Dick. It's gonna look like Frankenstein's creature, but it should work."

"Got it." Mike increased his pace enough to send shockwaves through Josh. It was still a stone's throw away from pleasure, but it was getting there. With a little more experimenting, he was sure they'd find what worked for both of them. Though there was no way he was going to come without some extra help.

As if reading his mind, Mike reached between them and grasped Josh's cock. He pumped it expertly in time with his thrusts. Didn't miss a beat. The dual sensations had Josh's head spinning. He doubted it would take him more than a minute to come if this kept up, and Mike showed no sign of stopping.

Damn, fucking a porn star has major benefits.

But then, Mike's thrusts grew erratic. A dozen or so pumps later, he moaned and tensed up. He slammed into Josh—which gave Josh all sorts of sensations, neither pleasant nor unpleasant—and cried out. Josh didn't need a handbook to recognize what that meant.

A few seconds later, Mike collapsed on top of him, breathing hard. "Fuck."

Josh was about to make a joke about it being his turn now, but he never got the chance.

"Cut! At last." Colette turned to the crew. "All right, people, that took way longer than it was supposed to. We need to hustle. Get the set broken down, and let's wrap this bad boy."

The crew members scuttled to obey before she'd even finished speaking.

Josh was flummoxed. "But wait. I didn't . . ." He looked to Mike for an explanation.

Mike didn't meet his gaze. Still panting, he wiped sweat from his brow. "I'm sorry. The bottom doesn't always get to come. Especially if time runs over."

Josh's mouth fell open. "What? Why?"

In lieu of an answer, Mike held the base of his dick and pulled out of him, taking the condom with him. Josh winced with every inch, and there were many, many inches.

"I have to take care of this." Mike indicated the condom. "Get dressed. You're gonna feel cold in a minute." Without another word, he stood up and made his way to the nearest trash can. Had this been anywhere in the vicinity of funny, Josh would have laughed to see a naked man strolling past buzzing crew members like it was nothing.

Right on cue, Josh shivered. He hadn't realized how sweaty he was until the air-conditioning hit him full force. Without Mike's body heat and the warmth from their sex, the room seemed freezing.

He scrambled to his feet and collected his clothes, pulling them on in record time. His legs wobbled with every step. He was going to have a hell of a time sitting on the bus later. All in all, however, the discomfort from his erection as he stuffed it into his jeans bothered him the most. Disappointment suffused him like an airborne contaminant.

What were you expecting? Fireworks and simultaneous orgasms? Mike told you a dozen times what this industry is like. You have no right to feel disappointed.

But he did. He might have expected treatment like this from Colette the ruthless business executive, but from Mike? He hadn't expected Mike to leave him hanging like that. Why else had he spent all that time talking dirty to him, preparing him, asking him if he was okay?

Then again, what could Mike do about it? They were off the clock. If he got Josh off now, it'd be because he wanted to, not because someone was paying him.

Gulp.

Josh was playing with fire, but there was something he had to know. Mike kept saying this was a job, but his words and actions didn't always line up. One second, he told Josh not to get attached. But the next, he took time they didn't have to prepare him, to tell him he was gorgeous. Was it all an act, or did Mike feel something for him?

When he'd finished dressing, Colette approached. She went over some details with him—how and when he'd be paid, when his video would be up on the website, and his deadline for reading the handbook—before dismissing him for the day. He would have loved some words of encouragement, but he supposed that was asking for too much.

After she left, he spotted Mike over by the table where they'd left their stuff. He'd pulled on his underwear and jeans but not his shirt. Josh couldn't blame him. With a body like his, where was the rush to get dressed? Mike was absorbed in his phone, perhaps texting someone. There was nothing to indicate he was interested in talking, but that'd never stopped Josh before.

He decided to bring Mike his shirt as a peace offering and see from there. He found it pooled on the floor by the couch. After scooping it up, he made his way over and stopped in front of Mike, waiting to be acknowledged.

Mike didn't look up from his phone. "What?"

"Here's your shirt."

"Thanks." Mike took it, slung it over his shoulder, and went back to texting.

Well, so much for the subtle approach.

Josh tried for a joke. "You owe me an orgasm."

Mike's head whipped up. The cagey expression on his face made Josh regret his words. "I don't *owe* you anything."

"Whoa!" Josh made a T shape with his hands. "Time-out. I was kidding."

Mike glanced at him askance. "Sorry. I've had some bad encounters with entitled assholes in the past."

There was a pun on the tip of Josh's tongue about the fact that Mike had recently vacated his asshole, but he swallowed it down. "So, that was filming porn, huh?"

"Yeah." Mike's expression was sympathetic. "Welcome to the glamorous sex industry."

"It's funny, you warned me so many times that it wasn't going to be what I expected, and yet I still wasn't prepared for it."

Guilt flashed across Mike's face. "I'm sorry the shoot went down the way it did. It's an unfortunate part of the industry. Be glad you're on the gay side of things. The ladies have to fake orgasms all over the place."

"I still had fun." He hesitated. "I, uh, hope you did too."

Mike's cautious expression was back. "Do you need something? Or did you just come over to chat? Because I have another shoot to get to tonight, and I'd like to go home and shower."

Already? Josh's stomach roiled. He didn't like the thought of that, and he *really* didn't want to examine why. He needed to think of something to say, fast. Mike was already turning back to his phone.

"I wanted some advice," he blurted out.

Mike looked skeptical. "You know that whole 'mentor' thing doesn't go beyond your first video, right? You've been pushed out of the nest and are now expected to fly on your own."

"Oh. Right. Well, I still thought I'd ask." An idea came to Josh. "I have to take the bus home, and I can't very well go out in public like this." He indicated the bulge that was clearly visible in his pants. "Any advice for how to deal?"

"I dunno. Think unsexy thoughts? Go rub one out in the bathroom? You wouldn't be the first. This is a work environment, but it's still a porn studio."

"Ah. Okay." It was then that Josh realized he'd been hoping Mike would volunteer after all.

"If it were me, though, I'd wait it out. Whatever you took should wear off soon. If not, you need to see a doctor."

Josh had followed along with his advice right up until the end. "'Took'? Huh?"

"Yeah. I dunno if you're a Viagra or a TriMix kinda guy, but regardless, I think you're at around the three-hour mark. If you're hard for much longer, you'll need to go to a clinic."

"I didn't take anything." Josh furrowed his brow. "I didn't even know that was a thing." Mike's unwavering erection from before flashed into his mind, and horror washed over him. "Wait a minute. Do *you* take drugs to stay hard? Is that why you never got soft while we were filming? You weren't actually turned on by *any* of that?"

In a flash, Mike seemed to realize he'd blundered. "Wait, I didn't—"

But Josh had already turned away, hands on his head. "Holy shit. This whole time I thought you were enjoying yourself, but all of it was fake. Like everything else around here. I can't believe I bought your act. You must think I'm the most gullible newbie ever."

Mike grabbed his shoulder and spun him around. "Don't freak, okay? I can explain."

Josh decided to earn the "brat" label Mike had given him and fire back. "I thought you had somewhere to be. No sense sticking around here. You're done mentoring me, remember?"

Mike made a frustrated noise. "I know I hurt your feelings, but there's no need to be like this. Especially considering I *didn't* take anything before our shoot. All my reactions were real."

That shut Josh up. For a second. "How do I know you're not just saying that?"

"Why would I lie?"

Josh ticked off reasons on his fingers. "To spare my feelings. To keep me from causing a scene. To shut me up so you can leave. To keep the peace with a coworker. To—"

"Okay!" Mike rubbed his temples. "Christ, you can talk. Look, I'm not lying. I normally do take Viagra before a scene because filming takes *hours*, and no one, not even a vet like me, can perform for that long without help. But when Colette told me I was filming with you . . ." He took a breath. "I shouldn't tell you this, but whatever. It's the truth. I don't have *any* trouble staying interested when it comes to you. I have no idea why, but there you have it."

For once, Josh was speechless. A little flicker of hope flamed up in him. Maybe Mike liked him after all. He'd just admitted he was attracted to him. That might not mean anything beyond the surface, but it was a start. Perhaps there was something here after all.

Questions swirled around in his head. There was so much he wanted to know. What he ended up asking was, "If you didn't want to tell me that, why did you?"

"I wanted you to believe me."

"Why? Why would you care? This is all business, right?"

That seemed to give Mike pause. "I'm not sure why. I guess because you've always been real with me. It's not often there's a genuine connection around here, so when it happens . . . It deserves to be acknowledged."

Despite himself, Josh's heart fluttered. *Yup. There's no denying it. I may not have a thing for gingers, but I do for one in particular.*

Great. Their situation couldn't be more complicated. They'd just had sex, for Christ's sakes, and pretty unsatisfying sex at that. He shouldn't want Mike after the epic disaster that was their first time. If he were smart, he'd go home and sort out all of his feelings before he said another word.

Once again, his mouth plunged forward without him. "Sorry I overreacted before. I know I don't need to tell you this, but I have no idea what I'm doing."

"Yeah, that much is clear. Do me a favor and don't quit your day job."

At that, Josh flinched.

Judging by Mike's widening eyes, he didn't miss the reaction. "You didn't. Did you?"

"Well . . ." Josh rubbed the back of his head.

Mike cursed under his breath. "Dude, are you self-destructive? What about your disastrous audition made you think that was a good idea?"

"I, uh, sort of quit before my audition." He swallowed. "I quit as soon as I found out I had one."

The look Mike gave him could have melted glass. "*Before* you knew if you liked this job? Before you knew if Colette was going to *offer* you a job? What were you *thinking*?"

"In hindsight, I realize it was . . . impulsive."

"Impulsive? That's so much kinder than what I'd call it." He scrubbed a hand down his face. "Do you know how few people make it in this industry as long as I have? Fuck, after the introduction to porn I just gave you, five bucks says you'll be a shooting star after all."

Josh frowned, remembering that term from before. "I'm not going to quit after one film."

"I can't imagine why not. From my perspective, it's been a miserable experience for you. If you were smart, you'd go back to your old boss and beg for your job back. Forget you ever came here."

Ice shot down Josh's spine, curdling in his gut. "You don't mean that."

Mike stared at him, eyes darting over his face. "Why wouldn't I?"

"You're only saying this because you feel guilty. You think you ruined my first time, but Mike—" he stepped closer "—you were the only good thing about it."

Mike sucked in a breath. "You shouldn't say things like that."

"Why not?"

"Because you're making me think this meant more than a paycheck to you."

"Maybe it did. Is that a crime?" Josh shut his mouth so hard, his teeth clicked. One of these days, he was going to think before he spoke.

But it was too late. Mike's face had shuttered like he'd closed blinds behind his eyes. He looked around. No one was nearby. "You know what I'm going to say, Josh. I've said it all before."

"I know. This is a job. Don't get attached. But there's something I need to know." *Am I really just a coworker to you?* The words were heavy on his tongue. He chickened out at the last second and swapped them for something safer. "Do you want to, uh, hang out sometime?"

Mike looked flummoxed. "What?"

"Hang out. You know. Get coffee, or dinner, or something."

"Like a date." Mike's tone was deadpan.

"No, like two friends hanging out. Or two coworkers. Doesn't anyone around here do anything outside of work?"

Mike studied his face with the attention of a cat watching a squirming mouse. "You want to be my friend?"

"Yeah. Of course." Josh had never told such an egregious lie. He wasn't totally crystal on what he wanted from Mike, but it wasn't friendship.

Mike was silent for a long moment. Then he sighed and held out his phone. "Give me your number."

Josh took it and programmed his number in, trying not to crow with triumph. *Mr. Doesn't-Get-Attached gave me his digits.*

His victory was short-lived. Before he could hit the Call button, Mike snatched his phone back. "Nope. If I want to contact you, I will. And *if* I do—note the emphasis—it will be in a strictly professional capacity. Capiche?"

Josh's heart crumbled into little shards that slid into his stomach, shredding as they went. Mike wouldn't even exchange numbers with him. He might have no intention of calling at all. Maybe he'd only taken Josh's number to shut him up. Josh must be the most pathetic person on the planet.

"Yeah, I get it." He swallowed around the glacier in his throat. "I guess I'll get going. Today was, um, informative."

"Bye." Mike paused. "Take care of yourself."

That sounds an awful lot like "Goodbye forever, loser."

Josh grabbed his things, turned away, and walked off, numb from head to toe. It was silly to be upset, but he needed to get out of here. Between Colette's criticism and Mike's rejection, he felt worse than he had in . . . God, maybe forever.

And to top it all off, he had no one to blame but himself.

CHAPTER 6

'm a terrible person, Mike thought as he posed—naked and oiled from head to toe—in front of a fleet of photographers. He'd been standing in one of Murmur Inc.'s first-floor photography studios for the past two hours, and while he could hold an uncomfortable position with the best of them, the hot lights were starting to make him sweat.

Next to him was a skinny blond man who didn't look a day older than nineteen. He bore no resemblance to Josh, other than the flaxen hue of his hair, and yet every time Mike looked at him, his erstwhile costar barreled into his thoughts.

I'm a bad, bad man. The lead photographer ordered them to switch to a new pose, and Mike heeded on autopilot.

A week had passed since his shoot with Josh, and every time Mike saw a blond head or a set of green eyes, he thought about him and what a clumsy job he'd done handling their situation.

If asked, Mike would say he loved his job. He loved getting paid to look good and make people feel good. But he was realistic about how tough porn was and the fact that it was a bad fit for some. Mike had spotted all sorts of warning signs that Josh wasn't cut out for this: the cockiness that didn't quite mask his insecurity, the waffling before showtime, and the way he'd clung to Mike like he was a life preserver. Mike had done his best to warn Josh about the pitfalls ahead of him; he'd even tried to guide him around them. And yet, they'd still ended up with hurt feelings and remorse.

The look on Josh's face when Mike had rejected him was haunting. He'd regretted snatching his phone away the moment he'd done it. He'd almost called out to Josh as he'd turned away, but a hoard of confused feelings had stayed his tongue. It had gotten too personal, and as much as he'd known he should have been stopping it . . . He hadn't wanted to.

It's because you like him, you mook. You're torn up about this because you wanted to lay him out and make sweet love to him, and instead you had to do a half-assed job of fucking him.

Damn.

He shouldn't have performed with Josh. As the more experienced partner, he should have made a judgment call, despite Josh swearing up and down that he wanted to go through with it. On some level, Mike knew it wasn't entirely his fault. He'd been following orders—doing his job, as he was so fond of saying—but he still felt responsible. In hindsight, he believed that Josh had wanted to have sex with him, but he didn't think Josh had wanted to film porn. Again, they were different things. Josh had learned that the hard way.

Mike hadn't made it an easy lesson, either. The fact was, his attraction to Josh scared him, especially since there was every indication that it was mutual. After what Josh had said at the end of their shoot—when he'd admitted that this meant something to him—there was no denying it.

Josh's attempt to claim he wanted to be friends had fallen flat. Mike had panicked and gone into deep-freeze mode when he should have been thinking about how this must all seem from Josh's perspective. One second, Mike was warning him away. The next, he was telling him he'd enjoyed their kiss. All those mixed signals would be enough to confuse anyone.

On Mike's end, he couldn't pretend it was simply physical either. Mike worked with some of the most beautiful people in the industry. If attraction were all he needed, he'd be having sordid affairs left and right. There was obviously something deeper about Josh that appealed to him. Mike had already copped to liking Josh's realness and his lack of filter, but those weren't qualities that made a long-time bachelor settle down.

Neither was Josh's petulant attitude. The man had *brat* written all over him. When he mouthed off, all Mike wanted to do was shut him up with a kiss. Leave bite marks all over his neck. Make him whimper and beg. Push him down ass-up on a bed and spank him until—

Okay, so there was a definite physical aspect to their attraction, but Mike still wanted to probe at what lay below the surface. To do that, he'd probably need to spend more time with Josh. That was the part that scared him.

After what happened, you'd be lucky if he gave you the chance to know him.

That was a sobering thought.

"Sean!" The lead photographer snapped her fingers. "You having some kind of fit?"

"No, sorry." Mike shook his head. "I drifted off for a second. What'd you say?"

"I said hold Blondie's chin like you're about to fuck his mouth."

Charming.

Mike got into position, with Blondie kneeling at his feet, mouth open an inch from the head of his swollen cock. He understood Blondie's appeal, on a superficial level, but the guy just wasn't doing it for him. Blondie kept talking dirty, for one thing. Telling Mike what a great cock he had and how much he wanted to suck it. That would have been fine if they were filming, but they were shooting stills. And the way he kept rolling his eyes back when Mike touched him was allegedly supposed to be sexy, but came across like a cut scene from *The Exorcist.*

You're being judgmental because you wish Josh were here instead.

Jesus, could he go two seconds without thinking about him?

No.

Mike sighed. This was what he got for being such a workaholic. He'd been single for so long, he was drooling over the first guy who'd caught his eye. It wasn't like he didn't *want* to date. It was just difficult to find anyone outside of the sex industry who was cool with what he did for a living. He wasn't about to lie, and when he announced over dinner that he was a well-known bisexual power top, things tended to go south.

He could date within the sex industry, of course, but the only people he ever met were ones he was about to have sex with, and it seemed creepy to hit on them then.

Except when it comes to Josh, apparently.

Which brought him right back to his initial problem: he'd struggled to keep his relationship with Josh businesslike, going so far as to hurt his feelings in the process, but Josh didn't seem to want to be professional. Now his phone number was burning a hole in Mike's pocket—or it would be if he were wearing clothes—and he had no idea where they stood.

Every decision he'd made since that fateful night Colette had asked him to stay late seemed to be the wrong one.

This just wasn't his month.

"Sean." The photographer sounded impatient. "Focus, please?"

"Sorry."

"Switch positions again." The photographer fiddled with the settings on her camera and then blinded him with a flash. "Sean, I need more variety from you. You're giving me the same pensive expression in every photo."

"My bad. My knees are starting to lock, though. Are we almost finished?"

She sighed. "Give me five more good frames—and I mean *good*, usable frames—and we can wrap."

Mike managed to pull his head out of his ass long enough to give some solid poses. Five cornea-frying flashes later, they were finished, and he was free to wipe himself down and collect his clothing.

He was sliding his belongings into the pockets of his black Saint Laurent jeans when his hand lingered on his phone, as had been happening more and more often of late.

Why don't you text him? End your suffering. You can act like you don't like Josh all you want, but you clearly do, and you're not doing anybody any favors by denying yourself.

What would he say, though? He could apologize, and they could do this right, without any cameras or an audience. Mike wanted that, and not just because he felt guilty. There was a whole list in his head of things he wanted to do with Josh, and a good portion of them involved that big mouth of his . . .

But how would that conversation go? *Hey, sorry the sex was so terrible. And that I pushed you away afterward. I'd love to make it up to you, but it goes against all my professional boundaries.*

He was willing to bet that wouldn't go over so well.

Mike's first time on camera had been a horror show as well. He'd fallen for one of the ads on Craigslist that had promised quick cash, and he'd gotten himself into a sketchy situation. He'd survived, but it had only been his college debt that'd kept him in porn. From then on, he'd refused to work with anyone but legit companies. He'd found Murmur Inc., and Colette's devotion to safety was what had convinced him to sign with her. The rest was history.

Though he wondered why Colette—who made a point of not pushing the newbies too far, too fast—had made the call she had with Josh. He trusted that she had a reason, but it didn't make him any less curious.

If Mike had any sense at all, he'd move on. Start thinking about his next film project. It'd been a while, and Colette should be calling him any day now to book him with someone else. Maybe the key to getting over his guilt involved getting on top of a new warm body.

Bullshit, Harwood. You're not going to feel better about this until you own up to what you did. Call Josh and apologize. Don't proposition him. Don't ask him out. Say you're sorry for brushing him off and see what he says. If you don't make this right, he might never come back to Murmur Inc., and then you'll never see him again.

The thought made his stomach acid coagulate. If only he had a reason to talk to him. Something to break the ice. Then he could apologize without it seeming weird.

He was still thinking about it as he waved goodbye to Blondie— who had donned a uniform that made Mike think he was a paramedic when he wasn't working here—and exited the set. Just as he was considering tracking down Colette and seeing if she could provide him with an excuse to call Josh, someone said his name.

"Sean. A word?"

Speak of the devil. Colette was leaning in the doorway of her first-floor office, which to his knowledge acted primarily as a quiet place for her to go when the phone sex operators on the third floor got too rowdy. Judging by her tapping foot, she'd been waiting for him to finish.

"I was about to come find you." He hustled over. As he walked, he noted her grave expression. She normally had a poker face that could make a Vegas dealer sweat. Something serious must be going on. "What's up?"

"Deep shit." She opened the door wider without preamble. "Come in, and close the door behind you."

Well, that confirmed his theory. He did as instructed, closing and locking the door behind him. Colette's office was small but tastefully furnished with a large, hardwood desk and soothing art on the walls. He sunk into one of the leather wingback chairs across from her and wished it weren't so supple. It didn't feel right getting bad news while sitting on a cloud.

Colette took a seat in the large boss's chair on the other side of the desk and steepled her fingers. "I'm afraid I have to be the bearer of bad news."

"The suspense is killing me." Worst-case scenarios ran through his head. They could be getting slammed with obscenity charges. The police were always giving them shit at the behest of conservative groups. Someone could have been caught with drugs on location, or they might have been prostituting on the side for extra money.

"There's no easy way to say this, so I'll be frank. Nickie Sixxy has announced she's positive."

Outside of the sex industry, that might have sounded like an inspirational message, but Mike knew otherwise. His mouth popped open. "She has HIV?"

"Yup. She broke the news on her Twitter this morning. Sent ripples of panic throughout the industry. She's been getting tested regularly, so she estimates she contracted it within the past month. The whole machine is grinding to a halt while everyone who performed with her is rushing to get tested. Good thing we recently held auditions, because I'm going to need a lot of new performers to fill the gaps. It's been a PR *nightmare*."

"I'm sorry to hear that." He meant it. An announcement like this always led to jobs drying up and a slow market. "But what does that have to do with me? I never fucked Nickie."

"No, but you fucked Diamond Rough ten days ago, and she did a scene with Nickie shortly before that."

"Shit! Seriously?" Mike tried not to overreact, but he couldn't keep beads of cold sweat from forming on his brow like icicles.

"Try not to panic. It's harder for women to pass HIV to other women, most of the time. It is possible, however, so you need to get tested."

Despite her words, the news slammed into Mike like a freight train. For several seconds, all he could hear was his own blood buzzing in his ears. Gradually, he floated down from whatever dark, cold place he'd been catapulted into and reemerged in Colette's office, clammy and shaking.

"Seriously, try not to panic." Colette's voice managed to reach him through the static clouding his brain. "Your chances of having it are low. Like, struck-by-lightning low. Nickie and Diamond didn't use protection, but you and Diamond did."

He remembered that. It was unusual. Straight porn hardly ever involved condoms, but Diamond didn't do cream pies without them. Mike had gotten paid extra to come in her. The condom reduced his chances of being positive by a *lot*. Thank fuck.

Colette continued. "We need to alert every Murmur Inc. employee you've slept with since Diamond to get tested. I have records of all your shoots, of course, but you should make a list of everyone in your personal life as well." She pulled a notepad and a pen out of a drawer and tossed them to him.

He stared at them, body growing rigid as realization dawned on him. "You have to contact everyone I've slept with in the past ten days? And everyone Diamond slept with, and Nickie, and then whoever those people went on to sleep with, and who they slept with? Not to mention group sex scenes, and threesomes, and gangbangs . . . We're talking *dozens* of people."

"Forty-eight, so far. I'm still counting. The number could break into triple digits by the time I'm finished tracking everyone down. How often do you get tested?"

"Every two weeks." It was the industry standard for anyone who had regular, condom-free sex, as most of the "straight" performers did.

"When was your next one going to be?"

"In three days."

"Well, I hate to disrupt your schedule, but I recommend skipping that one and waiting. The soonest you can get an accurate result is twenty-one days after exposure, but it's better if you wait the full twenty-eight. I hate to say this, but that means—"

"You won't be able to hire me for two weeks." Mike nodded. "I'd already figured that much out."

"I assure you that you'll still have a place here when you come back. Assuming . . ."

The unspoken end of that sentence punched Mike in the gut.

Colette cleared her throat. "This is just a suggestion, but no matter how low your chances are, you should still avoid all sexual contact until you have your results."

That'll be easy. I haven't slept with anyone recreationally in the past . . . Jesus.

"I think that's everything. You should receive an email from me later today. I'm sending it out to the whole employee database to explain what's happening—sans details, of course—so people don't panic. Well, any more than they already have."

God, this was a nightmare. Three years. Three years he'd managed to go without a major STI scare. He'd had an STI once, but that'd been an easy cure. A little penicillin, and he'd been home free. This was different. He would live with this for the rest of his life.

"You're going to be fine, Mike."

He glanced up. Colette almost never used his real name.

She offered him a small smile. "If you do have it, HIV isn't the death sentence today that it was for queer men in the eighties."

"I know." He blinked and was surprised to discover that his eyes had misted. "But it's still incurable."

"For now." She gave him a sympathetic look, which was her version of a hug. "You need anything from me?"

"Yeah." He hesitated. "You said you're going to contact every Murmur Inc. employee I performed with, right?" *That includes Josh.*

"Yup. Most of them will have heard the news already, but the ones who didn't perform with Nickie directly, like you, won't understand that this affects them too. I'm not looking forward to going through a whole month-long spider web of porn."

"I don't envy you." He paused again. "Sounds like you could use some help."

Colette looked at him askance. "Whatever you're not saying, say it."

He swallowed. This was a perfect excuse to get in touch with Josh. It wouldn't be under the best of circumstances, but while he had him on the phone, he could try to make things right.

"Well, I was thinking I could make one phone call for you. To, um, Josh. Or Dick Reams, rather."

Colette's eyebrows shot up. "You want to tell him yourself? I didn't think you two were close."

"We're not, but you did make me his mentor."

"That was only for orientation. You know that."

"I know, but I feel kinda responsible. To think he might have gotten an STI his very first time filming. That's like *The Lottery* levels of shitty luck, you know? I think he might take the news better if it comes from me, since we have a rapport and all. You don't want to scare the kid into becoming a shooting star, right?"

Colette pressed her lips into a thin line. "Is that your real reason?"

"Of course it is. What other reason could I have?"

She studied his face for a disconcerting moment before sighing. "Sean, I've been in this industry for a long time. I've seen my fair share of drama go down behind the scenes. Jealousy, scorned lovers, moral struggles, you name it. I've also known you for a long time, and it's obvious to me that Dick—"

"Josh," Mike corrected without thinking.

Colette's facial expression was a thing to behold.

Fuck.

"Sean . . . I know this is none of my business, but do you *like* Josh?"

He fidgeted. "As a colleague, sure."

Her frown said she didn't believe him. "Of all people, I never thought you'd fall in love on my set. I must say, it's about time you stopped working so hard and had some fun."

"I didn't *fall* for him." He sighed. "I don't know what I did. I need to talk to him."

"Far be it from me to tell a fellow adult what to do, but I think we both know Josh isn't cut out for this business. When I first met him, I thought to myself, *I give it a week.* I've been wrong before, but not often. Do you think it's wise to become invested in someone who could disappear tomorrow?"

I don't like this line of questioning one bit.

Mike huffed out an agitated breath. "Look, I appreciate the pep talk, but like you said, I'm an adult. I can make my own decisions. Let me talk to him, okay? My moral compass is telling me that's the right thing to do. As much as you like to play the role of the heartless CEO, I know you'll cave if I say it's important. So, I'm saying it. It'll be better for both Josh and me if I handle this."

Colette studied him for a few seconds before leaning back in her chair. "Very well. You can make the phone call. You realize, however, that I can't disclose his personal information, right? Like his phone number? You're not even supposed to know his name."

"Actually . . . I already have his number."

"Why am I not surprised? In that case, you're dismissed." She made a shooing motion. "Off you go. I have a lot of calls to make."

Mike scampered out of her office, shutting the door behind him. He shouldn't have mouthed off to her. Two weeks was a long time in the porn world, and at the end of it, he still needed to have a job. Thank fuck he had savings.

He exited the building via the side door and found his car waiting for him in the parking lot. It wasn't until he was behind the wheel that panic descended on him once again. He must be in shock, because it was hitting him in waves. Fuck, he might have HIV. The words rattled around in his brain like loose teeth.

To his surprise, hot tears stung his eyes. He took deep breaths and refused to blink. They fell anyway, staining his cheeks. He was being melodramatic. What Colette had said was right. His chances of having it were miniscule, and if he did, he wasn't going to die. There were all sorts of treatments nowadays, and positive people were living longer, healthier lives than ever before.

Part of his upset stemmed from the fact that he knew he shouldn't be so surprised. He was bound to come into contact with STIs eventually. It was a miracle he'd gone all these years of being sexually active without a major incident.

Mike had done his best to put the risks out of his mind. He got tested every two weeks and used protection whenever possible. At the time, he'd told himself this was his way of refusing to live in fear. If he'd spent the past few years being stressed out after every shoot, he'd never do anything else. And he'd been so *lucky*. He'd honestly started to believe he was invincible.

Well, his kryptonite had turned up in its own time.

"Calm down, Harwood." His hands shook as he gripped the steering wheel. "You're going to be okay. You'll get through this. You've gotten through so much already."

He ticked events off in his head: his parents' divorce, being bullied his whole life for his red hair and freckles, the angry teen years in which he'd joined the wrestling team and started working out, his parents throwing him out at eighteen—not because he came out as bisexual, but because he and Dad couldn't stop screaming at each other—putting himself through college with loans that kept piling up, and finally, turning to porn when it'd seemed like a miraculous solution to his problems.

In a lot of ways, it was. Porn had been good to him. He was successful. Debt-free.

And possibly diseased.

God damn. He shook his head to dispel that thought. He needed to remain calm. He'd have two whole weeks of unpaid vacation to wrap his head around the news, and by the end of that, he'd be ready for whatever happened. He'd face this like he'd faced everything else.

Though if he was positive, that would be the end of his porn career. Not because Colette would fire him, but because no one would work with him once he announced his status. And he'd have to announce it. He couldn't keep filming porn without disclosing it to his partners. Not just because it was a felony in most states, but because disclosing was the right thing to do.

His head was starting to spin from all the thoughts rolling around in it like a boat caught in a storm. One step at a time. Key into the ignition. Pull out onto the street. Drive home.

Fifteen minutes later, he arrived at the apartment he rented in West Hollywood. The building was set up like a series of two-story townhouses all crammed together in the manner of skinny books on a shelf. Mike almost never saw his neighbors, which was exactly how he liked it. He'd rented out his apartment to Murmur Inc. more than once, and he'd rather not have to explain why people in cheerleading uniforms and PVC vinyl catsuits were wandering in and out at all hours.

Unlocking his front door, he set his keys on the entry table, and swept through the apartment, crossing over hardwood floors. He passed the black leather sofas in the living room and a large kitchen full of shiny appliances, followed by the spiral staircase that led up to the loft. He headed all the way back to his bedroom.

The light-blue walls and simple furnishings soothed him. White curtains draped over the wide windows caught the afternoon light. He sat down on the edge of his bed, phone already in hand.

Josh's contact info stared back at him. Now that he was preparing to make this call, nervousness made his skin prickle. They'd left off on frosty terms, and they weren't going to get any warmer once Mike delivered his news. It might very well be the worst news Josh had ever received. Why had Mike been so adamant that he do this himself?

They'd had sex a week ago, which meant Josh—who, from what he'd told Mike, had quit his day job—would be out of work for two weeks, minimum. Two agonizing weeks in which he would probably be inundated with worry, and fear, and bills he couldn't pay. Plus, he'd have to call anyone he'd slept with since their shoot and tell *them* to get tested as well. To top it all off, at the end of all that stress, Josh might have HIV. What a perfect parting gift to mark the end of his single foray into pornography.

Josh will never forgive me. He's going to hate me forever.

The thought dripped misery into Mike's veins like an IV.

There was no going back now. He'd volunteered to call Josh. He had to do it.

With a final deep breath, Mike pressed the Call button and pressed the phone to his ear.

CHAPTER 7

"Well, well, well. If it isn't my former coworker. Joshua Clemmons." Sana was sitting on the counter at the Globe with her legs crossed, but the smug look on her face made it seem like she was on a throne. "Here for a social visit, or have you come crawling back?"

Joshua sighed and rubbed the back of his neck. "You're not going to make this easy for me, are you?"

"Oh, absolutely not." She uncrossed and recrossed her legs at the ankles, making her colorful floor-length dress flutter. It matched the bright-blue hijab covering her hair. "In fact, I had a feeling you'd be back, and I've prepared a speech to mark the occasion."

"Look, I realize what I did was wrong—"

"Wrong? After *years* of working here, you quit out of nowhere! No two weeks' notice, no warning, no phone call. You dumped the Globe through text message. I think you owe us both an apology." She gestured to the coffee shop around them.

Josh had come in at four o'clock on a Sunday for a reason. He knew it was their least-busy time, and he didn't want an audience for this conversation. "Sana, I—"

"That wasn't *wrong*. That was selfish, and immature, and irresponsible, and—"

"Okay!" Josh threw his hands up in a defensive gesture. "I get it. I'm the scum of the Earth. I should be tarred and feathered and made to walk through the streets while a weird nun rings a bell and shouts 'Shame!' behind me. I'm sorry."

Sana leveled him with a look that could boil water.

"I mean it! From the bottom of my heart, I apologize." He exhaled, looking down at his shoes. "I made a mistake. A big one. I hope you can forgive me." He peeked up.

Sana was studying him with her impenetrable brown eyes. After a moment, she pursed her lips and made a rude noise. "You know, if you'd asked for your job back before you'd asked for forgiveness, I would have kicked you out."

"How do you know I want my job back? Maybe I'm just doing the right thing."

"Oh puh-*lease*. You think I'm buying this whole contrite act?" She swished a hand at him. "I've known you for years. You may be a loudmouth, but you avoid confrontation whenever possible. You would never have come all the way down here if you didn't need something."

Josh pouted. "That was harsh. I'm wounded."

"Allow me to make it up to you." She hopped off the counter, walked around it, and riffled through a bottom cabinet. After a moment, she extracted one of the Globe's blue aprons and tossed it to him. "You can start tomorrow. As far as I'm concerned, you're a brand-new employee, so you have no seniority and no rank. Oh, and you're working a double shift."

Josh groaned, but at her sharp look, he swallowed it. "You may not believe me, Sana, but . . . thank you." He was about to head for the exit when Sana called after him.

"Hey."

He looked over his shoulder. "What?"

"Why'd you do it? Quit." She was leaning on the counter, head tilted to the side like a curious cat. "I came up with a handful of theories, but none of them seemed quite right."

Josh chewed on his bottom lip. "I can't talk about it here."

In lieu of a response, Sana took a long, pointed survey of the empty room.

"Yeah, I know, but someone could walk in."

"Why don't you just admit you don't want to tell me?"

Josh hesitated. Was he that transparent? It was nothing against Sana. He'd spent enough time rehashing what'd happened without doing it in front of someone else, and to be honest, as cool and fair as

Sana was, she wasn't his friend. They had a working relationship, on a good day.

She saw his hesitation and fixed him with a meaningful look. "Dude, there's something up with you. I can feel it. If nothing else, I need to know you didn't get mixed up in anything bad before I invite you back to work here."

Josh sighed. He supposed he owed her that much for giving him his job back. Plus, when their former coworker had come out as a porn star, Sana had been vocal in her support. Out of everyone he could talk to about this, she was his best bet.

"Fine." He walked back over and set the apron she'd given him down on the counter. "It's kind of a long story."

Sana rested her elbows on the counter and cupped her chin. "Spill."

It was like letting the air out of a tire. The story flowed out of him in a continuous stream. He told her *everything*, from the moment he'd started researching local porn companies to filming his debut. He spared no detail. Hell, he probably told her things she didn't want to know, like how hot he was for Mike and how disappointed he'd been by their lackluster sexual encounter.

If she were in any way disturbed, however, she didn't let it show. She listened without interruption until he was finished. After, he was shocked by how empty he felt, but in a good way. It was like the past few weeks had been building up in his chest, fighting to get out, and now the pressure had been released.

He ended his confession with, "I haven't heard from Mike since. I don't have his number, so I can't call him. I also haven't heard from Colette, but that's kind of a relief." He inhaled and exhaled. "If that's what porn is like with someone I'm attracted to, I can't imagine what it'd be like with someone I'm not. I don't think I can do it again."

Sana nodded. "So, you're going to be a—what was the term you used? A 'shooting star'?"

"Yeah, I guess. Porn is nothing like what I thought it would be."

"Did you get paid for the one movie you made?"

"Yeah. A fuck-ton. I mean—" He whistled. "Really, a lot of money. But even that didn't make me want to go back. So, here I am."

"Well, I don't think I need to tell you how thoughtless it was of you to quit your day job before you had a solid backup plan." She shrugged. "But if it helps, you still have a place here."

"Thanks." He looked down at the ground. "I'm sorry for what I did. I don't always make the best choices."

"Yeah, that's for damn sure." Sana leaned a hip against the counter. "So, what are you going to tell Colette?"

"I dunno. Nothing?"

The glare she leveled him with was nuclear. "Joshua Maurice Clemmons—"

"Er, my middle name is Allen."

"—if you think you can up and quit on another boss without a word, there will be hell to pay. Either you give her proper notice, or so help me, I *will* fire you."

"But porn isn't like other jobs. It's not on a regular schedule. You either get booked or you don't. It's not like I can give two weeks' notice. Besides, Colette hasn't called me. I kinda got the impression she was as disinterested in me as I was in filming again."

"I don't care. You go down there if you have to and tell her upfront that you've decided not to continue."

"It sounds easy when you say it, but you haven't met Colette. She's scary beyond all reason."

Sana pinched the bridge of her nose. "Buddy. Pal. My guy. Get your head out of your ass and learn to own up to your decisions. There's no shame in telling her it's not a good fit. As a fellow boss, I promise you she'd rather you didn't waste her time."

"Yeah, I guess you're right. I mean, what's she gonna do? Fire me? I'll go down there later today." Josh's phone vibrated in his pocket. He'd barely glanced at the screen before he gasped.

"What is it?"

"I don't recognize this number." *What if it's Mike?* Josh's heart thudded against his ribs.

Sana glared at him. "Oh wow, let me call the press!"

"It could be Mike, though."

"Not to be a pessimist or anything, but that's a bit of a reach. It's probably someone calling to say you won a free cruise that you never signed up for."

"Well, I won't know unless I—"

It went to voice mail.

Josh cursed. "I waited too long."

"So, call it back."

"Yeah." His finger hovered over the Call button. "Should I? What if it actually is him? Do I want to talk to him?"

"*Buddy.*" Exasperation radiated from Sana in waves. "I dunno if you can hear yourself when you talk about him, but it's clear you like this guy. After a week of you pining and waiting for his call, you might have gotten your wish. Of course you should call him back."

"But he told me our relationship can't be anything more than professional, and I decided to quit. That means we're not coworkers anymore." Josh bit his lip. "He might reject me again."

"Like you tried to say before, you won't know unless you try. Find out if it's even him. You might be freaking out over nothing."

He nodded and hit the Call button. It only rang once before a deep voice answered. "Hey, is this Josh?"

That's Mike all right.

Josh's eyes darted over to Sana. She mouthed a question to him, and he nodded his head.

"Hello?" Mike sounded impatient. "Are you there?"

"Yeah, I'm here." Josh cleared his throat. "Sorry about that. I'm, uh, at work."

"You're at Murmur Inc.? Can we meet up?"

He wants to see me. Josh's heart swelled like a hot-air balloon. "No, sorry. I'm at my other job."

"I thought you quit."

"I . . . changed my mind."

"Ah, okay. I guess we'll have to do this over the phone, then."

Josh blinked. "Do what? Actually, hold on a sec." Sana was waving at him. He pulled the phone from his ear. "What?"

"A customer walked in." She pointed at the door, where two women had in fact entered. "You're gonna have to talk somewhere else. But come back when you're done. I want to know *everything.*"

"Fine." Josh stuck his tongue out at her as he walked out the side door and into the balmy heat of a late Los Angeles afternoon. "Sorry again, Mike. I'm here now."

There was a pause. "Are you somewhere we can talk? You said you're at work, and I dunno if that will, uh, work."

Huh. Mike seemed flustered. That was a first. "Why, Mikey, I've never heard you sound so rattled."

Mike scoffed. "We talked about this, *Joshie*. Remember?"

"Fair enough. Yeah, I'm somewhere we can talk." The side door let out onto a little street off the main intersection. Josh leaned against the red brick, which was so sunbaked he heard his skin sizzle. He yelped and shoved away from it. "What's up? You miss me already?"

There was another pause. "Yeah, actually. If I'm being honest."

Josh was speechless. He'd meant that as a joke. He scrambled for something to say and came up empty.

Mike continued before he could recover. "That's not why I'm calling, though. I have some bad news. Colette was going to alert you, but I wanted to deliver it myself."

That didn't sound good. Josh's heart broke into a gallop. "What is it?"

"One of the perils of the sex industry, I'm afraid." There was a static sound, like maybe Mike had exhaled against his speaker. "What I'm about to say isn't easy. Please let me finish before you react, okay?"

"Mike, you're starting to freak me out. What is it?"

Another puff of air. "You know I'm a crossover, right? I perform with both men and women? And straight porn seldom involves condoms?"

"I guess." Josh brushed a bead of sweat off his brow. "I mean, I think I remember all that from orientation. Why?"

"A porn star announced she's HIV positive, and through six degrees of separation, I might be as well. Which means you need to get tested."

Mike kept talking, but Josh couldn't hear him. His ears filled with ringing, as if he'd walked from a loud room into a silent one. The sweat forming on his brow chilled despite the heat, and what felt like a year passed between his heartbeats.

"Josh. Josh? Are you still there?"

His mouth formed an affirmation, but no sound came out. He had to take several breaths before he could croak, "Yeah. I'm here."

"Like I said, try not to freak out. Your chances of having it are infinitesimal. They're even lower than mine, and mine are miniscule. I think if I for sure had it, you'd still only have a one to two percent chance, and I could very well be negative. And if you do have it, you're gonna be fine. I promise. Okay?"

Josh couldn't think of words. He made some sort of grunting sound, and then his lungs failed him. It seemed that was enough to satisfy Mike, because he kept talking in the manner of a babbling brook. Words and words and words, all jumbling around in Josh's brain. Mike explained that he needed to get tested in two weeks, and then again in three months, but all Josh could think was, *Someone has to be in that one to two percent. Someone has to be the one who gets fucked by probability. How do the people who work in this industry live with this kind of stress?*

He hadn't made it through a single film without running into a cornucopia of trouble. How did sex workers do this for *years*, like Mike had? Josh was starting to understand why the average shelf life of a porn star was three months. Or why some became shooting stars.

He checked back into the conversation in time for Mike to say, "I'm sorry to say you won't be able to work for two weeks. Colette won't risk booking you until she knows your status one way or another. Go down to Murmur Inc. as soon as you can and discuss your options with her."

"Oh no." Josh's tone was deadpan. "I can't film again for two weeks? Tragic."

"Is that sarcasm? I was expecting you to be devastated. You seemed so determined to make it in this biz."

"Yeah, well, I dunno if porn is for me after all. Like I told you before, I had no idea how complicated it was, and that was before all the politics."

Mike was silent for a moment. "I'm both relieved and disappointed."

"Disappointed in me?"

"No, not at all. I had a feeling from the start that porn wasn't gonna be good for you. I'm glad you figured it out before you'd gotten in too deep. Though I'm sure this STI scare is plenty deep for you."

"I'm legitimately trying not to think about it." He hesitated. "Why are you disappointed?"

Another long silence. "Because this means I won't get another chance with you."

For the second time in ten minutes, Josh's heart skipped a beat. "You want to film with me again? I thought I was a bratty newbie."

"Oh, you are. Make no mistake. But . . ." More static. "I feel terrible about the way your first time went down."

Josh shrugged to himself. "You weren't the one who ordered us to have sex, or who called cut before I got to come. That was Colette."

"Yeah, but I shouldn't have brushed you off afterwards. Part of the reason I called was so I could apologize for the way I treated you. I'm sorry. I was a complete jerk."

Josh sucked in a breath. "Yeah, you were."

Mike laughed. "Way to sugarcoat it."

"Well, it's the truth."

"Why don't you let me make it up to you?"

Josh bit his lip. "I won't lie, I have no desire to film with you again. The whole performing-in-front-of-people thing isn't my kink."

"I wasn't talking about filming again. I wouldn't ask you to do that."

"Then what did you have in mind?"

"I was thinking we could hang out some time. Like you wanted."

"As coworkers?"

"As friends."

Another bead of sweat rolled down Josh's face. He needed to get out of the heat soon. "I didn't think you wanted to be friends."

"I was wrong." Mike laughed, breathy and low. "Though, I must admit, the idea of being just friends with you isn't all that appealing."

Josh's breath caught in his throat.

Before he could recover, Mike continued. "If nothing else, then in two weeks, when we get our good news, we should go out and celebrate. I'll take you anywhere you want to go. My treat."

Josh started to say yes, but then a thought occurred to him. *He might be asking me out because he feels bad. I don't want to go on a pity date. Plus, he blew me off before. I bet he thinks I'll jump at the chance to go out with him. Maybe I should let him sweat a little.*

"I'll think about it." And with that, Josh hung up the phone. He could imagine the stunned silence that must be radiating from Mike. Maybe he was staring at his phone, slack-jawed with disbelief. *Serves him right.*

Josh headed back inside, breathing a sigh of relief when the air-conditioning hit him like an ice bath. He found Sana more or less where he'd left her, but now there was a customer at the counter. He waited, jiggling with impatience, while the man ordered a nonfat soy milk latte. By the time Sana made it and sent the customer on his way, Josh was ready to burst.

"All right—" she waved him up to the counter "—tell me what happened. Can I expect a Save the Date in the mail?"

"Not anytime soon, no."

For the second time that day, Josh poured his soul out to Sana.

When he was finished, she walked around the counter and threw her arms around him. Josh was almost too stunned to hug her back. Sana wasn't an affectionate boss. Her reaction made it harder for him to pretend like everything was okay.

After a moment, she pulled back. "I'm sorry you're going through this, Joshua. I know I said you're working a double tomorrow, but if you need to take some time off, I understand."

He shrugged. "What good will that do? I'll still have two long weeks ahead of me before I can get tested. After that, I'll have to go back again in three months. Working will keep my mind off things."

"Any way I can convince you to take some time off?"

"Thank you, but no. And thanks again for giving me my job back. And for all your support." God, he could only imagine how long the next fourteen days were going to be.

She patted him on the shoulder. "Get out of here. Go take a walk or get some ice cream or something. Try not to stress."

He shook his head. "I'm gonna go talk to Colette. Tell her I'm not coming back. I'm hoping she'll go easy on me. Maybe she'll have some advice."

"Good idea. Oh, and Joshua?"

"Yeah?"

"You can call me if you need to."

To Josh's embarrassment, his eyes prickled with tears. He gave her an awkward, one-armed hug and then scurried out the front door as if he could outrace his feelings.

He made it all the way to the bus stop before a tear slid down his cheek. Thank God there was no one around. He wiped it away with his T-shirt and took a deep breath. Over and over again in his head he repeated, *It's gonna be okay.* He kept it up all the way to his stop and through the ten-minute walk to Murmur Inc. He didn't stop until he'd climbed up the stairs to the third floor, where he hoped he'd find Colette.

Upon a quick scan of the bustling room, he didn't see her. He asked around, and a helpful middle-aged woman with a voice like a drunk sorority girl pointed him toward a wooden door. Colette's second office lay on the other side. Steeling himself, he knocked.

"Come in."

It swung open with a horror-movie creak. He found Colette sitting behind a large wooden desk, sifting through a stack of paperwork. She didn't look surprised when she glanced up and saw him there.

"Close the door behind you please."

Josh did. He sat in one of the chairs across from her without asking. "I got the news."

Colette stopped what she was doing. "How are you?"

"Fine." He paused. "Okay, I guess."

"That's better than I expected. Even seasoned pros struggle with the medical issues that come with the job. If it's any consolation, I've seen it all: pregnancies, prolapses, sprains in places you don't want to think about. In the end, everyone pulls through."

Josh nodded. *Doesn't mean I want to deal with it, though.* "I came down here because I thought you might have some advice for me. And because I need to tell you something."

"I dunno about advice." She indicated a card catalog on top of a filing cabinet. "I can give you some pamphlets, if you want. We can discuss your options. There are all sorts of medications these days."

"No, thanks." He took a breath and prepared to deliver the other half of what he'd come here to say.

Before he could speak, however, Colette reached across the desk and laid a paper in front of him.

He leaned forward to look at it. "What's this?"

"A new contract for you, if you want it. I know I can come across as harsh sometimes, but I care about my performers, and I take responsibility for my actions. You wouldn't be in your current predicament if I hadn't assigned you to work with Sean. I recognize that."

Josh shot her a confused look. "So, what does that mean?"

"I can't hire you for the next two weeks. Did Sean tell you that?"

Josh nodded.

"Well, I'm not going to leave you high and dry in the meantime. When I was your age, I worked for a company like mine, only if a performer got injured or pregnant or whatever, they were on their own. We were treated like independent contractors. That's not how things are here. We're a family. We need to support each other." She plucked a highlighter off her desk and made some notations on the paper. "That's why I want to invite you to try something different."

Josh read some of the highlighted bits. He saw the word *webcam* multiple times. "Different?"

"I think we can both agree that porn wasn't for you. Was it?"

Josh fidgeted and shook his head. "That's what I was coming down here to tell you."

"That's perfectly fine. You'd be surprised how many of my employees start out in one medium only to switch to something they like better. Just because porn didn't work out doesn't mean you have to quit."

A spark of excitement ignited in Josh's chest. "It doesn't?"

"Nope. In fact, I'd be surprised if you gave up that easily. One of the reasons I hired you was because of your attitude. You're stubborn, and you want to make money. I like that about you. I'm willing to bet you'd excel as one of my cam boys."

Holy shit. Josh perked up like a puppy who'd caught a whiff of bacon. "You think so? What do cam boys do? How are they paid?"

Colette laughed. "I'll answer the last question first, since I know that's most important. With other companies, cam performers get a cut of the private shows they sell, and tips, but that's not the case here. We pay ours by the hour, *plus* tips, *plus* a cut. The base wage isn't that much more than what waiters and waitresses make, but it'll keep you from starving. If you sell yourself and get some regulars, you can make good money."

Josh frowned. "I dunno. All that marketing crap was kinda what turned me off porn."

"You have to do way less than with porn. Murmur Inc.'s website advertises the cam channels already. All you have to do is get people who are already there to buy private shows from you. You can work as much or as little as you want, but I do recommend you log a minimum of fifteen hours a week."

Fifteen hours? I can do that around my regular job at the Globe. Have some extra money. Josh was starting to get excited about this. "What do I have to do?"

"Honestly? You're gonna masturbate on camera a lot. Clients may ask you to wear special outfits or act out their kinks. You're free to accept or decline on your own terms. We have some rules about what you're allowed to discuss with clients—do *not* talk about politics, for example, and for the love of God, don't give out your personal information—but otherwise, you have total control. You can make your own schedule and choose your own clients." Colette eyed him. "Are you interested?"

"Fuck yeah! It sounds like everything I liked about porn, sans all the stuff I didn't."

"I'm glad. I always joke that anyone can be a sex worker if they find what's right for them. One of my cam girls switched to phone sex the other day, and now she can't keep quiet about it. Literally. And that means there's an opening on our website."

Colette pushed the new contract his way and then added some more documents on top of it. "These are instructions, safety tips, and some rules and guidelines. Take 'em home, read 'em, and then give me a call when you've made a decision."

"Honestly, I'm ready to sign the contract right now. This sounds perfect."

Colette smiled, and for once, all the severity in her face melted away like butter. "I appreciate your enthusiasm, but promise me you'll read what you're getting into and make an informed decision. I may quiz you when you call to be sure."

"Okay." Josh stood up, gathered the papers into the crook of his arm, and then held out his free hand. "Thank you. I know you didn't have a whole lot of faith in me. I'm grateful for the second chance."

Colette stood up as well and gave his hand a firm shake. "Don't thank me too much. I owe you an apology."

Josh was so startled he dropped her hand. "Huh?"

"I shouldn't have pushed you on your first shoot. Obviously there's no way I could have prevented the STI scare that's currently rippling through the community, but I think I could have given you an easier first time on film."

Josh hesitated. "Why didn't you, if you don't mind my asking?"

She shrugged. "Because I misjudged you. Your résumé gave me an idea of you that didn't end up being the truth. Whenever I get 'joke' résumés like yours, it's always from snotty rich kids from the Hills."

"Oh, trust me." Josh waved his hands. "I am *not* rich."

"I realize that now, but I didn't know at the time. Every now and then a trust-fund brat will waltz in here for a laugh, or on a dare, or because they're bored, and it's insufferable. A lot of the people who work for Murmur Inc. are trying to make better lives for themselves. This is one of the few industries where marginalized groups—queer people, people of color, et cetera—can make real money, and even then they end up being fetishized. It's not easy. So when you sashayed into that audition, all cocky and acting like you thought it was a laugh . . ."

Realization settled in Josh's chest like lead. "You thought I was just another kid doing this for kicks. Wow. Looking back, I can't blame you for thinking that."

"Yeah. That still doesn't excuse how hard I was on you, but I hope you can understand where I was coming from."

"No, I get it. You were testing how serious I was, and as it turns out, I wasn't serious about porn at all." He flexed his fingers on the papers he had nestled against his chest. "But I think I could be serious about a side job in cam work. I'll let you know once I've read all this."

"I look forward to your call. Oh, and Dick?"

"What?"

"Pick a different stage name, or I'm pulling out the pink slips."

CHAPTER 8

Three days into Mike's new, abstinent existence, he was already starting to itch.

He hadn't realized how much he'd come to rely on having regular access to sex. He hadn't thought of porn as being in the same genre as sex. It was work. A perfunctory task he performed along with things like going to the grocery store and getting his tires rotated. It was analogous to how a waiter who spent all day on their feet might not consider that a workout.

But by the fourth day, his itch had developed into a full-blown rash. It'd gotten to the point where he'd started being hyperaware of how much sex was in advertisements. Every time he saw a billboard with a naked torso on it, he twitched. Plus, without work to fill his schedule, he was left with more free time than he'd had since his college days.

He did a decent job of occupying himself at first. He got reacquainted with his apartment complex's pool. Tanning wasn't an option, due to his freckled complexion, but it was good to get some vitamin D. He tried new protein shake recipes, and he meal-prepped enough chicken and brown rice to feed him for a week. He even delved into the depths of his Murmur Inc. email account and got to some long-overdue responses. But when all that was finished, he was still left with far too much time to sit around with his own thoughts.

This had led him to an uncomfortable realization: over the course of the past three years, his life had come to center around Murmur Inc. When he wasn't working, he was thinking about work. He'd previously spent his free time going to the gym to keep his body in peak form and marketing himself online. He had every kind of social media there was, and he interacted with his fan base daily.

His handful of friends were also in sex work, and while they were sympathetic when they heard news of his quarantine—the sex industry's rumor mill was one of the greatest in the world—none of them volunteered to pop by with chicken soup.

He couldn't blame them. The last time he'd shown up for a night out, Rio had been hosting the World Cup. He detested clubbing, and that seemed to be all anyone in this town wanted to do.

Still, he needed to do *something*, or he was going to get cabin fever in his own apartment. He was so restless, he almost considered calling his parents. That was the definition of "desperate times." They'd never even been to his place. He could imagine his dad's snide remarks about how Mike had forgotten his trailer-trash roots and was too fancy for them now.

I'll take a rain check on that particular conversation.

That wasn't the worst result of his sabbatical, though. The more time he had to think, the more he realized how often he thought about Josh. It'd made sense before, when they were working together, or when Mike was concocting a tactful way to deliver bad news to him, but now it was getting ridiculous. He thought about him when he was cooking, and he wondered what sort of food Josh liked. He thought about him when he was getting dressed, and he remembered Josh's terrible Christmas sweater with odd fondness. And most alarmingly, Mike thought about him before he fell asleep at night.

His musings were split into two camps. Part of him was still racked with guilt every time he thought about the situation he'd put Josh in. There was a chance Josh was never going to speak to him again after this, supported by the fact that he'd hung up on him the other day. Mike knew Josh must've been in shock, but he still thought it was further proof that Josh was a grade-A brat.

Another part of him, however, wanted to see Josh again so badly he ached. And not just because Josh was the last person he'd slept with before he'd been condemned to celibacy. Though that certainly played a role in it. Josh might not ever get a chance to star in one of Murmur Inc.'s blockbusters, but he'd had a starring role in Mike's fantasies every night.

Whenever Mike closed his eyes, Josh was there. Spread out over a mattress, naked and panting and flushed. Sometimes he was on his back with his cock jutting straight up from his body, quivering and leaking. Sometimes he was on his stomach with his legs spread wide enough for Mike to kneel between them, whimpering while Mike fingered him into a quivering mess. But most of the time, Mike's fantasies took advantage of Josh's light build and had Josh straddling him, riding Mike's cock while his thighs flexed and his back arched, moaning and crying out and shaking when he—

Mike, who had been in the process of scrubbing his already-pristine kitchen counters, dropped the sponge with an exasperated sigh. He was wearing sweatpants, thank God, because for the third time that day alone, he was hard. Fuck. If he kept masturbating at this rate, he was going to give himself a friction burn.

He took a deep breath, picked the sponge back up, and willed his erection to go away. It worked. For one whole minute. Then Josh sprang back into his thoughts, and the cycle began anew.

"What is it about him?" he asked his empty apartment.

It was a question that had plagued him from pretty much the moment they'd met. The more he interacted with Josh, the more he thought he was zeroing in on an answer. Ever since the HIV scare, Mike had learned something new about the blond-haired center of his attention. He'd learned Josh was steady in a crisis—or at least, as steady as could be expected—and that he was not above brushing Mike off.

There had been a part of Mike that had hoped they'd bond over their mutual worries in the time between now and when they got tested, but he hadn't heard a peep from Josh since their phone call. He could only pray the very experience that he'd hoped would bring them together wasn't about to drive them further apart.

That might be another part of why he couldn't get Josh out of his head. It'd been a long time since Mike had gotten rejected. Not since he started working out in high school and got the confidence to match his new body. Plus, he'd *never* been rejected by someone who'd seen his dick. Josh was full of surprises.

"You're acting like a lovesick puppy," he muttered to himself as he washed off his hands and dried them on a kitchen towel.

Something had to give. All this pining with no action behind it wasn't his style. If he were certain Josh wasn't pissed at him, he'd call him up and ask him out again. But the ball was in Josh's court, and so Mike was stranded on Lovewreck Island until Josh made a move.

Doesn't mean you gotta stay home and sit by the phone. You still have your pride, Harwood. You're not gonna wait around for some guy. Get off your ass and find a good use for your time.

With a sigh, he finished up in the kitchen and climbed the spiral staircase leading up to the loft. There, his little home office awaited him. He sunk into his squishy office chair, fired up his desktop, and opened a multi-tab browser window that had all his usual sites ready and waiting.

Mike had majored in marketing in college, before he'd ever given porn a shot. Once upon a time, he'd had dreams of going into advertising. Now, he used his social-media savvy to ensure his new head shots got at least a thousand likes on Instagram.

It's funny how life works out.

Mike had already hit his marketing goals for the day, but he burned an hour going through new Facebook likes and comments. He had some threads going on Murmur Inc.'s Facebook, but there was also his personal page to peruse.

When that was finished, he moved on to the task he'd been dreading: checking his voice mail. He'd gotten several phone calls from people he'd performed with pre-Nickiegate. He was willing to bet Colette had delivered the news to them, and they weren't taking it as well as Josh had. What happened to good old-fashioned killing the messenger? Why'd they have to blame him?

Sure enough, three of the voice mails were from Aaron Cooper, a gay-for-pay straight guy that Mike had done a barebacking scene with. And he was *not* happy. Mike hadn't heard that many gay slurs since the last time he'd been in a locker room.

Mike deleted the voice mail halfway through, listened to the rest, and did the same. Then he moved on with his life. There was nothing else he could do. If an edge of guilt still gnawed at him, it was overshadowed by how many of his own worries he had to deal with.

When he'd checked everything he could check, he navigated to Murmur Inc.'s website. He wanted to see what new faces Colette had gotten to fill in while a chunk of her usual roster was out of commission.

Sure enough, when the homepage loaded, there was a big flash banner at the top announcing the arrival of Murmur Inc.'s newest stars. Several of them were faces Mike recognized from the most recent orientations. Others must have been bandage hires, because he'd never seen them around and their head shots weren't up to Colette's usual quality standards.

Mike scanned the list twice, looking for one face in particular, and frowned. Josh was absent from the lineup.

Did he already quit? I remember he talked about it, but I didn't think he'd just . . . disappear.

Mike's stomach sank. Even if Josh *had* quit, his videos should still be up. Colette would never throw out good footage, and porn stars quit all the time. Had Josh asked that she take them down? If he'd made a piteous enough case, she might have taken the loss. Mike knew of a couple of occasions where a shooting star had begged for their footage to never hit the internet, and Colette had obliged. Her frozen CEO heart was capable of bleeding.

Why would Josh do that, though? Mike supposed it was none of his business. If that was the decision Josh had made, it was his own. There was something unsettling, however, about having every trace of their time together erased. Mike had planned on watching their videos. For research, of course.

Liar.

He gave himself a small shake, trying to dispel the ennui that had crept over him. If Josh's videos were gone, and he'd quit Murmur Inc., there was nothing left tying them together. Josh could ghost him, and that would be the end of that. It'd be like they'd never met at all. The disappointment that seeped into Mike was so cold it burned.

Jesus. When had he gotten so damn maudlin?

He forced himself to move on, checking the announcements on the front page and the new releases. Several big summer blowouts were available, including a few Mike wanted to see: *Lesbian Vampire Strippers*, *My Best Friend's Boyfriend*, and *Heat Wave*. All of them promised to be huge hits.

There were a couple of his own new releases on the site as well. He watched the teasers for them with mild interest. Most people who worked in film claimed that it was always an experience to see themselves how the camera saw them, but that wasn't the case for Mike. When he filmed a scene, the majority of his mannerisms were affected. He did whatever looked good on camera, and after three years, he had it down to a science.

He checked the time. He'd only managed to kill two hours. With a sigh, he pulled his phone out of his pocket and placed it on the desk next to his wireless keyboard. If anyone else called him to throw a fit, he might answer out of sheer boredom.

There were plenty of parts of Murmur Inc.'s site that he never ventured on. He could take a tour while he had time to kill. He clicked on the Live Cam portion of the website first. Despite some obvious resemblances, porn and cam acting were so different, Mike avoided the live streams. Didn't want to pick up on any bad habits. It'd be like asking a mime to teach him to juggle—similar, but not the same thing. Though he supposed it couldn't hurt this once.

In fact, it might do him some good to see how his fellow sex workers earned their keep. A handful of the channels had free general chats where prospective clients could talk with the stars before deciding to buy a private show.

When the page loaded, the most popular cam girls popped up front and center. Their channels featured photos of them in obscene poses with brief biographies. Mike recognized a few of the big names in the industry, but he'd never worked with any of them.

He spent a minute or two scrolling through the available women's channels before toggling over to the other gender options. He selected *men* and then checked his phone while the new page loaded. He had a handful of Facebook notifications and a Snapchat from another male porn star. Nothing of real interest.

The site loaded, and Mike glanced at it. For a second, he didn't process what he was seeing. Then understanding crystalized in his brain.

There were three new male webcam models, and one of them looked decidedly familiar.

Mike stared open-mouthed at a memorable photo of a clean-cut blond man standing next to a horse. And not just because it was an unusual choice for a cam model's cover photo. Josh would have stood out in the sea of shirtless, ripped men even if Mike hadn't recognized him.

Colette must not have had time to take head shots of him, or maybe she'd decided to roll with the wholesome, shined-shoes Americana thing he had going on. Now that Mike was looking at the photo again, he remembered it was what had first attracted him to Josh. There was something so pure about it, so guileless. If that was Colette's marketing angle, it wasn't a bad one. Plenty of people went for that whole boy-next-door thing.

Yeah, people like you.

This answered some of Mike's questions. If Josh had chosen to go into cam work instead of porn, then his absence from the main website made sense. A newbie couldn't try to corner both the porn and cam markets at the same time. It split their focus, and clients didn't tend to cross from one to the other, so his fan base would get split as well.

It raised some questions too, though. Cam stars didn't work from location like porn stars did, or from the office like the phone sex operators. They could work from anywhere. Josh might be the only one on Murmur Inc.'s page who was from LA, which made it strange that Mike could see him at all. Cam stars had the ability to block viewers by geographic location. The smart ones blocked their entire home cities so no one they knew would stumble upon them by accident.

Why then was Josh—

Mike didn't finish that thought. "Fucking newbie."

He scrubbed a hand down his face. *Of course*, Josh was too green to block the city where he lived. He might not even know that was an option. Colette would have explained it to him, or at least given him some info packets describing how to use the feature, but Mike would bet money Josh hadn't thought it was necessary. Of all the irresponsible, reckless—

He took a breath.

He forced his eyes away from the photo to the name of Josh's channel. It said it starred Bret Monty. So, Dick Reams had gotten the ax. Thank God. Mike suspected that was Colette's handiwork. She'd done it at the right time too. If Josh had gone public with his other name, he would have been stuck with it. Since he was new, he could still do things like switch names and mediums without losing all brand recognition.

So, the moral of the story here is Josh is still with Murmur Inc. He's become a cam star.

Mike's eyes drifted to the green "live" light next to Josh's channel, indicating that he was online right now. If Mike wanted to, he could see him again without having to leave his home.

The mouse was in Mike's hand before he could think about it. His computer had the room up and loaded in seconds, but it felt like a lifetime. A screen popped up, displaying the camera feed and the chat box where clients could chat with the star and each other.

Sure enough, that was Josh.

He was smiling—bright, white, and wide—and for a moment, the sight of his unguarded expression stunned Mike. Josh's mouth moved, and Mike realized his sound was off. He scrambled to turn up his speakers just in time to hear Josh say something.

"Yeah, I'm from LA. I've never lived anywhere else."

He must have been responding to a client's question. Mike checked the chat box. There were thirteen users in the channel, and several of them were shooting rapid-fire questions at Josh—or Bret. Personal ones.

"Damn it, Josh," Mike muttered. "You're not supposed to give away information about yourself."

Mike typed that into the comment box and hit Send. Josh was oscillating between reading the messages and looking into the camera. Mike watched his eyes dart down to the chat, and a little frown worked its way onto his brow.

Did he read my message?

"Oops," Josh said. "Sorry guys, I just remembered I can't answer certain questions about myself. You can ask me other things, though."

That confirmed it. Man, it felt good to talk to Josh again, even if it was anonymous.

Of course, the predators in the channel were none-too-thrilled by Mike's interference. Comments poured in.

Let Bret tell us what he wants.

What are you, his mom?

Spoil sport. :P

"Fucking creeps." Mike sat back and ran a hand through his hair. Speaking of creeps, what the hell was he doing?

You're looking out for him. And good thing too. Knowing Josh, he probably would have told these guys his social security number, if they asked.

It still felt weird. Here he was, watching Josh same as the rest of the clients. Or potential clients, as it were. None of them had paid for a private show from Josh yet, or he'd have gone offline. Josh would have to entice them into it. Most of the cam stars put on mini-shows, like stripteases or small sex acts. The thought made Mike go from irritated to turned on in a flash.

Watching Josh on the cam, he understood why Colette had chosen such an organic cover photo for him. He was sitting there, relaxed and natural, in a tiny room that was probably his bedroom. He hadn't even put on sexy clothes. Just jeans and a T-shirt that somehow looked flawless on him. Hell, his *hair* was wet, like he'd recently gotten out of the shower.

A hard-core porn consumer would think Josh was a genius. He had not-trying-too-hard nailed to the wall. But that was the funny thing. Mike knew he genuinely wasn't trying. This wasn't Josh putting on a brilliant show of being natural. This was him having no clue what he was doing. And it *worked.* It especially worked on Mike, who was watching a bead of water slide down his temple like it was rapturous.

Judging by the comments, the other people in the channel were eating it up too.

ur so hott

Did u just get out of the shower?

tell us more baby

Mike watched the comments stream by for a moment, half listening to Josh's responses, before peering at what he could see of the room behind Josh. There was a TWENTY ØNE PILØTS poster by Josh's head, a pile of dirty laundry on the floor, and peeling paint on the walls. Mike could also see the corner of a stack of books that looked like textbooks. Josh had never mentioned school, but he was twenty-one. It was possible he was enrolled in college, or he'd at least completed some of it.

A lot of cam stars had separate spaces that they used for work. Josh wasn't slick enough for something like that, but he could be in a friend or roommate's room. Though the room felt like him, somehow.

The things in it—the bands and the books and the laundry—seemed like things he would own. If this was his room, and these were his belongings, then Mike had gotten his first inside peek at Josh's home life. Mike had a sudden, burning desire to know for sure.

His fingers were on the keyboard in an instant.

Is this your bedroom, Bret?

To everyone in the chat room, including Josh, it would sound like another suggestive message. And indeed, that was precisely how it was received.

"Yeah." Josh grinned. "In all its glory. Pardon the mess."

That inspired a slew of comments that even Mike found obscene about what sorts of messes Josh made in his room. A strange emotion swirled in his stomach as he watched all the anonymous people clamoring for Josh's attention.

For a horrifying second, he thought it was jealousy, but the more he probed at it, the more he realized it was deeper than that. He didn't care that other men were talking to Josh. Josh was working, same as Mike did. They all had bills to pay, and if these chat room guys wanted to pay them, so be it.

It was more . . . the way Josh looked. So serene and laid-back. His inexperience couldn't be more obvious, but he still seemed a hundred percent comfortable. Way more comfortable than he'd ever seemed when he was filming porn. With Mike.

That was it. Understanding settled on Mike like cold sweat. That was what was bothering him. When they'd filmed together, Josh had been a jittery mess. He'd never been at ease, even when they were fucking. Mike had made a lot of mistakes with Josh. He'd recognized that almost immediately, and he'd done his best to atone for it. But the biggest one he'd made was thinking Josh wasn't cut out for this business. He was. He just wasn't cut out for *porn*.

It seemed Mike's time would have been better spent not mentoring him on how to be a porn star, but how to be in this business in general. And how to block your own damn city from getting your channel.

There was also a special irony to the fact that Mike had schooled Josh on professionalism and separating business from pleasure, when here he was, in Josh's channel, being decidedly unprofessional.

It was becoming harder and harder to tell himself that he didn't have it bad for this guy.

His phone found its way into his hand before his brain registered the movement. He found Josh's name in his contacts and stared at it as a plan solidified in his head.

Before he let himself like Josh—for real like him, no denying it or acting like he was doing his job—he had to know if Josh shared so much as an inkling of his feelings.

It was a long shot, but he had an idea that might allow him to find out.

Josh had hung up on him the last time they'd spoken. If Mike called him right now, even Josh wasn't inexperienced enough to answer the phone during a session. But what if Mike texted him? If Josh's phone was near him, Mike might get to see, in real time, how Josh reacted to getting an unexpected text from him. The thought made him salivate.

This is beyond creepy, Michael Harwood.

I know, he answered his own mental voice, *but I have to know.*

He composed a simple text message, asking how Josh was doing. He seldom used emojis, but Josh seemed like the sort of person who would like them, and so he tagged a winking face onto the end and hit Send.

Not three seconds later, Josh paused after answering a question and reached into his pocket. His hand reappeared with his phone clutched between long fingers.

Mike held his breath. He leaned forward in his chair and watched as Josh's green eyes roved over the single line of text. And then, like a golden dawn sweeping over a grassy knoll, Josh's face broke out into a smile.

Not just any smile either. Possibly the most beautiful smile Mike had ever seen. Soft and damn near radiant. Mike wasn't the poetic sort, but he could write a verse or two about the look on Josh's face. It . . .

Well, fuck. If Mike didn't know any better, he'd say it looked a little bit like love.

It was gone in an instant, a candle flame flickering out. Josh put his phone back in his pocket without answering. Mike experienced a brief twinge of rejection, but it wasn't as if Josh could respond while he was working. The clients in the chat room were already commenting about him checking his phone at all. Mike would have to be patient and see if he responded to him later.

It occurred to Mike that in all this time, no one had paid for a private show with Josh. That wasn't unheard of, but Josh was also doing nothing to draw them in. Cam channels weren't meant to be like interviews. The clients had only been entertained this far because Josh was new, and they wanted to know about him. When Josh failed to do anything more interesting than sit there, they'd get bored and move on.

Mike knew from his handful of friends who did cam work that Murmur Inc. gave cam stars a base pay, but it was a pittance. If Josh was going to make any money, he'd need to learn the ropes. And he *needed* to make money to keep Colette from firing him. All her employees had goals and metrics they were held accountable to. She wouldn't keep paying Josh to run a free channel that never landed any clients.

Mike was done being a pseudo-mentor to Josh, but there was one surefire way he could still help him. He could get him off the ground and keep Colette off his back. At least, until Josh figured things out for himself. Which he was sure to do, judging by what a natural he seemed to be.

Mike pulled his wallet out of his back pocket and took out his credit card. If he was going to be a creep, he was going to do it thoroughly.

CHAPTER 9

"It's been *years* since I've been out." Josh leaned his head back and breathed in deep. "Nothing like getting some fresh air."

Monica chuckled next to him. "If this is your idea of fresh air, *papi*, you've lived in the city too long."

Her words were almost drowned out by the pounding bass pouring from the nearby speakers. Twist—the gay club they'd made their home for the night—was packed wall-to-wall with bodies. Even for a Saturday, the turnout was fierce. They'd managed to snag a pub table to stand around, but now they were holding on to it for dear life. Darius and Ashley had made a trip to the bar while Josh, Monica, and Josh's roommates guarded their real estate.

"I don't understand why we always have to go to gay bars," Will huffed. In camouflage cargo pants and a Lakers jersey, he stuck out from the sea of glittery club wear around him like a neon *I'm Straight* sign. Which was ironic, considering the camo.

"No one forced you to come." A.J. threw a beefy arm around him. "You might as well enjoy yourself." His eyes moved from Will's face to a group of nearby guys who were staring at his flexed muscles. Rather than lower his arm, he brought his other one up to join it, posturing like a peacock.

"Dude, you're straight," Chris said, pushing his black bangs out of his eyes. "Why are you always showing off your body when we come here?"

"Is it so wrong of me to want all my hard work to be admired?" He finally removed his arm from around Will, but he moved at a snail's pace so the guys could get a good look. "I spend five days a week at the gym, and by God, I am going to get hit on tonight."

Chris shook his head. "I worry about you."

Ashley appeared next to Chris. "We come bearing alcohol!" In her arms were three beer bottles and a glass of red wine. She set the drinks on the table, paused to peck Monica on the cheek, and then distributed the alcohol. "Darius should be right behind me."

"I'm here, sug." Darius, who had opted to show some beautiful dark skin with a pink mesh top and black sequin booty shorts, glided up to the table. "Enjoy, ya lushes." He had two more beers, which he divvied up between Ashley and himself, and a wine cooler that made its way to Josh.

"Thanks, guys." Josh took a generous swig.

Monica made a sour face, but the effect was diminished by the bright-pink kiss mark her girlfriend had left on her brown cheek. "I don't know how you can drink those things. Just thinking about it gives me a hangover."

"What can I say?" He shrugged. "Tastes like candy, whereas beer tastes like fermented piss."

"You're the last person in the world who needs to be sugared up."

"Stop judging me."

In truth, Josh was too embarrassed to admit the real reason he was drinking these: they were cheaper than cocktails, and he was broke. He hadn't been back at the Globe long enough to get a paycheck yet, and cam work was harder than he'd thought it would be. He'd only booked a handful of private shows in the entire week he'd been at it. He had to be doing something wrong.

I bet Mike could give me some pointers.

Not for the first time that evening, Josh's thoughts turned to his former costar. Ever since Mike had texted him out of the blue, all Josh seemed to do was think about him. The text had been simple, and yet Josh had still managed to overanalyze the fuck out of it.

Was Mike checking up on him in general? Was he seeing how he was doing after the bad news he'd dumped on him? Why had he chosen to send a *winking* emoji? Josh had never been the academic sort, but he was quite certain he could write a dissertation on that five-word text.

After hanging up on him, Josh had planned to let Mike stew for a few days before he reopened communication, but the surprise message had startled him into having a brief but pleasant exchange.

Mike had seemed different somehow. Smoother, in the sense that some of his rough edges had been sanded down. He'd seemed genuinely interested in how Josh was doing, and not just in terms of sex work. He'd asked about Josh's family and friends and if he had any plans for the weekend. It was . . . normal. The first normal thing that Josh could claim had happened between them.

It also reaffirmed in Josh's head that there was something between them. Something worth exploring, even after the handful of disasters they'd been through. He didn't know what Mike's intentions were toward him—and one text conversation did not a relationship make—but he wanted to find out.

Darius waved a hand in front of his face. "Did the sugar short-circuit your brain or something?"

Josh snapped back to the smoky pink and blue reality that was the club. "Sorry, I was thinking."

"About what?"

"His new boyfriend," Chris cut in.

Josh spat some of his drink back into the bottle. "What?"

"I share a wall with you, dude. I've heard you talking to someone at all hours of the night."

Oh fuck, he's heard me doing webcam sessions. How much did he hear?

Chris continued. "No clue what you're saying, but the only person you'd spend that much time on the phone with is a boyfriend."

Josh's heart started beating again. "Oh, no. That's not what you think." As soon as the words were out of his mouth, he wanted to shove them back in.

"Then what is it?"

Ashley and Monica both turned to look at him. Darius leaned on the table, propping his chin on a fist. Even Will stopped scowling long enough to give him a curious look.

Fuck my life and my big mouth.

"It's nothing." Josh took another sip to calm his nerves, which had frayed like fine rope in the span of ten seconds. He hadn't planned on telling his friends about his secret double life. It wasn't like he was *ashamed* or anything. But he wasn't sure he wanted them to know. And he *definitely* didn't want to answer the hundreds of probing questions they'd ask him. Plus, there was a chance his roommates wouldn't like the idea of him performing sex acts for an audience under the same roof as them.

Fuck. It would have been best if he'd kept his trap shut, but now that they'd scented blood in the water, they weren't going to leave him alone. He had to give them something.

"All right. You caught me." He set his bottle down on the table and raised his voice over the new, much louder song that had started playing. "There is a guy, but he's not my boyfriend." He went in for the kill. "Not yet, anyway."

The collective gasps from his friends were every bit as overdramatic as he'd expected. Monica even pretended to swoon into Ashley's already-waiting arms. Relationship goals.

"Tell us about him." Darius shimmied with excitement. Bent over the table as he was in his tiny shorts, the movement attracted plenty of attention. But when a man screwed up the nerve to approach, Darius shooed him away and looked back at Josh. "Spare no detail. What's his name? How did you meet?"

Oh shit. I didn't think this through.

"Um, his name is Mike. We met online." It wasn't a total lie. Murmur Inc.'s website was what had brought them together. "It's not as serious as I made it seem, though. We haven't been on a date yet."

Ashley's eyes gleamed. "Have you hooked up?"

Shit. Can't get anything past her.

"Well . . ."

More melodramatic gasping.

Will clapped his hands over his ears. "If you're gonna talk about butt sex, I'm leaving."

"Not me." A.J. held up his beer. "I'm here for you, bro. Bring on the gay."

"Seconded," Monica and Ashley said in unison.

Josh frowned. "I don't want to talk about it. Hell, I don't know *how*. It's—"

Darius groaned. "If you say complicated, I'ma smack you."

"Well, it is."

"Tell us what he's like, then." Monica waved a manicured finger at Darius. "Tall? Dark? Handsome? Nice? Funny?"

"Kinda cranky, to be honest. The way he talks sometimes, you'd think he was in his fifties instead of his twenties. He's cynical too. And proud. But protective, in a weird way. He gets all gruff when he's worried you're gonna hurt yourself. Like a muscular, red-headed bear. A sexy one." Josh eyed his drink. "I might have had too much."

"Does he treat you well?"

"That's . . . kind of a tough question."

Monica's dark eyes flashed like a blade's edge. "*Papi*, if he's not being good to you, I volunteer to hunt him down."

"I didn't mean it like that. It's just, when I first met him, I thought he was all business. Total ice king. But the more time I spent with him, the more I realized he was trying to help me. In fact, pretty much everything he did was to keep me from getting hurt."

Ashley frowned. "Hurt? By him, or what?"

Josh swallowed a frustrated sound. Explaining this without explaining it was beyond him when he was three drinks deep. "Never mind. Forget I said anything. The point is, he's a good guy, and I'm hoping I'll get to see more of him." *Though I've seen a lot already.*

"Well, I'm confused." Darius shrugged. "But if you like him, I'm sure we will too. When do we get to meet him?"

"Um . . ."

In a paragon of perfect timing, someone knocked into Josh's arm. Josh stumbled over his clubbing boots but caught himself before he went sprawling.

"My bad. I'm sorry." A dark-haired man reached for him as if to help him up. "Are you okay?"

"Yeah, I'm fine. No worries." Josh's eyes widened as they dipped down the guy's body and darted back up to his face. *Holy shit, he's hot.*

The guy must've noticed Josh scoping him out, because he grinned. "Let me make it up to you. I'll buy you a drink."

Free booze. Score. Josh turned away from his bottled sugar with glee. "Sure. I was about to get one myself." He made it all of three steps before someone yanked him back. "Ow! What the—"

"What do you think you're doing?" Monica hissed in his ear. "You told us you're into someone else."

He lowered his voice. "It's not like that." After years of clubbing, Josh's brain was hot-wired to accept free alcohol without question. Especially since he'd been too young to buy it for himself until recently. "I'll be good, okay? I just want the drink."

Hot Guy raised a thick eyebrow. "Everything all right?"

"Yeah." Josh pulled out of Monica's grasp. "Lead the way."

They cut through the pulsating crowd with minimal resistance. The bodies melded around them, welcoming them into the hot, sweaty fold. It wasn't until they reached the bar that they encountered resistance. It was *slammed*.

Hot Guy brought his lips to Josh's ear, purportedly so he could hear him. "While I flag down a bartender, why don't you tell me your name? And what you'd like?"

"Josh, and I'll take a . . ." He racked his brain for a cocktail he'd never pay for on his own. "Manhattan."

"*Ooh*, que fancy. I'm Ray." Ray managed to snag the attention of a bartender and placed their orders, bending over the bar to be heard. Josh took the opportunity to sneak a peek at his ass.

Yup. Definitely hot. But not Mike.

Orders placed, Ray faced him and smiled. "You from around here?"

Josh nodded. "Born and raised. I'm an LA devotee. You?"

"I'm from your cocktail."

Josh's alcohol-infused brain trundled its way through that sentence. "You're from Manhattan?"

"Yup. You know how you can tell if someone's from New York?"

"How?"

"They can't go ten minutes without saying they're from New York."

Josh laughed so hard he teared up a little. The bartender appeared with their drinks.

Ray paid for them, scooped them up, and handed Josh's to him. "Did you come here with those people I saw you with?"

"Yeah, those are my friends and roommates. Are you out with friends?"

"No, I came here by myself." Ray gave him a smile that was dripping with suggestion.

Josh, who spoke fluent gay, didn't need a decoder ring to figure out what that meant. *He's looking for a hookup.* Josh took a sip of his drink to mask his sudden nerves.

As he was struggling not to blurt out something awkward, Ray stepped closer.

"I'm not usually this forward, but I'm having a rough night, and you're hot. What do you say we ditch your friends and get out of here?"

Josh blinked. "Wow, that was direct."

"Sorry. I got dumped the other day, and I haven't dated in a long time. But I've heard the best way to get over someone is to get under someone else. Up for it?"

Josh opened his mouth only to close it again. Two weeks ago, he would have said hell yeah. But now, all he could think about was Mike. It was ridiculous, of course. They weren't dating. Hell, they weren't anything. But he couldn't help it. Sleeping with Ray would feel like a betrayal, and not just to Mike, but to his own feelings.

What was he going to say, though? *Sorry, I can't. I have a non-boyfriend.* Ray would think he was blowing him off, and he didn't want to hurt the guy's feelings. Maybe there was another excuse he could use. Hadn't Colette said he shouldn't sleep with anyone until he got tested?

He seized onto that with both hands. "I'm sorry, but I can't have sex for at least another week."

Ray furrowed his brow. "Is it Lent, and no one told me?"

"No, I need to get tested. I might have HIV."

The effect his words had was instant and explosive.

Ray backed away from him, eyes wide. "Holy shit, dude. What the fuck?"

Josh bit his lip. That reaction seemed a little extreme. "What's the big deal? I'm just being honest." He held out his hand. "Friends?"

Ray looked like Josh had offered him a bomb. "Don't touch me. I don't want to catch anything from you."

"You can't get HIV from shaking—"

But Ray had already turned away and was pushing through the crowd. It seemed like he was trying to put as much distance between them as he could. Josh didn't chase after him. He was caught between confusion and rejection. Ray's reaction was way over the top.

It reminded him of how the jocks in high school would react when he told them he was gay. Back then, it'd seemed like they hated him, but Josh understood now that they were scared of shit they didn't understand.

It's not personal. It's not about you. He needs to work through his own ignorance.

It was true, but it didn't make him feel less like a mutant.

Josh trudged back over to the table. Monica, Will, and A.J. were missing—it was their turn to get drinks, no doubt—but the others were still there. Ashley took one look at him and pursed her neon-pink lips. "What's wrong?"

"Nothing. I'm just exhausted all of a sudden."

"What happened to that guy?"

"He left. Good riddance." Josh took the drink Ray had bought him and knocked it back, as if to destroy the evidence that he'd ever been there.

Darius looked between him and the empty glass. "Whatever you say."

Chris touched his shoulder. "You wanna go home? We can split a cab."

"Home sounds phenomenal. Do you think Will and A.J. will be pissed?"

"Nah, they found some straight girls having a bachelorette party. They'll be fine. I'll go get us a cab. Meet me outside?"

"Right behind you." Josh glanced at his friends. "Will you tell the others where I went?"

"Sure thing," Ashley said. "But you know Monica's gonna call you later, right? She'll expect full details."

"And that's why God invented the Reject Call button." He pecked her on the cheek. "Enjoy the rest of your night. You too, Darius."

He slipped away before they could ask any more questions. It was a cool, clear night, though this far into city center, stars were never visible. Josh was wearing one of his tamer club outfits: tight faux leather pants and a slashed black shirt. It provided almost no insulation against the wind. Good thing this was California. Even at night, it was hotter than noon in New York.

Don't think about New York.

Chris was standing by the curb with a cab idling next to him.

Josh hurried over. "I dunno how you always manage to find a cab in two seconds flat no matter where we are."

Chris opened the back door and climbed in. "We're in the nightlife district. The cabs know this is where the drunk people live."

Josh laughed, giving their address to the cab driver between giggles. Chris wasn't the chatty sort, which was perfect. He didn't ask Josh about Ray or make small talk. Fifteen minutes later, they were home. Chris invited Josh to play some *Call of Duty* with him, but Josh declined, claiming he was exhausted. In truth, after the rejection at the club, he was looking for a nice hit of self-esteem, and he knew exactly where to get it.

When he got to his room, he didn't bother changing out of his clothes. His club outfits were always a hit with the clients. He glanced at the clock on his nightstand. It was after midnight, which for most jobs would be slow, but as Josh had discovered, it was prime time in the sex industry.

He switched on a lamp for some mood lighting, flopped onto his bed, and opened his laptop. The portal he used to log in to his channel was already loaded. A few minutes later, a screen popped up, showing his account information and a window with his camera feed. He checked himself out. Sweaty and a little disheveled, but his clients would like that.

When he was ready, he set his status to *online*. Within seconds, people popped into his chat. He grinned as he watched his channel fill up. Colette had told him that when he was no longer a new face, he'd have to rely on repeat customers, but for now, he loved seeing all these people clamor for his attention.

Their comments were exactly what he needed too.

u look hot tonight bret

Very sexxi. Did u go out?

bet you got hit on, dressed like that

It had taken Josh some time to get used to how everything worked, even with Colette's instructions. He logged in to Murmur Inc.'s website with his employee ID, he loaded the chat, marked himself as available, and boom. His webcam turned on, and hopefully so did his clients.

Anyone who logged in to the free public chat could see and hear him, but Josh couldn't see them. If the clients wanted to communicate, they had to type in the chat box, or buy a private session with him. Josh could type too, but that option was used by people who didn't speak English well or flat-out didn't want to talk. As it just so happened, Josh loved to talk.

"Hey, guys." Josh affected the deep, sexy voice he used when camming. Remembering what his roommates had said earlier, he kept his volume down. "I was out at a club tonight. Wanna see more of my outfit?"

That got a round of affirmations. Josh climbed off the bed and stood back so most of his body was visible in the cam window. He did a slow turn, pushing his ass out and lifting up the hem of his shirt like he was going to take it off. He couldn't read what his clients were saying, but judging by the speed with which responses were flying up the screen, they liked what they saw.

Josh grinned. Cam work had its ups and downs, like any job, but it was always good for a confidence boost.

A moment later, a notification pinged on his screen. Someone had bought a private show with him. Jackpot.

Josh hurried back to his laptop and clicked Accept. The chat screen minimized while a new screen popped up. Josh squinted at the process. He was still getting used to how it worked. If someone bought a show from him, it put him offline and opened a new window. The client—or clients; group shows were an option—could then choose to turn on their webcam or simply type to Josh, depending on what they wanted.

The handle of the person who'd bought the show flashed onto the screen: gingersnap93. Josh knew it well. It belonged to a man who called himself "Martin." He was the closest thing to a regular that Josh had, and he was ... Well, he was a bit odd.

Josh had given a dozen private shows since he'd started doing cam work, and he'd learned that clients wanted one thing: to watch him get off. Sometimes they got off with him, ordering him to watch them masturbate, or they wanted him to use toys on himself. But at the end of the day, it was always the same thing.

Except with Martin, a mild-mannered LA native who only ever wanted to talk.

Josh didn't know if he was ugly or shy or what, but Martin never turned on his cam. He never asked Josh to strip or touch himself or talk dirty to him. Nothing. They just had regular conversations for hour-intervals at a time.

Josh had never thought that there would come a day when talking to a man would seem odder to him than getting off with him, but that was the case here. Martin was an enigma wrapped in a mystery.

Stranger still, Martin had claimed he was in sex work as well. He'd never said what kind, but it was clear he was knowledgeable about the industry. And he was from LA as well.

Josh had spent a whole session with him talking about his disastrous foray into porn, and Martin had listened with infinite patience. He'd even offered Josh some tips on how to be safe and successful in cam work. Josh now knew how to hold shows for multiple customers at a time, and that if a client harassed him, he could boot him from the chat. They might get blacklisted by Murmur Inc. if what they'd done was bad enough.

Josh appreciated Martin's insight, but he couldn't figure out what the other guy got out of their chats. They seemed to benefit Josh way more than they did him, and they weren't cheap. Josh had offered no fewer than a dozen times to do *something* for him, but Martin refused every time.

There was a chance Martin was simply lonely. Either way, Josh wasn't complaining. He was a cool guy, and the money was great. Plus, they'd talked about *everything*. Books, movies, their favorite foods, what albums they'd take with them to a deserted island. Even their families. Martin had a complicated relationship with his father, to say the least, and Josh couldn't remember the last time he'd sat down and called his mom.

It was strange, but although he had no idea who Martin was or what he looked like, Josh almost had a little crush on him. But then, everything he said about himself could be a lie, and Josh was still hung up on Mike. Sigh. He'd never thought that one day he'd be so committed to a nonexistent relationship with a prolific porn star who might have given him HIV.

What *was* his life these days?

The screens finished arranging themselves, and the private show began.

Josh greeted Martin as he always did. "Evening, Martin. How was your day?"

An ellipsis popped up, indicating that Martin was typing.

Long. Hard. And yes, those are innuendos.

Josh laughed. "Why don't you tell me about it?"

Sometimes talking to a complete stranger for any length of time was trying, but Josh was comfortable with Martin. They had a rapport. A routine.

This time, however, Martin deviated from it.

Tell me about yours instead. You look stressed.

"You know me too well. I just got back from Twist with my friends."

Twist?

"It's a gay club I like. I go there so much, I feel like I owe them rent." Josh was about to say more, but a response from Martin popped up.

Bret, we've been over this. Don't tell people things like that. What if I were some obsessed stalker? I could go to Twist and track you down.

"Oh, right. Sorry." Josh gave the camera his best contrite expression. "Though I don't think that would be so bad, if it were you. I like you." Josh must still be in the overly honest stage of being drunk.

There was a long pause.

Very smooth. I almost thought you meant that.

"I did mean it."

I'm in sex work too, pal. We all have to fake interest in our clients to keep them coming back for more.

Josh rolled his eyes. Martin could be such a cynic. Josh wanted to argue with him, but after the night he'd had, he didn't have it in him. "Anyway, like I was saying, I went to the club, and some guy rejected me. Kinda put a damper on my night."

He waited for a response. No ellipsis popped up. Josh waited a minute and then checked his internet connection. He was online, and so was Martin. Had Martin stepped away from his keyboard?

"Hello?" Josh tried. "You still there?"

Yeah, sorry. I was getting some water. So, you hit on a guy, huh?

"No, he offered to buy me a drink. I wasn't all that interested, but he was hot, and free is free."

Why weren't you interested?

Josh bit his lip. Another of the general-knowledge tips Martin had given him was to never mention outside lovers or relationships unless the client had a cuckolding kink. It could make them jealous enough to stop spending money on you. But Martin had asked him a question, and he was in sex work too. Surely he would understand?

"There's this . . . guy that I like."

Sounds juicy. How'd you meet?

Josh shook his head. "You're gonna think I'm such a sucker. I've literally seen him twice in my whole life, and both times were at work. I shouldn't be so hung up on him, but . . . I dunno, I can't stop thinking about him."

Martin's response was immediate. *If you really like him, you should go for it.*

"Go for what? I don't know if the guy likes me back. Well, okay, I'm certain he's attracted to me, but that doesn't mean anything. We've seen each other twice, and we've texted once. That doesn't sound like an epic romance in the making to me. Although"—Josh tapped his chin—"he did ask me out once."

I'm positive he likes you back. How could he not? You're gorgeous and funny and fun.

"Thank you." Josh crinkled his nose. "But you don't know the guy. He's not the shy type. If he liked me, he would have done something about it by now."

Josh's phone buzzed in his pocket. "Do you mind if I check that?"

I insist.

Josh pulled it out. "Speak of the fucking devil. It's a text from him."

Read it to me.

"It says 'Do you want to go out sometime?'" Josh gasped. "Holy shit. It's like he read my mind."

I told you he likes you back.

"I guess you were right. What a weird coincidence."

Are you going to say yes?

"It'd be silly for me not to, right? I just said I like the guy."

I can't give you advice on this one. Do what feels right.

Josh stuck his tongue out at the screen. "You're no help at all. Dunno why you've chosen now of all times to keep your opinions to yourself." He composed a quick reply. *What did you have in mind?*

Within seconds, Mike texted back. *I was thinking we could go out dancing. Maybe hit a club.*

"Damn. That's spooky. He wants to go to a club. I didn't think he was the clubbing sort." *I would love to. When?*

When are you free?

Thursday is my day off.

I'll see you Wednesday night.

Holy shit. He had a date with Mike. His heart was pounding. His cheeks ached, and he realized he had a smile stretched all the way across his face.

"Martin, you won't believe this. I have a date for Wednesday." Josh glanced at his laptop. A second later, he frowned.

Martin had logged out of their session early. Josh's first instinct was to panic, thinking he'd pissed him off by texting while they were in a show. But then a dialogue box popped up, indicating how much money Josh had made from the session.

Martin had left him a twenty-dollar tip.

CHAPTER 10

Standing outside of Twist on the night of his date with Josh, Mike actually checked his feet to make sure he wasn't walking on clouds. Ever since Josh had accepted his date invitation, it was like his insides had been replaced with helium. He felt light and dizzy and excited in a way he hadn't since . . . Shit. Since the last time he'd been in love.

When he'd first started masquerading as Martin, he'd done it to help Josh out. He'd had no idea it would be the key to them setting up a long-awaited first date. But it had, and now Mike was finally going to get his chance to do this right.

Thank fuck a bout of insomnia had prompted him to log on that night. When Josh had said he'd been rejected by a guy, Mike had panicked. He'd been too stunned and disappointed to respond. For a blinding, white-hot moment, he'd thought he'd waited too long. He'd planned on asking him out again when they got their test results. It hadn't occurred to him that Josh might not wait around.

But then Josh had explained he was into someone else . . . The look on his face had stolen Mike's breath away. He'd known Josh was talking about him even before Josh confirmed it. That was the final push he needed to make his move. He couldn't wait any longer. With every passing day, he became more certain that he wanted to be with Josh.

And now he knew for certain this went way deeper than a physical connection. That was another unexpected bonus of the time he'd spent posing as Martin: they'd gotten a chance to talk.

Mike had never intended to use his secret identity to have sex with Josh. He'd never deceive another sex worker like that. There were enough creeps and scammers out there without them screwing over each other. It was a consent issue. Josh couldn't give informed consent if he thought he was performing for a stranger, but was actually performing for someone he knew. Sex was so far off the table, it was in the backyard.

But they'd had to spend the private shows Mike had bought somehow, and so they'd talked. Mike had been delighted to discover they had an honest-to-God connection. He'd known he liked Josh, but he hadn't realized how much they had in common, once he got past the big mouth and the bratty attitude. Oh, and the fact that Josh liked clubbing. That was a bullet Mike was gonna have to bite. It was worth it if he got to bite Josh a little too.

They both preferred *Scarface* to *The Godfather*. They listened to all the same music. They both wanted to buy a house someday and get a dog, though they argued about what breed. (Mike was the pit bull to Josh's golden retriever.) It was nice having someone else to talk about being in the sex industry with too. Josh listened to Martin, thank God. Mike had almost had a heart attack one time when Josh had talked about what school he'd attended in the public chat. Josh had the survival instincts of a blind baby mole.

Which brought Mike to the other thing he'd refused to do while acting as Martin: use his influence to get Josh to go out with him. Spying was slimy enough, but urging Josh to say yes to his invitation would have been crossing a line. Josh trusted Martin. He followed all the advice he gave him. If Martin had said to go out with Mike, Josh would have done it.

Mike had done the right thing, but now he had a new moral conundrum: he'd been lying to Josh. Getting to know him while pretending to be someone else. It was a lie by omission, but a lie nevertheless. It didn't help that through their chats, Josh had given him the exact instructions he needed to seal the deal.

Now here he was, standing in front of the entrance to Twist, a gay club he never would have looked twice at otherwise, waiting for a guy he felt like he'd been waiting for all his life. He'd never been this nervous before a date. The thought of seeing Josh again added to the helium feeling inside him until he thought a light breeze would be enough to send him flying.

There was still one thing worrying him, though. Should he come clean that he was Martin right away or wait for an opportune moment? There was no question he was going to tell Josh. He just wasn't certain he should drop the news on their first date. Josh might start to associate him with getting bad news, and that was the last thing he wanted. But would Josh be angry later when he found out Mike hadn't told him sooner?

Part of him wished he'd turned on his camera when he had the chance. He could have shown Josh it was him. But he hadn't, and he knew why: he was afraid Josh would freak and cancel their date. At least this way, if everything went awry, he got to see him one more time.

You're a fucking coward, Michael Harwood.

Mike didn't have long to dwell on it. He spotted a blond head weaving toward him through the crowd outside. Mike started to meet him halfway, but as soon as he saw Josh's outfit, he stopped dead in his tracks.

"Wow," he said when Josh was close enough. "Why not roll in some glue and then dump glitter over your head? It would have been easier."

Josh held his arms out and spun around, almost smacking a bystander. "But not more fun!" He was wearing shiny silver pants—like *chrome* shiny; Sisqó's hair shiny—and a tight green shirt. His black sneakers sparkled like the pavement at noon. It wasn't Mike's idea of fashion at all, but it worked on Josh somehow. His pants also featured zippers running all the way from hip to ankle. If they worked, Josh could be naked in three seconds flat. Now *that*, Mike liked.

Mike had opted for more traditional club clothing: nice jeans and a designer button-down shirt. He didn't often feel underdressed, but standing next to Josh in all his glittery glory . . .

"If I'd known you were gonna go full peacock on me, I would have worn something else."

Josh looked down and then peeked up at him in a shy way. "I think you look great."

Mike's heart thumped hard against his ribs.

"You two are adorable, but can we get inside already? I wanna see my girlfriend."

For the first time, Mike noticed the girl standing behind Josh. "Oh, hi."

"Mike, this is Ashley. Fair warning, she has no filter. Ashley, meet Mike."

Ashley stuck out a hand. Four of her fingernails were painted seashell pink, but her ring finger was silver, like Josh's pants. "It's a pleasure. Josh has told me so much about you."

Mike took her hand. "I can't say Josh has ever mentioned you."

She glared at Josh, and he recoiled like a cornered animal. "Rude."

"Sorry. Why don't you go inside, and we'll be right behind you?"

Ashley whirled around and marched up to the bouncer by the door, who let her in after a fraction of a glance at her ID.

Mike raised an eyebrow at Josh, a question on his face.

"We come here a lot. I know the bouncers by name." Josh waved. "Hey, Darnell."

Darnell nodded once before turning back to the person he was attaching a wristband to.

"Gotcha." Mike fidgeted. "So. You brought friends with you. On our date."

Josh looked sheepish. "Yeah, I'm sorry about that. Like I said, we come here a lot. I found out after I made plans with you that they were going to be here, and I didn't want to cancel, but I also couldn't ignore them. Besides, Ashley wanted to split a cab, and I'm not making enough money yet to turn that down."

"I wish you'd told me. I could have picked you up."

"I didn't know you have a car. Most people who live in the city don't."

Mike nodded. "Well, Ashley seems nice enough."

"We could go somewhere else." Josh stepped closer. "I'll go anywhere you want to go."

Again, Mike's heart took note of Josh's proximity. In fact, his whole body did. The closer Josh got to him, the more Mike seemed to heat up. "No, it's fine. I want to meet your friends." He smirked. "Apparently, you've told them about me. I bet if I buy them a couple of rounds, I can get them to tell me what you said."

Josh blanched. "Well, this has been fun, but I think I'll go crawl in a hole now."

Mike laughed. "C'mon. Let's go inside."

They approached the bouncer. Mike pulled out his wallet, but before he could do more than hand over his driver's license, Josh caught his arm. "I got your cover." Mike started to protest, but Josh shook his head. "It's five dollars."

"Yeah. Trust me, I can afford it."

"No, I mean, it's *five dollars*, specifically. We had a bet."

Mike blinked. "Huh?"

"You don't remember?" He looked around and then lowered his voice. "After we had sex. You said, 'five bucks says you'll be a shooting star.' I thought at the time I was gonna prove you wrong, but so much for that."

Mike was actually a little touched. "I can't believe you remember that."

"It was a memorable day." Josh waggled his eyebrows.

"You know, that bet wasn't serious. You never agreed to it."

"In my head, I did."

"Fine, but I'm buying your first drink."

"Deal."

They got their wristbands and made their way inside. It was early—and a Wednesday—so the club wasn't packed, but there was a healthy crowd at the bar. Mike didn't drink on first dates as a rule, but if he was going to stomach a night at a club, he didn't see how he had a choice. Good thing he liked dancing. And Josh.

He pointed to the bar. Josh nodded and gestured for him to lead the way. True to his word, when they flagged down a bartender, Mike bought Josh and him a drink. He'd asked Josh what he'd wanted, but in a move that surprised Mike, Josh had said to order for him. Mike made a mental note to ask him about it later and then ordered them both a beer for lack of a better idea.

Drinks in hand, they moved out onto the floor, where a handful of people were already dancing. Random striations of light roved over their writhing bodies. Mike had to admit, this club had a decent atmosphere.

He leaned into Josh under the pretense of being heard over the music. "Do you see your friends?"

"Yeah." Josh nodded toward a series of tall tables on the other side of the club.

Mike didn't have to ask which one he was indicating. Even in the dim light, he could see a group of twentysomethings staring at them. A beautiful black man wearing next to nothing waved.

Mike started to wave back, but Josh caught his hand. "Don't encourage them. They *will* come over here."

"What's so wrong with that? You don't want me to meet them?"

"No, I do. But . . . not right now." He took a gulp of beer. "I need at least one drink in me first, and I want us to have some alone time. There's something I wanna talk to you about."

Mike's anxiety ratcheted up from a six to a sixteen. "Should I be worried?"

Josh glanced at him and did a double take. "No. It's nothing serious, I swear. Well, I mean, it's kinda serious. But it's nothing bad."

"Well, now I'm really curious." Mike took his hand, giving him time to pull away if he wanted. "Let's grab one of the booths along the wall, out of sight of your friends."

Josh laced their fingers together in lieu of an answer and tugged him toward one of the black velvet alcoves in question. They were circular, like scoops that had been taken out of the walls, with upholstered benches and little tables. It wasn't in the proximity of privacy, but at least they were facing the dance floor instead of the other tables.

Mike scooted into the booth, leaving enough room for Josh to sit a comfortable distance away from him. Josh did, but then he touched their knees together under the table. Warmth spread through Mike from that little bit of contact.

"I was gonna ask you about your day and all that, but then you dangled that carrot in front of me." Mike set his beer on the table. "What did you want to talk about?"

Josh looked down at his beer, rolling the bottle between his palms "You know how the last time we talked, I said I was thinking of quitting porn?"

"Yeah."

"Well, I went down to Murmur Inc. and talked to Colette with the intention of quitting, but she offered me another job. As a webcam star."

Mike wished there was a camera on him. He did a masterful job of sitting up and widening his eyes. "Did she now? And you accepted." Stating facts as if they were questions wasn't technically lying, right? As long as he wasn't outright false, he could circumvent his moral compass, which was spinning out of control.

"I did. And I love it. Well, maybe not love, but I'm way better suited to it than porn. The thing is, though . . . my friends don't know about what I do. Or the porn we filmed. I'm not ready to tell them. I dunno if you're out or whatever, but I wanted to let you know what the deal was before we went over there."

"You thought I was going to out you?" Mike frowned. "Do I seem like the sort of person who would do that?"

"No! No." Josh set down his beer and waved his hands. "I was just making sure. I knew that if I brought you over there, they'd ask how we met or what you do, and I wasn't sure if you were prepared to answer those questions. A lot of people assume that because I'm so extroverted, I must be open about everything, but I'm not. I didn't come out as gay until I was eighteen and living on my own."

Mike leaned back in his seat. "Wow, that is surprising."

"Yeah. Anyway, it's not like I'm ashamed of what I do—what *we* do—or anything like that. I just wanna tell my friends in my own time, you know?"

"What if one of them goes online one day and finds your channel?"

"Trust me, my friends would *never* pay for porn. Not because they're against it or whatever, but because they're broke and there's plenty of free shit. The chances of them deciding to check out some local cam sex channels are astronomical." He paused. "Though come to think of it, I found my old coworker on a porn site. That's how this whole thing got started. I saw an ad for one of his videos, and it led me to Murmur Inc."

"There you have it." Mike took a sip of his beer. "It's more likely than you think."

"Well, if that happens, I'll deal. But in the meantime, I'd rather not tell them."

"What should I say if they ask me what I do for a living?"

"Lie?" Josh grimaced. "I bet you hate lying."

"Not as much as you'd think." At Josh's raised brow, Mike elaborated. "I'm not out as a porn star. I lie to people about what I do every day. I usually say I'm in real estate. They ask how the market is. I tell them interest rates are going up, and everyone leaves the conversation happy."

Josh grinned. "Real estate? You're serious?"

"Don't act so surprised. With the number of strangers' houses I've been in during the course of my porn career, I picked up all sorts of shit. I know a sundeck from a patio."

"That reminds me of something I wanted to ask you, out of curiosity. How'd you get into porn in the first place?"

Mike studied his face for a moment before cracking a smile. "Well, with a last name like Harwood, I figured it was fate."

Josh snorted. "No, seriously."

"I am serious. My nickname in high school was Hardwood. It started out as an insult, but then I wore it as a badge of honor. I came out as bisexual when I was a sophomore, so I had to grow thick skin in a hurry. Plus, I had red hair and freckles, and I didn't get my last growth spurt until senior year." He shrugged. "Anyway, the nickname stuck, and people were always joking to me that it should be my porn-star name. Then one day, when I was fresh out of college and struggling with student loans, I came across Murmur Inc. The rest is history."

"You ever think about doing something else?"

"Oh, all the time. But I've made a name for myself, and a *lot* of money. Turning away from that is going to be tough." Mike noticed Josh's eyes had widened. "What?"

"It's *'going* to be tough'? As in, you're for sure going to quit?"

"Of course I am. Some day. We don't have to talk about work right now, though."

Josh put his elbows on the table and cupped his chin, directing his full attention at Mike.

"Very well. No one stays in porn forever. I always knew one day I'd decide I'd had enough. I didn't realize how disillusioned I'd gotten until . . . well, until I met you."

"Disillusioned?"

"When I was telling you about what porn is like, and when I participated in your fiasco of a first time, it made me realize I talk about my job like I hate it. Which, for the record, I don't. I maintain that I'm realistic about it. But since I haven't been working these past two weeks, I've gotten the distance I needed to realize how tired I am. The scare itself put some things in perspective for me too."

"Like what?"

"I'm about to be twenty-six. I know that's not old, but the closer I get to thirty, the more I think about my life. I'm tired of faking it. I'm tired of spending all my time acting like I'm into strangers instead of forming real relationships with people. I'm tired of having to look a certain way and of pretending to be enjoying myself when I'm not." He gave Josh a wry smile. "Though sometimes I enjoy myself very much."

The blush that spread across Josh's cheeks was lovely. "Me too. Well, I enjoyed my audition. Our second round of filming kind of sucked."

Mike reached across the table and placed a hand on one of Josh's. "I hope I get to make that up to you someday."

Josh's blush turned into a full-face flame. "I'd like that." He looked like he was going to say more, but instead he cleared his throat. "I think now would be a good time for me to introduce you to my friends."

"Lead the way."

They grabbed their drinks and wove through the crowd to where a group of five people were gathered around a metal pub-height table. As soon as they approached, a brown-skinned girl wearing a cute white dress elbowed the scantily clad black guy in the ribs.

"Ouch, Monica! Why—" He spotted them. "Look who finally decided to join us."

"Hey, Darius." Josh nodded to him before turning to the others. "Monica. Ashley. Chris. A.J. This is Mike."

"Nice to meet you all." Mike waved.

"The pleasure is all ours," Monica said with a pronounced Spanish accent. "We've heard a lot about you."

"So I've been told." Mike shot Josh a wicked grin. "What sorts of things?"

"Oh God," Josh groaned. "Here we go."

Darius threw a muscular arm around Josh. "We tease because we care. And because your boy here is *cute*. Where can I get me one of those?"

"I'm so sorry." Mike put on a somber face. "My parents only made one. I have a cousin who's my age, but he broke my aunt's heart when he came out as straight."

"I like him," Darius said to Josh in a stage whisper so loud it could be heard over the music. "He's funny."

"We're Josh's roommates, by the way," said a guy wearing eyeliner and all black. If Mike remembered correctly, Josh had called him Chris. "There's one other, but he couldn't make it due to a severe case of being an uptight straight guy."

"I used to have a bad case of that," said the toned, Abercrombie-looking one who had been identified as A.J. "Pretty hard to cure, but I think exposure helps." He looked at Josh. "You should invite your boyfriend over for one of our roommate dinners sometime. Maybe Will isn't a lost cause."

"A.J.," Josh hissed. "He's not my boyfriend."

"Oh, sorry." A.J. looked between them. "You guys seemed so cozy."

Mike played it cool, though at *boyfriend*, his heart had decided to match the fast tempo of the club music. "This is our first date, actually, and I think it's time for us to knock out our first dance." He touched Josh's elbow. "Come with me?"

Josh nodded, though he shot a venomous look at A.J. "I am so putting peroxide in your shampoo."

"Do it, bro. We'll be twinsies."

Mike took Josh's hand and tugged him away. There were more bodies on the dance floor now, but they had no trouble finding a spot. Mike closed his eyes and sunk into the beat with ease. Dancing was just like having sex, in his opinion. A lot of hip action, and rhythm was everything. Of course, having a good partner helped as well.

He opened his eyes again and found Josh staring at him. "What?"

"Nothing. You . . ." Josh's cheeks had colored again. "You, uh, dance good."

"Very eloquent." Mike pulled him closer. "You dance?"

It was like a word faucet turned on. Mike pressed their bodies together, and Josh started babbling. "Oh yeah. All the time. It's half the reason I go clubbing so much. But, you know, I'm usually dancing with the girls, or Darius, or with guys I've met. Not that I meet a lot of guys when I go out. Anyway, I only mentioned it because you looked like you knew what you were doing, and—"

Gently, Mike pressed a single finger against Josh's lips. He stopped talking. Mike pulled it away.

"—I was wondering if you're naturally good at it, or if you took lessons, or—"

Mike giggled and pressed his finger against Josh's mouth again. "Why are you like this?"

Josh's throat bobbed. Mike dropped his hand, and Josh said, "I can't seem to stop myself. I think it's some kind of cosmic joke. I'm just not sure who it's on."

Mike laughed again. "If this is making you nervous, we don't have to dance." They were standing so close, it was nothing for Mike to brush his cheek against Josh's. "Feels nice, though."

Josh's answer was almost too soft for him to hear. "It feels right."

The sea of people around them were all moving to the fast pace of the music, but Mike was content to sway in place, feeling the heat from Josh, smelling his soap-and-laundry-detergent scent. "There's something I want to ask you, if I can have a turn."

"Shoot."

It was a question that had been in the back of Mike's mind for over a week now. "When I invited you out the first time, over the phone, why'd you hang up on me?"

Josh bit his lip. "I thought it was a pity invite."

Mike was so surprised, he jerked back a few inches to look Josh in the eye. "What?"

"You asked me out after you'd told me I needed to get tested *and* I was out of a job. I thought you were trying to make me feel better, or maybe make yourself feel better."

Mike almost couldn't speak. "That's the reason? For real?"

"Well, this is me we're talking about." Josh grinned. "Part of it was to be coy. I wanted to play hard to get after you were so cold to me. But yeah, when it came down to it, I thought you were being nice." His smile faltered. "Are you mad?"

"No, of course not. It's just . . ." Mike swallowed hard. When he spoke again, his voice had roughened with emotion. "How, even back when we first met, could you have doubted my interest in you?"

Josh looked down at his feet. "It's not like you told me or anything. On that note, why'd you take so long to ask me out in the first place?"

"If you haven't noticed, I'm kind of a cynic. I had to get to know you before—" Mike stopped short. Josh didn't know everything Mike had done for him. Helping his cam channel get off the ground. Giving him advice as Martin. Spending hours talking to him. Should he come clean?

That might scare Josh off. This was their first date, and looking back, Mike realized it sounded kind of intense. He studied Josh while he debated with himself. This wasn't the time or the place to drop that sort of news. In fact, it occurred to him that Josh was a grade-A drama queen. He wouldn't appreciate a frank confession. He'd want a big reveal. Maybe he could . . .

"You know," Josh said when Mike failed to speak, "they say if you look someone in the eye for five seconds or longer, you either want to kill them or fuck them."

Mike scoffed. "'Or'?"

"*Ooh*, kinky." A cheeky smile slid over Josh's features. "Joke all you like, but you more or less gave me a love confession right here on the dance floor."

"I said I'm interested in you. Not that I love you."

"Semantics." Josh moved away from him and did a little spin. "There's no taking it back. You want me. You need me. It's the pants, isn't it?"

"I know what you're doing." Mike moved closer. "You did the same thing at your audition. You act out when you're nervous."

"I'm not nervous." Josh tried to prance around him, but Mike caught him in his arms and held him tight. Josh swallowed. "Why would I be nervous?"

Mike leaned up until their mouths were brushing. The air between them crackled. "Because you think I'm about to kiss you."

"Well . . . are you?"

"Maybe, but that depends. I think I'd like a confession of my own. Are you interested in me?" Mike was certain he knew the answer, but he wanted to hear Josh say it.

Josh's eyes were losing their focus. "Interested in what way?"

Mike lips skimmed Josh's jaw. "If you tease me right now, I'll remember it later."

Josh shivered in his arms. It was beyond hot. "I'm not teasing you. I'm having trouble putting my thoughts together." He leaned into Mike's touch. "You smell good."

"What was it you said? Like citrus, right?"

"Yeah. Makes it hard to think."

"Then let me ask again: are you interested in me?"

Josh wet his lips. "I have been for a long time. Maybe not when I first met you, but I think it started when I first kissed you."

"Kissed?" Mike mouthed Josh's neck. "Like this?"

Josh made a small sound. "Yeah, like that." He stretched his head back, making his throat nice and long.

Mike slid a hand up his chest to cup his jaw. "Part of me can't believe this is finally happening. I've wanted to get you all to myself for so long now."

"We're not alone, though. We're surrounded by people."

Mike slipped his hand into Josh's hair. He buried his fingers in it and squeezed like he wanted to grab a handful. "Has that ever stopped us before?"

Josh's reaction was *delicious*. He moaned under his breath and pressed against Mike. At some point, he'd gotten hard, and as he pushed their hips together, Mike realized he had as well. "No."

"Do you want me to stop?"

Josh let out a ragged breath and met his gaze. "No."

Mike used the hand in Josh's hair to pull him in for a bruising kiss.

The first time they'd kissed, they'd been strangers. It had been intense, but there'd been no real emotion behind it. Now, kissing Josh felt like standing on the precipice of something. Mike didn't know what, but somehow, the idea of falling didn't seem scary at all.

Especially if it felt anything like Josh's lips. Warm and soft and sweet. Josh melted against him, like he couldn't get close enough. And the little sounds he made. Mike couldn't hear them—goddamn loud club music—but he could *feel* them: hot, wet breaths against his skin.

Maybe it was because it had been so long since Mike had felt like this about someone. Maybe it was because he'd been lusting after Josh for weeks now with no real satisfaction. Maybe it was because

Josh made him feel like his lungs were two sizes too small. Whatever it was, Mike went from being kinda turned on to wanting to fuck Josh on the floor of the club in the span of a *kiss*. He was a porn star. Kissing was like shaking hands to him. But not with Josh.

"Fuck, I want you," he mumbled without thinking. He was more drunk from touching Josh than he was from the half a beer he'd had.

"You can have me." Josh was panting, wide-eyed and disheveled.

Mike pulled back and looked at him. "You mean it?"

"Yeah."

"It won't be like before. We were working then. Playing our roles. If we do this—" Mike swallowed "—it'll be because we want to. They'll be no one to call cut. No one to please but us."

"I know. That's what makes me want it so bad." Josh said the one word that Mike couldn't resist: "Please."

A frisson of pure, electric want shot down Mike's spine. "You asked for it."

CHAPTER ⚫ 11

Josh barely managed to lead them off the dance floor and into one of the single-stall unisex bathrooms before Mike pounced on him. His back ended up closing the door with a *bang* so loud, he was certain it could be heard over the music. He fumbled with the lock, and managed to turn it as Mike kissed him like he was oxygen. This was as close to privacy as they'd ever gotten, not that Josh much cared with a sexy man ravishing him.

"Want you so bad," Mike said against his mouth before biting his bottom lip.

Josh gasped as the little burst of pain mixed with the pleasure of having Mike's hard body pushed up against his. He managed to say back something like, "Murff," but coherency was impossible. And then, Mike slid a thigh between Josh's legs.

Josh had known he was turned on before, but Jesus, having Mike pelvis-to-pelvis with him added sharp pleasure to his haziness. He almost couldn't see straight, there were so many sensations to sort through.

If he'd known at the beginning of the evening that he'd end up having sex in the bathroom, he wouldn't have worn such tight pants. He was going to bust a seam any minute.

Mike's lips found the soft skin below his ear and kissed it. "We don't have to do this here. You can come back to my place."

Josh shook his head and whimpered. "Look me in the eye, and tell me you can wait another minute."

The smile that played across Mike's lips was sinful. "Touché." He rolled their hips together, and Mike's erection nudged up against his. "I have everything I need right here."

Josh caught his kiss-swollen bottom lip between his teeth and chewed on it to distract himself from how good everything felt. "Then do something about it. I think you mentioned making last time up to me."

"Oh, I intend to." He picked Josh up and deposited him on the edge of the sink like he weighed nothing.

"Holy shit," Josh murmured, stunned. "That was hot."

"Not as hot as it's about to be." Mike slipped his fingers under Josh's shirt and dragged blunt fingernails down Josh's stomach.

Josh whimpered, especially when Mike's fingers continued their slow creep downward. "Fuck, please touch me."

Mike laughed, breathy and low. "I'm a sucker for when you say please." His hand reached Josh's pants, but instead of sliding under the waistband, it ghosted over the front, palming his erection. Josh gasped and canted up into the touch, head back, torso taut. He hadn't realized he'd spread his thighs until Mike sunk between them.

Josh grabbed Mike's shoulders and squeezed as Mike traced the outline of his dick through the fabric with a single finger. Fuck, he should have specified *how* he wanted to be touched. He'd bet money that Mike would be content to do this for hours. Under normal circumstances, Josh would love that, but he was tired of being patient. He'd had enough of foreplay. He wanted to get fucked.

And he knew exactly how to get Mike to hurry up.

Josh took a breath and scraped together his ability to form sentences. "Remember when we first met, and I told you I was a top?"

Mike's mouth found his neck again, and, *fuck*, did he have talented lips. "I remember."

"I've changed my mind." Mike stiffened against him, and Josh plunged ahead. "Ever since I met you, all I've wanted to do is take your cock. I want you to fuck me, Mike. Please."

Josh felt rather than heard Mike's reaction. A deep, rumbling growl rose from somewhere in his chest, more vibration than actual noise. He didn't ask Josh to turn around. He grabbed him again and flipped him over, shoving him against the sink. Josh braced one hand on the wall with such force, the mirror rattled. Mike draped himself over his back, and his reflection appeared next to Josh's.

Lips brushing against his ear, Mike looked him in the eye. "Forget everything you think you know about sex. I'm going to show you how it's done."

Josh whimpered. "*Please.*"

Mike slid his hand down the small of Josh's back, between their bodies. For a second, Josh thought Mike was going for his ass, but then he heard the sharp, metallic click of Mike's belt buckle coming undone. Shit. He hadn't known that sound could be so erotic.

There was something he needed to ask, because any second now, he was going to be too far gone to think.

"Do you have a condom?" Josh was almost breathing too hard to speak, but he got it out. He usually brought condoms with him, but he didn't have pockets. His wallet and phone were in Monica's bag. *I am so never wearing these pants again.*

Mike blinked at him for a moment, and then the arousal haze cleared from his eyes. "Condoms."

"Yeah. I don't have one on me."

Mike stepped back. The loss of his warmth was tragic. "Shit."

"What's wrong?"

"We can't have sex." Even as Mike said that, he moved closer again like he couldn't handle the distance between them.

"What? Why not?" Josh whirled around. A pang of rejection resonated through him from head to toe before settling in his stomach. "We've already had sex, remember?"

Mike shook his head. "I know, but that's not the point."

"Whatever I did, please tell me." To his chagrin, his voice cracked.

Mike had him in his arms so fast, Josh didn't realize what had happened until he was pressed up against a warm, hard chest. "It's nothing you did, baby. Don't think for a second I don't want to be with you. This is all my fault."

Something about that pinged in the back of Josh's mind. His heart fluttered in his chest, but he couldn't identify why. He'd have to think about it later. "What's your fault?"

"We can't have sex until after we get tested. Our two weeks aren't up yet."

Josh sucked in a breath, understanding washing over him, cold and stark. "Since we don't know if either of us is positive . . ."

Mike's mouth twitched. "Let's be real, we don't know if *I'm* positive. You were negative before we filmed together, right?"

"Well, yeah. I'd gotten tested right before, and it had been a while since I'd had sex with anyone."

"Then if I'm negative, you're negative. But if I'm positive, and you didn't get it from me the first time, then having sex now would be another shot at me infecting you. You'd have to wait three more weeks to get tested and start the whole mess over again."

"Oh." Josh frowned. "Wow, yeah, I didn't think of that."

"Trust me, I'm as disappointed as you are. I wish I'd remembered sooner, but I guess I got caught up in the moment."

"So, we can't do *anything*?"

"I'm afraid not. Any exchange of fluids would be a risk." Mike cupped Josh's face, brushing a thumb along his jawline. "We should go back to the club. Find your friends. Assuming you're still in the mood to hang out. If not, I can take you home."

"No way, I want to finish our date. I do, uh, have a bit of a problem, though."

"What's that?"

Josh's eyes dipped down to Mike's groin. "See, you made the decision to wear jeans. A wise decision. Your erection isn't that visible. In the dark, no one will notice, and you can just wait for it to subside. But in my case . . ." He gestured at his pants. The tight fabric might as well be transparent, his cock was so obvious. "I know this is a gay bar and all, but I don't think anyone out there will appreciate me walking around like this."

Mike's eyes latched on to Josh's dick and stayed there. It was hard to tell, since his irises were so dark, but Josh thought he saw his pupils dilate. "You raise an excellent point." Mike palmed Josh through his tight pants.

Josh cried out and grabbed his shoulders, fighting the urge to rock up into his palm. "Mike, that's not going to help me get soft anytime soon."

"I know. I have a better idea." Mike's wicked smile was back, and Josh's dick pulsed at the sight. "It occurred to me, we shouldn't do anything *together*. No swapping fluids, just in case. But that doesn't mean we can't still get off."

Josh was struggling to think while Mike's hand was on him. "It doesn't?"

"Stay against the sink." Mike stepped back, taking his wonderful, talented hand with him, and Josh almost whined. "Keep some space between us, and take your dick out." Mike reached for his belt buckle again.

What was about to happen finally clicked in Josh's head. "Oh, I am so down for this." He wriggled his tight pants down to his thighs—no underwear—and had his cock in hand in seconds. "But what if we get something on the floor or whatever? It's safe?"

"Yeah, someone would have to be barefoot with an open wound. But try not to make a mess anyway. It's bad form." Mike shuffled backward until his shoulders hit the tiled wall. He was only about two feet away, but to Josh, it felt like miles. Mike seemed to read his face. "I know it's not ideal, but—" he unzipped his jeans and pulled his cock out "—I'm right here. With you. And for the record, this isn't the first time I've touched myself while thinking about you. But I bet this time's gonna be so much better."

Josh shivered and gave himself a squeeze. "Oh God. Tell me more."

Mike licked his palm and then stroked himself from head to base. "You got under my skin somehow. It was like an itch. After we filmed together, all I could think about was you. I tried to pass it off, pretend it was because I wasn't allowed to have sex, and you were the last guy I fucked. I was wrong, though. The more I fantasized about you, the more I realized it was because I wanted *you*."

Josh's breath hitched in his throat as he started stroking himself to the same rhythm as Mike. "What did you fantasize about?"

"Fucking you, in every position you can think of, all over my apartment. I had you in the shower, in my kitchen, splayed over my dining room table while I pulled your hair and pounded into you." Mike's head fell back as a shiver worked through him. His hand started moving faster.

An answering ripple of arousal swept through Josh. He sped up his movements, keeping time with Mike. He didn't need to spit on his hand or anything. His cock was leaking pre-come freely. "That's so fucking hot, I'm dripping."

Mike cracked an eye open and zeroed in on his cock. Josh pumped himself shamelessly. The expression on Mike's face—like he wanted to *devour* him—made everything feel that much more intense. "Good, Josh. Just like that. Keep going."

Josh moaned. "Feels so good. I'm not gonna last."

"Me neither. I never could last all those times I fucked my own fist thinking about you. My favorite times were when I was in bed, and I pictured you there with me, on top of me, naked and sweaty. I thought about kissing bruises into your neck while you rode me, your thigh muscles flexing, your hole clenching around my cock because you still weren't used to how big it is."

"Oh fuck, *fuck.*" Josh was suddenly right on the edge. He'd never been a size queen, but then, he used to only top. The image of riding Mike's cock, taking it at his own pace, letting it fill him, was too much. "Mike, *ah*, I'm—I'm—"

"You're close?"

Josh nodded, too far gone for words.

"Me too." Mike swallowed loud enough for Josh to hear it, breaths coming in pants. Mike's hand was moving faster now, and with the last of his cognizance, Josh matched the rhythm. In a way, it was like Mike was fucking him by proxy, dictating how he was touched. "I'm right there too. I wanna see you come. You're so sexy. I wish you could see yourself right now. With your lip caught between your teeth like that, light eyelashes over your beautiful eyes. They look black right now, you're so turned on. I wanna turn you around and make you watch yourself come in the mirror."

Josh moaned, loud and needy, and hoped his message was clear. *Don't stop talking. Shit, please don't stop.*

Mike must have understood somehow. "You're so gorgeous, baby. So hot. Let me see you fall apart. When you do, I'm gonna come too. Seeing you come is going to *wreck* me."

Josh orgasmed so hard, his knees buckled. It was a good thing he'd braced himself against the sink, because that was the only thing holding him up as his climax swept through him, stealing the air from his lungs.

He wasn't sure what he shouted—some garbled mixture of vowels and Mike's name—but a second later he heard an answering shout from Mike. He didn't open his eyes, as much as he wanted to watch Mike come. He didn't think he *could* open them. For what felt like a week, his muscles locked up with the vestiges of his orgasm. Only after the last shockwave had crested and fallen away was he able to move. His head hit the cool mirror behind him, and he went boneless.

In all his years, he'd never had an orgasm like that, and he'd had a *lot* of orgasms. He had no idea how he was still on his feet. Magic, or something, because his muscles sure as hell weren't working.

"Holy shit," he muttered, still in a daze. It felt like his heart was never going to stop pounding.

"I agree." Mike's voice was nothing but a rough rasp, like morning stubble.

Josh lifted his head—a Herculean effort—and looked blearily at Mike. One of his hands was flat against the tile wall like he'd been blown back. The other was still in the vicinity of his flagging erection. It seemed as though he'd caught his ejaculate in his hand. Josh inspected his own sticky fingers. To his surprise, he'd gotten most of his as well.

When he could move again, he flopped over and washed his hands in the sink. Then he pulled up his pants, splashed some water on his face, and dried off with paper towels. He glanced in the mirror to see if he was in the vicinity of decency and caught Mike watching him.

"Sorry for staring." He smiled. "I've never heard you be so quiet."

"I think I used up my quota of being loud for the day." Josh stepped aside and gestured at the sink. "You want a turn?"

Mike nodded and came over. Josh moved enough to give him room but otherwise stayed close. When Mike had finished cleaning up, he tossed the used paper towels in the trash, turned to Josh, and kissed him.

The kiss was magnetic, even without any heat behind it. Slow. Deep. Nothing but lips moving together. Josh couldn't stop the small, wanting sigh that poured from him.

Mike kissed him once more and pulled away. "I gotta go."

Josh's head popped up. "What? No, you don't."

"I really do, baby."

Josh nuzzled his neck. "No."

"I'm serious. I'm exhausted now. Besides, if I stay near you, we're gonna be in here all night. Especially now that I have the fantasy of what we just did to replay over and over again. It's a miracle no one's knocked on the door yet."

"Let 'em."

Mike held Josh at arm's length. "You wanna get kicked out of your favorite club?"

Josh pressed his lips together into a thin line. "No."

"Exactly. Go find your friends and enjoy the rest of your night."

"Can I come over to your place tonight?"

Mike echoed Josh's earlier words. "Look me in the eye and tell me you could come to my house, where my bedroom is, and not have sex. Because we couldn't control ourselves in *public*."

Josh frowned. "I guess you're right."

"I don't like it any more than you do, trust me. Now, I'm gonna go home and pine for you." Mike placed a gentle, almost chaste kiss on his lips before moving over to his ear. "Three more days. Then you're mine."

With that, he unlocked the door and slipped out into the dark club with only the brief crescendo of the music to mark his passage.

Three more days, Josh repeated in his head. *In three days, our two weeks will be up. We can get tested. We can be together. Whatever that means.*

What *did* it mean? When Mike had said, *"Then you're mine,"* did he mean physically, or did he want something more?

Josh felt reasonably confident that Mike was into more than just his body, but that didn't mean he wanted to be boyfriends. But then, did *Josh* want to be boyfriends? He hadn't known Mike that long. After what had gone down between them, there was a part of Josh that thought he could handle being fuck buddies if it meant he got to have sex that good. But his chest tightened at the thought of never getting to be more with Mike.

He shook his head. They'd only hung out in person three times, and each time had been sexual in some way or another. If Josh was going to let himself develop feelings for Mike—real feelings that had nothing to do with his dick—he needed to spend some legitimate time with him.

Not that the sex wasn't legitimate. Because holy shit.

Someone pounded on the door, and Josh almost jumped onto the ceiling like a cat. "Are you fucking done in there yet? You've been in there forever!"

Shit. Josh spun around. One look in the mirror told him he was going to look like sex no matter what he did. Might as well face the music.

He opened the door and walked out with a sheepish grin on his face. There was a line six people long, and all of them were glaring at him.

"Sorry," he called as he scooted past them. "Don't eat the cocktail cherries they have up at the bar!"

He found the table his friends had been at before, but only Monica and Darius were there. "Hey, guys."

"Don't you 'Hey, guys' me," Monica said. "Where were you this whole time? We were looking for you."

"Oh, you know, I was off with Mike. Talking." He schooled his expression into a look of neutrality.

One of Monica's thick eyebrows arched up. "'Talking,' huh? Translation: you were getting it on with the hot ginger."

"You think he's hot?" Josh asked. "You never think the guys I like are hot."

"Wow, you didn't even *try* to deny it. Where is he anyway?"

Josh sighed. "He had to go. Where's everyone else?"

Darius rolled a shoulder. "Ashley's outside having a smoke. Chris is getting us some ill-advised shots. A.J. went trolling for chicks half an hour ago and somehow ended up in an all-male conga line. He's now shirtless and dancing on that platform." Darius pointed to one of the stands where the club's dancers gyrated for tips.

Josh's jaw dropped when he spotted A.J. booty-dancing in his underwear with two other dudes. And looking happy to do it too. "Are we . . . *sure* he's straight?"

"Don't you stereotype him. Straight men can be comfortable with their sexuality too."

"Fair enough." Josh's beer was still on the table where he'd left it, but he didn't reach for it. In fact, he discovered he wasn't interested in drinking at all. He kinda wanted to go home.

"Don't even think about it."

He blinked at Monica. "What?"

"You had your 'I wanna go home' face on. No way. Not until you dish."

"Dish?"

She looked heavenward and sighed. "About your new man, babe."

"I second that," Darius said. "If he's gonna join our little family, you should tell us more about him."

"I dunno if he's going to do anything yet. We've only hung out a few times. We haven't talked about what either of us wants yet. For all I know, he just wants something physical."

Monica gave him a pointed look. "Honey, nothing about tonight said 'just physical.' He made an effort to introduce himself to us even when you kept dragging him away, he made us laugh, and I saw you two dancing together. You were so absorbed in each other, it's like the other people in the room ceased to exist."

Josh's face heated up. "You mean it?"

"Big time. You two might not be anything right now, but I bet it won't stay that way for long. Mark my words." She nudged Darius. "Back me up here."

"She's right. I was dancing near you at one point, and you didn't so much as glance my way." Darius grinned. "The moony look on your face was adorable. And Mike had his eyes on you the entire time he was here. I dunno if you noticed, but more than one guy tried to get his attention, totally in vain."

Josh hesitated. "That's sweet. Really, it is."

"But?" Monica prompted.

But as much as I like Mike, I don't know how I feel about his job. Our job. If they started dating, there was no expectation whatsoever that Mike would quit porn and be monogamous with him. Josh wouldn't ask him to either. Porn was his job. Josh wouldn't ask anyone else to quit their job for him. He was going to have to do some soul-searching to decide how he felt about Mike sleeping with other people and the very real possibility that this might not be their last STI scare. Until he answered that, he couldn't date Mike. It wouldn't be fair to either of them.

But that was a question for another day. Right now, he had two loving, pushy friends to assuage.

Josh cleared his throat. "Mike and I are not as serious as you guys think. There's a *lot* we have to learn about each other. Don't go buying us monogrammed towels until I know who he voted for and how he likes his eggs."

Monica and Darius stared at him.

Josh looked between them. "What?"

"That was so . . . adult," Darius said.

"Yeah," Monica said. "Like, super mature and level-headed. You didn't make a single dick joke. You've changed."

Josh couldn't deny that. He'd noticed how much everything he'd been through in the past month had impacted him. And he'd been through a *lot*. Quitting his job only to have to go crawling back. Trying porn and hating it. Running a webcam channel and discovering he enjoyed it. The STI scare. And yes, being with Mike.

He hoped it wasn't all going to culminate in him getting his heart broken.

"I know you told me not to, but I think I am gonna go home. I'm beat."

To his surprise, Monica gave up without a fight. "Okay, *papi*. Be safe. Tell your boyfriend we say hi."

He didn't have the energy to correct her. She handed over his belongings, and he managed to tuck his wallet and phone into the waistband of his pants. His keys he would have to hold. He hugged them both goodbye and then found Chris at the bar. Chris had gotten a round of shots and was in no way interested in leaving, so Josh swung by where A.J. was dancing, instructed him not to leave without making sure the inebriated Chris got home safely, and called for an Uber.

His thoughts swirled as LA melted by his window. As muddled as he felt about some of the turns his life had taken, one thing was clear: Mike made him feel things he hadn't known were possible.

When he got home, the first thing he did was shimmy out of his pants with the intention of burning them posthaste. But then he checked his phone. His heart leaped up into his throat. He had a text from Mike.

I had a great time, but clubbing isn't my idea of a proper first date. Give me a chance to do it right? Have dinner with me?

Josh smiled so hard, his face hurt.

I'd love to.

CHAPTER 12

After the night they'd had together, Mike had expected Josh to accept his dinner invitation. He had not, however, expected Josh to send him a flood of kissy-face emojis, along with some disturbingly suggestive fruit and vegetables. Mike was left staring at his phone, perplexed but also grinning.

The date was set for the day after their results would be in. They were going to have dinner, and—with any luck—celebrate their good news together.

Mike had already made an appointment to get tested. He couldn't wait any longer. If he was negative, that would mean Josh must be too. If he wasn't—

He stopped that thought short. He hadn't allowed himself to think about what it would be like if he'd given Josh HIV. Or what it would mean for their relationship.

Josh hadn't said anything to him about being nervous, but there was no way he wasn't. If Mike could remove the burden he'd placed on him, he'd do it in a heartbeat. But for now, he was going to go forward with his plans. Woo Josh. Get to know him. And most importantly, tell him the truth.

Before they went on their real first date, Mike had to come clean about his secret identity.

And he knew exactly how he wanted to do it.

That was how he'd come to spend the entire morning trolling Murmur Inc.'s website, waiting for Josh's channel to come online. He'd abused the refresh button on his keyboard to the point where it now made an ominous clicking sound every time he touched it. He had to have reloaded the list of gay channels a hundred times, with no sign of Bret Monty.

Morning rolled into afternoon. Mike had eaten two full meals sitting at his desk in his loft, his patience growing thinner than spun glass.

"I swear," he muttered to himself as he hit F5 for the hundred-and-first time, "if his blond ass is hungover and still in bed, I'm gonna lecture him so hard."

But then, Josh had another job, didn't he? What if his boss had called him in on his day off? He wasn't a full-time sex worker like Mike. Or at least, like Mike had been before he'd been benched.

It'd been so long since Mike had done anything else with his life, he sometimes forgot that other people had things like schedules and managers and hours of operation. What would Mike even put on a résumé at this point? He'd worked a glut of part-time jobs when he was in college, but that wouldn't help him now.

Why was he fretting about this? He wasn't going to quit porn anytime soon. No matter how much this break from it had made him look at his life. Or how tired he'd realized he was. Or how much he didn't want to go back—

Uh-oh.

As if sensing his tumultuous thoughts, Josh's channel appeared at the top of the Live Now list. Mike almost knocked his mouse across the room in his haste to click on it. When prompted, he typed in the pseudonym he'd created for Martin and drummed his fingers on his desk as he waited for the chat room to load. Knowing his luck, someone else would buy a private show with Josh before he ever got a chance.

But as it turned out, luck was on his side. The camera feed loaded, and there was Josh, with mussed hair and faint pillow marks on his cheek.

I fucking knew it.

Without pausing to say hi in the chat box, Mike bought a private show. A new screen popped up with a toggle at the bottom that would allow Mike to turn on his own camera and mic if he wanted to. He left those off as per usual. For now.

Josh appeared in the new window a moment later. He was smiling from ear to ear. "Hey, Martin! I was hoping I'd hear from you today."

There was a part of Mike that resented how pleased Josh seemed to be to talk to Martin. He was seldom so cheerful with Mike. But, then, Mike *was* Martin, so in a sense . . .

He gave himself a little shake and typed, *Hey, Bret. You look tired. Rough night?*

"No, last night was great. It's this morning that isn't agreeing with me. I definitely stayed out too late, but it was worth it. I had a blast."

That made Mike smile. *Oh? Were you out partying?*

"Nah, I think I had half a beer. It was more the company I was with that made it fun." Josh looked off into empty space, and his smile warmed. Mike could almost see Josh replaying bits of their night together in his head. Mike's pulse couldn't decide if it wanted to race or skip.

He typed, *Were you with that guy you told me about? The one you like?*

"Yeah, and it was . . . amazing." Josh blinked and refocused on the camera. "But you don't want to hear about that."

Mike had never typed so fast in his life. *No, go on. I'm nosy.*

Josh laughed. "Well, if you insist. It's funny, I never would have pictured myself with someone like him, but he's checking boxes I didn't know I had. Funny, smart, sexy as hell. The whole package. And I dunno what it is, but I feel *safe* with him, you know? Like, I can tell that every time he does something, it's to protect me. I know that sounds odd, but it's true. I can't imagine him ever doing something to hurt me."

Well, fuck. Josh's words, sweet as they were, reminded Mike what he was here to do. And how creepy it was that he was having a conversation with Josh about himself while pretending to be a client. Mentally, he added that to the list of things he needed to apologize for.

He took a breath and wrote, *There's something I need to tell you.*

"Are you cheating on me with another cam star?" Josh winked.

No, it's much worse than that, I'm afraid.

Josh sobered instantly. "Did I do something wrong? Is it because I was talking about other guys?"

No, it's not you. You've been great. This is on me. I don't really know how to tell you, so I'm going to show you. I'm going to turn on my webcam.

Josh's fine eyebrows shot up. "You never turn on your cam. I gotta admit, I'm curious to see what you look like."

You already have.

And with that, Mike hit the toggle that activated his webcam. A second, smaller screen came to life next to the big one that showed Josh's feed. It took a second to load, but when it did, the look on Josh's face would have been comical had the situation been any less serious.

For a full ten seconds, Josh stared at him, eyes wide, jaw slack. Mike remained silent. There was nothing he could say right now that would make this any easier, and he wanted to give Josh time to process. Though the silence made his ears ring worse than the speakers from the club last night.

Finally, Josh wet his lips. "Mike."

Mike waved. "Hi, Josh."

"You're Martin."

It wasn't a question, but Mike answered anyway. "Yes."

"You've been Martin this whole time?"

"Yes, I have."

Josh was silent for another interminable moment. Then he asked the question Mike had been dreading. "Why?"

"At first, it was to help you. I felt bad for putting you out of work and being so hot and cold toward you. I paid for some private shows to get you and your channel off the ground. Of course, that meant we had all that time to fill. We couldn't have sex, because that would be a huge ethical violation, so—"

"So you spent it talking to me," Josh finished. "Getting to know me."

"Yes." Mike drew a sharp breath. "I know I shouldn't have pretended to be someone else, even if I had good intentions. It was still a lie. But for the record, everything I said about myself as Martin was true. I only changed my name."

Josh didn't speak, so Mike continued. "It seems so silly now. This was before I knew I had feelings for you. I didn't think for a moment we were going to end up here. And after we filmed together, I thought I'd be the last person you'd want to talk to. But I saw you giving out personal information, and I *had* to say something. Plus, it was such an easy, no-pressure way to get to know you. You opened up to Martin, and I got sucked into it." He paused. "Are you angry?"

"I don't know what I feel. I think I'm still processing." Josh studied him through the webcam. "Why didn't you tell me sooner?"

"Well, it's not like I was being subtle about it in the first place. I picked another *m* name, for Christ's sake, and my username has the word 'ginger' in it, along with my birth year. I was kinda expecting you to figure out it was me. I wanted to come clean last night, but I thought you'd prefer a grand reveal." He gestured around himself. "And so, here I am."

To his surprise, Josh gave him a small smile. "What in the world made you think I'm smart enough to figure something like that out?"

"Hey." Mike frowned. "You're plenty smart. You don't want to admit it, for some reason, and lord knows you have no control over what comes out of your mouth—"

"Are you trying to get me to forgive you or break up with you?"

Mike's heart stilled in his chest. "'Break up'?"

Josh's expression turned grave. "Yeah, break up. I know we're not technically dating, but this right here"—he waved a hand at Mike—"is the sort of big lie that ends relationships before they begin."

Mike swallowed, throat tight. "You are angry. I was waiting for that."

"Wouldn't you be? Mike, it's not just that you lied to me. You *kept* lying to me. And then you talked about yourself to me as if you were someone else. You got me to tell you things I might not have told you otherwise. I think I have every right to feel however I want to feel about this."

Mike was silent for a long moment. He dropped his gaze to his keyboard. "I think you do too."

Josh made an exasperated sound. "I need some time to think about this. It's a lot to process, and I don't want to say anything rash out of anger." He paused. "But as of right now, our date is off. When I've come to some sort of decision, I'll let you know."

Mike flinched but nodded. "That's fair. Take all the time you need."

There was no response. Mike glanced up.

Josh had signed out of their private show. His channel was gone as well, meaning he'd gone offline entirely. The website prompted him to leave a tip, but he exited out of the window. It wasn't appropriate to give Josh money anymore; it could be construed as bribery.

Now that Josh was gone, the full force of Mike's emotions swept through him, making it difficult to breathe. Remorse, panic, and embarrassment warred within him until fear swooped in and stole the show.

He didn't want to lose Josh. Not like this. Not ever.

To his surprise, his eyes stung, as if he were about to cry. Jesus. He hadn't cried since he was a kid. He blinked until it went away, though it did nothing to change how he felt.

For a long time, Mike stared at his computer screen. He hit the refresh button again on impulse, but Josh's channel didn't pop back up. Not that Mike had honestly expected it to.

Two more days. If they had made it two more days, they could have had their date. But no, that wouldn't have helped anything. Mike still would have had to confess, and Josh would still have been angry. Rightly so.

Mike understood why he'd done what he'd done, but as he stared in the face of the consequences, it was hard to not wish he could do it over. He'd go back to the audition, and from the moment Josh entered his life, he'd never let him go.

Sighing, Mike climbed to his feet. He couldn't torture himself like this. It could be days before Josh contacted him—if he ever did.

That was a horrifying thought. If Mike had fucked this up forever, he'd never forgive himself. A fresh gush of panic slithered through him and coiled in his gut.

He needed a distraction, or he was going to work himself into a froth. But what could he do? He still couldn't work. His address book contained nothing but porn stars who wouldn't want to see him right now. TV or reading wouldn't hold his attention for long, social media would be agony, and he could only clean and work out so many hours a day.

It occurred to Mike, as if through a fog, that his life was pretty damn empty. He lived alone in an apartment that was too big for him, paid for by a job he was no longer passionate about, and he'd potentially lost the one person in over a year who'd made him feel . . . awake.

And every single one of these things, he'd brought on himself.

How had he not noticed before how lonely he was?

"This is what happens when you live with your head up your own ass," Mike muttered to himself. "You miss what's right in front of you. And, apparently, you start talking to yourself."

He turned to his computer with the intention of shutting it down. Instead, he hit Refresh one more time.

Josh's channel popped up right at the top of the list. Mike stared at it, wondering if he'd somehow conjured it there by sheer force of will.

That was ridiculous, though. Josh was probably finishing out his shift. They might be fighting, but Josh still had to work.

The desire to see him was potent, but there was no way in hell Mike could go in his channel. That would be a huge violation of the space Josh had asked for. Mike went to close out of Murmur Inc.'s website entirely. Before he could, his phone—which he'd placed on its usual spot on his desk—lit up.

He glanced at it. His breath caught in his throat. He had a text from Josh.

He snatched his phone up so quickly he half expected to send it flying into the wall.

Come back into my channel and buy a private show.

Mike stared at the message, reading it over and over, convinced he was misunderstanding it. His first thought was that it had to be some sort of mistake. Josh had sent this earlier, and due to a bad connection or something, it'd only gotten delivered now. But hadn't Josh been asleep earlier? And why would he have asked Mike to buy a show from him? He hadn't known that Mike was Martin and that he'd been visiting his channel. It didn't make any sense.

Mike hit Reply with the intent of getting some answers, only to drown in the deluge of things he wanted to say. Why was Josh talking to him already? Why did he want Mike to come back into the channel? What the hell was going on?

A paranoid part of Mike wondered if this was some kind of test, but what would be the point? Regardless, Josh wasn't the sort to play games. He'd never been anything but straight with Mike.

Well, maybe that wasn't the best choice of words.

Mike put his phone back down, retook his seat, and entered Josh's cam channel. No matter how wrong it felt, Josh had asked him to, and he didn't want to piss him off further by ignoring his requests.

As soon as the feed loaded, he saw Josh eagerly scanning the left side of his screen, which Mike knew from experience was where the list of users in the channel was.

"Ah, gingersnap93," he said. His eyes nipped up to the camera, and he seemed to look right at Mike. "Just who I was waiting for."

Well, that clinched it. Josh had really asked him to come back. Pushing aside his trepidations, Mike bought a private show. This time, he set it so that his mic and cam would turn on right away.

When the new screen appeared, he blurted out the first of his many questions. "Josh, why did you ask me back here?"

"Because you're a shitty tipper." Josh had switched positions so he was leaning back against the headboard, laptop balanced on his knees. "Zero percent? Seriously? A lot of us cam stars live on tips, you know. Twenty percent is the new fifteen."

Mike stared at him in disbelief. "Dude, if this is some kind of joke, it's not funny."

"Not at all. I take my tips very seriously." Josh seemed to sober somewhat, however. "Sorry for the back and forth. I wanted to talk to you, but I had to finish out my shift. I thought I'd kill two birds."

"You can't be serious. You want to talk already? It's been like five minutes."

"Twelve minutes, and what can I say? I'm decisive."

Mike was still half in shock, but it occurred to him that this didn't bode well. If Josh hadn't needed long to think, that might mean he was so furious, he couldn't even consider forgiving Mike.

There was no sense in delaying. Mike braced for impact. "What did you decide?"

Josh chewed on his lip. It would have distracted Mike under normal circumstances, but now he wished he'd spit it out already.

"I want to go on our date."

Mike took a quick breath. "You do? You mean it?"

"Yeah. I think it's something that we need to do. Though make no mistake, Mike Harwood." He stuck up a single finger. "You get one more chance. *One*. Think of this date as a test. If it doesn't go well—if you don't prove to me that you're sincere—it's over."

That should have scared Mike, but he was too busy being relieved. "What made you decide to give me another shot?"

Josh shrugged. "I like you. After everything we've been through, it seemed like a shame to give up on this. Before, when I called off the date, I felt . . . sick. Like, nauseated. It made me realize how much I'd been looking forward to it."

Mike smiled. "I know what you mean."

"It's funny, I know I should be angrier, but the lie you told, it was such a *you* thing to do."

"What do you mean? I swear that's the only time I've ever lied to you."

"I believe you. I mean the fact that you were watching out for me." Josh flicked a hand at his computer. "Helping me get my channel off the ground. Giving me all that advice about how to stay safe and get clients to book shows. You've been doing this from the start. Teaching me. If I didn't know better, I'd think you were a big ol' mama bear inside."

Mike grinned. "Nah, I'm just a know-it-all. I wanted to impart my wisdom."

"And I understand that part of what you did. The bit that still weirds me out is all those conversations we had about you while you were Martin."

Mike flinched. "Yeah, that wasn't the best move I've ever made. I tried not to influence your decisions. When you asked Martin whether or not you should go out with me, I didn't say either way."

"I remember that, but you also used Martin to find out how I felt about our date, and *that* is creepy. You could have asked me yourself."

There was no denying it. "You're right. I'm so sorry. I got carried away. Hearing you say such nice things about me made me realize how wrong that was. But if I can beg you to believe me, what you said before was true. I would never hurt you on purpose."

Josh looked away and rubbed his chin. His expression was unreadable. Mike overanalyzed every micro twitch of his facial muscles.

After an eternity, Josh nodded. "All right, you convinced me that I made the right decision. You're still on probation, but we're definitely going to have that date. Oh, and Mike?" Josh winked. "That sappy speech you just gave was *priceless*."

Mike glared at him. "Brat."

"You know it."

"All joking aside, I'm thrilled you decided to give me another chance. You won't regret it."

"See that I don't." Josh stuck out his tongue. "Although, to be honest, if the roles were reversed, I dunno that I would have acted any different."

"What do you mean?"

Josh shrugged. "It's natural to be curious. If I'd had an anonymous way to find out what you really thought of me when we met—or anytime after that—I would have jumped on that so fast. And I did enjoy the big reveal. I'm a sucker for drama. Not that this means you're off the hook or anything, but I do think I understand."

"Well, I swear I'll never do anything like that again. I'm gonna make it up to you."

"Are you?" Josh's expression grew mischievous. "How?"

"Name it."

Mike might have imagined it—Josh's cam didn't have the best quality—but he thought he spotted some color in Josh's cheeks. "Before, when you were Martin, I always wondered why you never asked me to do anything sexy."

Mike shook his head. "You couldn't consent. You thought you were performing for Martin, not for me. I would never have crossed that line."

"Yeah, and I think you made the right decision, but it's also . . . kind of a shame." Josh glanced down, like he was too embarrassed to make eye contact. "Last night, I learned what a gift you have for dirty talk. We could have been enjoying that this whole time."

Mike had a suspicion he knew where this conversation was going, and his cock was already taking a pronounced interest. "You bring it out in me. Everything I said, all the fantasies I talked about, were true. Ever since I met you, I can't seem to get enough."

Josh looked up again. His eyes were dark with desire. "Well, we're here now, and you did book this private show. We have to fill the time somehow."

Mike's body made what it wanted very clear to him, but he had to ask, "Are you sure this is what you want? You haven't forgiven me yet."

"If there's one thing I know for sure, it's that I always want you. I haven't stopped thinking about last night. All those things you said to me, describing how you wanted to fuck me, and watching you touch yourself . . ." Josh shivered. "I think that was some of the best sex I've ever had, and it was technically masturbation. I can only imagine what it'll be like when we can fuck for real, and I imagine it a *lot*."

The last of Mike's reservations crumbled away. "Liked that, huh? Hearing me talk about how badly I want to fuck you? All the ways I'd do it?"

Josh nodded, shifting on the bed. Mike was positive his pants were getting tight. "That was so hot. I can't believe how hard I came. If you really want to make it up to me, I wouldn't mind another orgasm like that."

"It'd be my pleasure. How do you want to do this?"

Josh's eyes blazed like green fire. "When I'm being Bret Monty, guys tell me to do all sorts of things to myself, and I have to pretend to be into it." He reached for his pants and undid the button, slid the zipper down. They didn't come off, though. He gave Mike a little peek at the blue boxers he had on underneath. And the impressive erection straining against the fabric. "But in your case, I think I'd *really* enjoy being told what to do."

That pushed every single button Mike had all at once. His hand moved to his groin, and when it brushed his cock through his jeans, the pleasure that jolted through him from that indirect contact was so intense, he hissed. He couldn't believe how turned on he was.

"Would you like that, Mike?" Josh's smile was a sinful mixture of coy and cocky. "Watching me touch myself in all the ways you want to but can't?"

"Tease. If I were with you right now, I'd kiss that smug look off your face." Mike took a deep, shuddering breath and unbuttoned his jeans. "We still have two days left on our sentence. I suppose this'll have to do for now."

"You say that like you're not loving this." Josh pushed the flap of his pants open and fingered his boxers. "Like you're not every bit as hard as I am."

Mike salivated but teased him back. "Maybe I'm not."

"Oh?" Josh's eyes tracked down to where the camera cut off his view of Mike's lower half. "Prove it."

Mike scooted his chair back, which brought his hips and the tops of his thighs into the frame. He watched the screen that showed his feed as he arranged himself: legs spread, one hand resting casually next to his groin. "Is that good?"

"Almost. Looks like you've got something in your pants there. Why don't you unzip them and show me?"

The zipper slid down easily, helped along by the pressure from his erection. As soon as it was down, his cock sprang up, tenting his underwear. Josh's eyes locked on to it. His expression was so wanting, so downright *hungry*, it made Mike's breath catch.

"If you're satisfied, I'd like to make a couple of requests of my own."

Josh dragged his eyes back up to Mike's face in a reluctant way. "Please do."

"Get on your feet and strip. Slowly. Turn the camera around so I can watch."

Josh almost fell over himself in his haste to comply, and *that* was mega hot. There was a blurry moment as the laptop swiveled, but then it stopped on a view of a small, cluttered bedroom. Mike took in details in an instant: worn paperbacks on the dresser, the same posters on the walls that he'd noticed before, and a pile of laundry with, bewilderingly enough, what looked like the shredded remains of the pants Josh had been wearing last night.

Mike was more interested in the man standing in the room, however. He was visible from head to mid-calf. His long fingers were toying with the hem of his shirt, giving Mike little peeks at his stomach.

"You want me to take this off?" A smile curved Josh's mouth.

"Oh yeah." Mike had told him to strip slowly, but now he kinda wished he hadn't.

Josh slid his shirt up to the bottom of his rib cage. "Like what you see?"

"Very nice." Mike leaned closer. "Did you start working out?"

"How kind of you to notice." He flexed, and his stomach— which had been toned before but not exactly ripped—divided into a faint six-pack.

"You've got abs now. Very nice."

"You like?"

"I do, but honestly your whole tall, leggy look does it for me any way you want to serve it up. Always has. Did Colette tell you she showed me a photo of you before your audition?"

"She didn't. I had no idea."

"I wasn't going to perform with you, but when I saw your photo . . . I knew I had to have you."

Mike wondered, not for the first time, if Josh had a bit of a praise kink, because the compliments seemed to charge him up. He dropped the hem only to reach behind him and pull the shirt off his back. He tossed it aside with the ease of a professional stripper.

Mike whistled. "That was some *Magic Mike* shit right there."

"Maybe I missed my calling." Josh hooked his thumbs through his belt loops. "What now?"

"Pants off. And I'm thrilled you decided to wear skinny jeans. I want to watch you work them down those thighs of yours."

Josh's pants were already unzipped, so he slipped his thumbs between them and his underwear and pushed them down one tantalizing inch at a time. He made a relieved sound when his cock was freed that Mike could listen to all day.

"Better?" Mike asked.

"You have no idea. I'm so hard, it *ached*." He paused to run a hand over his clothed erection.

He stopped when Mike made a dissenting noise. "No touching yet. Pants off first."

Josh did indeed have to work them down his thighs. Mike loved every second of watching it. When they reached his ankles, Josh pulled them off and threw them aside. "What now?"

"Underwear."

Josh pouted. "So, I'll be totally naked, and you'll still be dressed?"

"Good point. That doesn't seem fair, does it?" Mike peeled his shirt off and tossed it over his shoulder. Showing off, he flexed his stomach and ran a hand down the sharp cut of his abs. "Now we're even."

"Much better." Josh slipped his underwear down. His cock bobbed up when it was free and stood straight out from his body. He let his boxers fall to his feet and swept them to the side with his toes.

Mike made an appreciative sound. "Turn around."

Josh did, moving without a hint of tension, like there wasn't an uncomfortable bone in his body. When his back was to Mike, he folded his arms behind his head. It might have been to get them out of the way, but it emphasized the curve of his broad shoulders as they sloped into his narrow waist.

"Fuck," Mike said under his breath. Josh had clearly learned how to make himself look good on camera, which wasn't hard, considering he had a great canvas to work with. Louder, Mike said, "You're beautiful."

"Gonna compliment me all day?" Josh glanced over his shoulder. "Or can we get this show on the road?"

Mike smirked. "I bet I could make you come by complimenting you."

Josh flushed. "After last night, I believe it."

"Come back to the bed. Sit against the headboard, and put the laptop between your legs."

"Like this?" Josh got into the position Mike had described, angling the camera and slumping so he fit in the screen. Mike had the most delicious, obscene view between his legs.

"Yeah, that's perfect." Mike lifted his hips and started to push his pants down.

"Wait." Josh bit his lip. "Push 'em down just enough, yeah? To get your cock out, but otherwise keep everything on."

Desire pulsed between Mike's legs. "You have a clothed-sex kink?"

Josh nodded. "No idea why."

"I can imagine." Mike lowered his voice to a deep rumble. "People don't take their clothes off all the way when they're dying to fuck. They pull down or lift up the bare minimum so they can get to it. It's frantic and messy and hot."

Josh made a soft noise. "Sounds about right."

"I've done that to you before, in my head. The other day, I was looking at my dining room table, and suddenly all I could picture was bending you over it, fumbling between us to shove our clothes out of the way, and fucking you. I swear, I could hear you moaning and picture your hands slipping as you tried to brace yourself."

"Shit, that's good." Josh's hand started to reach for his cock, but he paused. "Can I touch myself now?"

"You remembered. Good boy. But not just yet, I'm afraid." Mike pulled his pants and underwear down enough to free his cock, like Josh had asked. "If I were there right now, no way I would have taken the time to have you do that striptease. I would have had you on the bed, ass up in seconds. I doubt I would have done more than get my cock out before I absolutely had to fuck you."

"Oh *fuck*." Even through the webcam, Mike could see pre-come leaking from the tip of Josh's cock. "That's . . . fuck, so good." Josh's cock was straining against nothing, begging for contact. "Please let me touch myself. I'm so hard."

"Since you asked nicely. Start at the head. Make a loose fist and go slow. I don't want you coming too soon."

Josh fisted the head of his dick, but when he stroked himself, his pace was fast. Mike growled at him. Josh whimpered but slowed his movements.

"That's right, baby. Exactly like that. Enough to keep you gagging for it but not enough to make you come."

"Jerk." Josh let his head fall back, and it hit the headboard with a soft *thud*. "I can't believe you called me a tease earlier. You're the tease."

"Oh baby, you haven't seen anything yet. One of these days, I'll lay you out and spend hours fucking you open with my fingers. I've wanted to do that for a long time, feel you tremble and moan from the inside. You'll beg me to fuck you, but I won't until you're almost sobbing with need. And even then, I'll draw it out. Long, deep thrusts that feel so good but leave you wanting more. By the time I'm finished, you'll come like you never have before."

Josh's cock spilled so much pre-come, Mike thought he'd orgasmed, but he didn't stop touching himself. "Holy shit, Mike. I want that. I want you." His hand sped up, seemingly against his will. "Sorry. I need—"

"It's okay. Keep going. Tight and fast." Mike spit on his palm and started touching himself too, but slower. If he went as fast as Josh, he'd come in no time. He didn't think he'd ever been this turned on from doing so little. "That's good, Josh. So good."

Josh lifted his head, opening one eye to look at Mike. Mike gave his dick a long stroke and spread his legs until he couldn't any more.

Josh moaned. "Perfect. Stay like that."

"Tell me how it feels."

"Amazing." Josh shuddered. "So much better than jerking off in the shower or whatever. Last night, I thought it was because of what you said, but now I know it's you."

"What's me?"

Josh's eyes were lidded, but he made an effort to look at Mike. "Sex is so much more *intense* with you. You turn me on so much, I can't think. It's like drowning, but wanting to drown."

Fuck. Mike was suddenly right on the edge. With extreme force of will, he pulled his hand off his dick, fearing it might be too late. He felt one mini pulse, but it seemed he'd stopped in time. His orgasm hovered over him, or maybe it was buried under his skin. He couldn't tell. The precipice was back, and he was dangling over it.

Josh's mouth had gone slack. "Do you feel it too, Mike?"

Mike's voice was nothing more than a rasp. "I feel it."

"Gonna come. Are you close?"

"I'm there. I wanna watch you come. Would you like that?"

Josh nodded, mouth forming the word *yes* as if he lacked the strength to speak.

"Do one last thing for me, baby. Take your other hand and slide it down to your hole. Touch yourself there and think about me fucking you."

Josh sobbed. "I can't. It's too much. Want you so bad. I—" He mewled and arched his back, hand working his cock furiously. "Can't wait any longer."

"Almost there, baby. You're doing so good." Mike wasn't going to push Josh to finger himself, but to Mike's surprise, Josh's free hand slid down a second later, past his balls, down his perineum, where a single finger found his hole. Mike let out a low moan. "Fuck yes. Touch yourself right there. Can't wait to put my cock there."

Josh barely swiped his hole before he moaned, loud and broken. "Ah, oh God, Mike!" He dissolved into orgasm. It was stunning to watch. His body went rigid, and his eyes clenched shut. He pumped his cock a few more times before his hand stilled. Undoubtedly, the stimulation had reached critical levels. There wasn't much come—surprising, after all that pre-come—but a glob slid down the underside of his cock beautifully.

Mike took himself in hand again and managed to stroke himself half a dozen times before he toppled into pleasure so intense, it blacked out the world around him. Shockwaves ripped through him; he couldn't tell if he was shouting or was silent. All he knew was that when he returned to his body, his hand was a mess, and so were his pants. Good thing he kept tissues on his desk.

Josh was panting, eyes closed, slumped against the headboard. He looked like the life had been drained out of him through his dick. "Fuck."

"I agree." Mike took a deep breath to try to corral his wild pulse. It continued to pound like waves slapping against rocks. "You okay?"

Josh slurred something that sounded like "I'm fucking fantastic" before he pushed himself up. "God, I can't wait for our date. Though part of me is worried that since this is so good, the actual sex will be terrible."

"I'm not concerned. That first time notwithstanding, I have the utmost faith in us." Mike smirked. "Although, who says we're gonna have sex after our first date?"

"After? Fuck that. I was thinking before. And possibly during, as well. Don't take me anywhere you want to go back to."

Mike laughed. "Deal. As fun as that was, I have to get going. I spent half my day waiting around for you, and now I have things to do."

Josh looked hesitant. "Before you go, there's something I want to ask."

"Anything. But can you put some clothes on first? With you all naked and sweaty, I'm having trouble focusing."

"Hell no. I'm not standing anytime soon. But here." Josh grabbed his tangled sheets and spread them over his lap. "Better?"

"Marginally. What's up?"

"I guess I, um—" Josh scratched behind his ear with his clean hand. "Well, I was wondering . . . There's something I've been meaning to talk to you about."

"I don't think I've ever seen you tongue-tied before. It's refreshing. But whatever it is, you can ask me. I promise."

Josh took a breath. "Once we go on this date—assuming that everything goes well, and I forgive you and all that—are we, you know, dating? Like, do you want to be a couple, or is this casual to you?"

Mike's stomach flopped at the word *couple*. Not in a bad way. "You always ask boys what their intentions are before a first date?"

"When I've had sex with them three times already, yes. But truth be told, I've never been in a situation like this before. I don't know what the protocol is. We have to get tested before we can be together, and then there's the fact that we're both in sex work, which brings a whole other set of complications to the table, and I don't know if our anniversary would be the day we first had sex or the night we went to the club, or should it be when we have dinner, or—"

"Baby. Your mouth. It's big."

Josh looked sheepish. "Sorry. I tend to babble."

"I've noticed. After some debate, I've decided it's charming." Mike grabbed a handful of tissues and cleaned up. He needed a distraction while he said this next part. "In all seriousness, Josh, I like you. Obviously. But I'm not a hundred percent sure what I want right now. I think I do, but I'm afraid to say it before we've figured some things out. You said it yourself: this date is a test. I don't want to make any decisions until we see if we pass or not."

Josh nodded. "I'm kinda scared too. Is that weird?"

"If it is, we're both weird. Why don't we take this one step at a time? Let's have our first official date. We can worry about it after that, assuming we're both still in this."

"I like that plan."

Mike paused before plunging ahead. "For the record, though, I have never quit porn over a boyfriend in the past. I might quit for other reasons, when I'm good and ready, but I'll never quit for you. Just like I wouldn't ask you to quit any of your jobs for me. Can you deal with that?"

Josh paused before answering, making Mike squirm.

"Honestly, I have to think about it. I don't love the idea of you sleeping with other people, even though I know it's your job. It would take getting used to."

Mike supposed that was all he could expect for now. "I can be patient. For the record, I haven't slept with anyone else since you, and not just because I'm waiting to get tested. Though if I go back to porn, I would be doing my job, just like when you go on your cam channel and masturbate while people watch."

"I get that. I wouldn't quit my channel if you asked me to." Josh smirked. "Unless you wanna make me your kept man."

"Don't tempt me. I could keep you handcuffed to the bed."

Josh shivered. "Keep talking like that, and I'll make you buy another hour."

"Two more days, Josh. We can make it." Mike blew him a kiss. "I'll talk to you later, okay?"

"Okay. Hey, one more quick thing."

"Yeah?"

"How do you like your eggs?"

Mike blinked. "Scrambled with salt and pepper. Why?"

"Just curious. I'll text you later. Bye."

Mike signed off and watched as Bret Monty went from offline back to on. He was only there for a second though before his channel disappeared again. Mike couldn't be sure if he'd logged off or if someone had immediately bought a show with him. He hoped it was the former, if only to give Josh's poor cock a rest.

Two more days.

In two days, he might have his first boyfriend in over a year. It was scary to think about. But also exhilarating. For the first time in a long time, Mike was ready for a taste of something real.

But there was a phone call he needed to make first.

CHAPTER 13

J osh thought his skeleton might be trying to rattle its way out of his skin. That was the only explanation for how badly he was trembling as he waited out in front of a little Japanese restaurant in Pasadena. He fiddled with the buttons on his shirt to distract himself, but his hands were shaking too.

Calm down, Clemmons. It's only a date.

But his nervousness refused to ebb. He'd hardly slept since the night Mike had texted him the name of the restaurant and time, along with the message, *I'll show you mine if you show me yours.*

Despite his dirty mind, Josh had gotten the joke immediately. It was a flirty invitation that didn't quite mask the seriousness of the request. If they wanted to, they could disclose their test results with each other during their date. Mike had said he'd made an appointment, and Josh had gone to his the day before. He was beginning to get the feeling that Mike liked dramatic reveals as much as he did. Why else couldn't they have texted each other the good news? Or at least, in Josh's case, it was good.

Josh had tested negative for HIV.

The relief he'd felt when he received the phone call was profound, but also strangely anticlimactic. As soon as the nurse had told him he was negative, it seemed as though he'd known all along that he would be. What was that called? Hindsight bias. But he liked to think it was a sign that all the good turns his life had taken lately were going to continue.

Of course, the nurse had advised him to get tested regularly for pretty much the rest of his life, but for now, Josh felt safe. Like he'd dodged a bullet. He was still glad he'd taken the plunge and tried porn, but this experience cemented in his head that he wasn't cut out for it.

It'd been worth it, though. To meet Mike. Even if this date went poorly and Josh decided he couldn't forgive him after all, he was still glad they'd met.

Mike was actually off to a bad start, though. He was late, and it was giving Josh far too much time to think about everything that had happened in the past month. The ups, the downs, the changes he'd seen in both himself and Mike, and the whole uncertain future sprawling ahead of them. *If* they had a future together. That was one of many things Josh intended to find out tonight.

First and foremost, he wanted to know if Mike had tested positive. Josh wouldn't demand that Mike disclose his status, but he was pretty sure Mike would tell him either way. And if he was positive, Mike had some big decisions to make. He'd probably need space to deal, consider his options, and decide on a plan. Josh would be supportive no matter what, but he'd need to make some decisions as well. He'd have to decide if he still wanted to date Mike.

A month ago, he might have reacted the way that one asshole at Twist had. Josh couldn't say if he would have considered dating someone with an STI back then. But he'd been ignorant, and he was a big enough person to admit it.

It helped that he'd done his research. There were plenty of people with HIV who never passed it to their partners, or if they did, they managed it together. Mike would take certain medications, and there were ones for Josh as well, all of which had excellent rates of success. And they could use condoms for the rest of their lives.

The rest of our lives.

When had Josh started thinking about Mike in terms of absolutes? Jesus. He needed to remind himself that they'd never so much as shared a meal together before. They had a lot of ground to cover before they got serious. It was funny, though. When it came to Mike, Josh had no trouble imagining a future together.

But was that wise? If Mike stayed in porn, he was going to sleep with other people while they were dating each other. Not that Josh had much room to talk. He was a cam star. He masturbated while dirty old men watched him do it. Was there a way for them to be monogamous while they were both having sex with other people?

Josh wasn't sure. Despite all the experience he'd gained since that faithful day he'd auditioned for Colette, there was still a lot about the sex industry he didn't understand.

He knew two things for certain, though: he wanted to be happy, and he was in serious danger of falling in love with Mike. However inadvisable that might be, he had to see if there was some way to make this work.

"Lost in thought?"

Josh shrieked. He spun around, heart racing, and found himself inches from Mike Harwood.

Mike looked like he was struggling not to grin. "Sorry. Didn't mean to scare you."

"No, I'm sorry." Josh took a deep breath. "I'm a little nervous."

"What for? It's just me." Mike gestured to himself. Josh absorbed him in a sweep. He looked *good*. White shirt with a black flight jacket thrown over it, dark jeans, and the fancy shoes Josh always saw but didn't know the name of. It all fit him beautifully, too.

Josh must have stared for a second too long, because Mike chuckled. "Guess I picked the right outfit. You don't look bad yourself. I've never seen you all cleaned up before."

Josh had scrounged together the only nice clothes he had. He'd bought them for an interview when he was twenty and hadn't worn them since. Never heard from the job either. It was nothing fancy, but he thought the light-green button-down brought out his eyes.

"Well—" he cleared his throat "—my mom says you can't go wrong with business casual for a date."

"You called your mom for dating advice?"

"Yeah." He rubbed the back of his neck. "She's been married three times, so I figure if anyone knows how to land a man, it's her."

Mike laughed again. "But as for staying with one, I hope you won't take any advice from her." He held out his arm. "Shall we? I'm sorry I'm late, by the way. I had to make a trip down to Murmur Inc."

Josh started to ask what for, but he stopped short. If Mike had gone to a shoot, then he didn't want to know. "Lead the way."

The restaurant, which was called Zen according to the cut-out metallic sign out front, had two large aquariums adjacent to the entrance, in which colorful fish swam amongst towers of fake coral.

To the left was a hostess stand, where a pretty woman with dark hair and eyes greeted them. She seemed to recognize Mike, because she led them to the sushi bar without asking for a name.

"You come here a lot?" Josh seated himself on one of the barstools, which all had red seats and black metal backs.

Before he could answer, a sushi chef shouted, "Hey, it's Mike!" He waved, knife in hand, from where he was cutting vibrant purple tuna into sashimi. "How's life?"

Mike waved back. "It's fine, Genzo. Same old."

"Be right with you."

Josh looked between them. "I guess that answers my question."

"I eat a lot of fish," Mike explained. "It's a good, postworkout protein source. My gym is near here, so I come in maybe once a week." He slid his jacket off, hung it on the back of the barstool next to Josh, and took a seat. Their knees touched. With anyone else, Josh would have assumed it was an accident, but with Mike, he knew better. The light touch—a gentle reminder of Mike's affection—sent a ripple of warmth through him.

"I'll defer to your expertise, then." Josh picked up the paper sushi menu left by his place setting and handed it over. "You pick."

"Are you adventurous?" Mike flashed a smile. "When it comes to food, I mean."

"I'm not picky, but don't order me anything that still has eyes."

"Got it."

While Mike made tallies next to various kinds of fish, Josh settled into his seat and observed him. So far, this seemed like a regular first date, and he appreciated that Mike had dressed up. Mike always looked good, but there was a clear delineation between his street clothes and what he was wearing tonight.

It hadn't escaped Josh's notice that the jacket he'd chosen had a series of decorative silver zippers. Had he worn it because he'd thought Josh would be into it? If Josh were a betting man, he'd put money on yes. That was the sort of attention to detail he'd come to expect from Mike.

So far, so good, but what now? He didn't want to launch right into the STI talk, but he wasn't sure what else to say. He knew what people normally talked about on first dates—their families and what concerts they'd been to and what movies they liked—but he and Mike had already covered all of that via Martin.

"Something on your mind?"

The question forced Josh back to the present. His gaze had moved from Mike to the white tile floors. When he looked up, he found Mike studying him with raised eyebrows.

"What?"

"You seem pensive. Is there something you want to talk about?"

Well, that's one way to start a tough conversation. "Yes, to be honest, but I was also thinking about what an unusual first date this is."

"Really? I thought sushi was pretty standard."

"No, I mean because of our history. If you were anyone else, I'd be asking you what your favorite food is, or if you like musicals. But thanks to Martin, I already know it's lasagna and that your iPod has the soundtrack to *Hamilton* on repeat."

He was expecting Mike to smile, maybe crack a joke, but instead he blanched. "Let me apologize about that again. I didn't mean to—"

"No!" Josh held up a hand. "I wasn't trying to start anything, I swear. Obviously, we'll talk about that at some point, but I was more saying I'm glad we don't have to go through all that small talk. It's my least favorite part of first dates. When I've recently met someone, learning their favorite color isn't my top priority." He paused. "Though out of curiosity, what's yours?"

Mike answered without hesitating. "Orange."

Josh crinkled his nose. "I hate orange."

"A lot of people do. I love it, though. It's vibrant and energetic. Makes me think of fresh fruit."

"Is that why you wear the cologne you do?"

"Yeah, it's orange blossom. I was surprised when you picked up on it. Most people think it smells flowery."

"Well, we were in pretty close contact."

Mike pressed his knee against Josh's. "Yeah, we were."

Genzo appeared. "Sorry for the wait." He reached over the clear partition to shake Mike's hand. "Have you decided on something for you and your . . .?"

"Date." Mike handed over the marked sushi menu. "We're going to try a bunch of different things, if that's all right."

Genzo took the paper with a sly smile. "Ordering for your date is a little old-fashioned, don't you think?"

"Oh yeah," Josh quipped. "We're a very traditional couple."

Laughing, Genzo left to start on their order. Mike stared at him. "What?"

"'Couple'?"

Damn. Josh kept doing that. "I didn't mean—"

Mike giggled like a schoolboy and touched his shoulder. "It's okay. I don't mind. Actually, I like the sound of it."

"I felt the same way when you called me your date."

Mike gave his shoulder a squeeze before letting go. "So, what did you want to talk about? Don't think that bit of misdirection made me forget."

Damn. Part of him had been looking for an excuse to avoid this.

"I think there are some things we should get out of the way. I know this is our first 'proper' date, or whatever, and we should be enjoying it, but I think I'll be a lot more relaxed if we clear the air."

Mike swiveled in his seat to face him. "Okay. I think I can handle that. Does this have to do with our test results?"

Josh took a quick breath. "Yes and no." He looked around to see if anyone was listening, but the other diners were absorbed in their own food and conversations. He lowered his voice to be sure. "I have no problem telling you my status. I tested negative."

Mike's lips quirked up. "Me too."

Josh let out a breath despite himself. "That's *great*. You must be so relieved."

"I am. When a waiter comes by, I'll order us some champagne."

"I'm down to celebrate, but you realize this isn't over, right?"

Mike's face clouded over like an overcast day. "What do you mean?"

"We both have to keep getting tested. Hell, you have to get tested every two weeks."

"It's the same for everyone who's sexually active, though."

"Not exactly. Most couples who are monogamous can stop getting tested after they've been together for a long period of time. Because of what you do, your risk is higher, and it never goes away. I don't mean that in a judgmental way. If I'd stayed in, uh, the business, I'd be in the same boat."

"Porn." Mike didn't bother to lower his voice. "My business is porn. You can say it."

Josh looked around. No one had so much as glanced their way, but paranoia crept over him like a figure standing just over his shoulder. "Dude, we're in public."

"So? I'm not ashamed of what I do. I'm a porn star. I'm in the sex industry. So are you. I may not be out to my family, but I don't care if a bunch of strangers know."

Josh took a deep breath. Clearly, he'd struck some sort of nerve. "Mike, I'm not ashamed either. I just don't want to invite any spectators into this conversation. There's a table of guys right over there getting drunk on sake. I've had experiences before where I talked about being gay in public, and some jock types decided to take notice. Okay?"

That seemed to lower Mike's hackles. "Fair enough. I'll keep my voice down."

"Thank you. Anyway, what I'm getting at here is that so long as you're in porn, this could happen again. And if we're together, then I'm at risk as well."

The tension in Mike from before sprang right back up again. "So, what do you think the solution is?"

Josh sensed somehow that this was a trick question, but he didn't want to answer it with anything other than the truth. "I can't ask you to quit porn any more than you can ask me to quit my jobs. It's your livelihood. You have bills to pay, and believe me when I say I get that. But if we start dating, then I want you to start using condoms when you film. Every time."

He paused for Mike's reaction. Mike had gone wide-eyed, but he didn't speak, so Josh continued. "I know straight porn doesn't usually use condoms, but I'm sure you can find people who will work with you regardless. There have to be women out there in your same boat. Or maybe you can exclusively film gay porn? I don't know. I haven't thought it all the way through yet, and it occurs to me that it might be too soon to talk about this, but now you're not talking, and it's freaking me out. Please say something."

Josh bit his lip to stop himself from babbling.

Mike blinked, as if coming out of a trance, and looked hard at him. "You're not gonna ask me to quit my job?"

"No. I won't lie, part of me wants you all to myself, but I would never ask that of you."

"Why?"

"Lots of reasons. Namely, we're not together. Who am I to barge into your life and demand you rearrange everything when for all we know, we won't last another month? Plus, working for Murmur Inc. opened my eyes. Now that I'm a sex worker too, I get it. This is a job. It has ups and downs, same as any nine-to-five. It'd be hypocritical of me to ask you to quit, even for health reasons. I wouldn't ask a construction worker to quit their job because they might get hurt. Or a realtor, if you prefer." He winked.

Mike continued to stare at him for another long moment before he reached over, cupped the back of Josh's neck, and drew him into a kiss. It was chaste compared to their usual kisses, but the emotion behind it left Josh's breathless.

"Wow," he said when Mike pulled away. "What was that for?"

"For being amazing." Mike stroked his neck with a thumb before letting go. "Sorry I was acting all cagey for a minute there. That wasn't what I was expecting you to say."

"What were you expecting?"

Their sushi arrived then, along with a waitress who brought them water and asked if they needed anything else. It seemed the restaurant didn't have champagne, but they did have sparkling wine, so Mike ordered that instead.

When the waitress left, Mike grabbed his chopsticks and pointed to a decorative sushi roll. "Try that one. I'll answer while you chew."

Josh broke his chopsticks and clumsily navigated a piece into his mouth. It was surprisingly salty at first, but then something mild neutralized it. Avocado?

"It's really good. What's the salty part?"

"Salmon roe."

Josh gave him a quizzical look.

"Fish eggs."

Josh made a face. Mike silently took the plate from him before sliding over some beautiful sashimi in its place. Josh tucked into that with delight.

"To answer your question, when you started talking about risks and all that, I thought for sure you were gonna ask me to quit. When I first started in the industry, I tried dating outside of it, and without fail, everyone I met couldn't handle it. They judged me, or they tried to 'rescue' me, or they gave me ultimatums. Sometimes all three. After a while, I swore I'd only ever date fellow sex workers. That was better, but I still encountered problems from time to time."

Josh swallowed a bite. "Like what?"

"Remember what Colette said at orientation about the shelf life of a porn star?"

Josh dipped a piece of yellow tail into a little dish of soy sauce and tossed it into his mouth before nodding.

"Well, once I dated this girl who was only in porn for a week. When she quit, she expected me to quit with her. I refused, and that was the end of that. Happened again with a guy who was in phone sex. When we got serious, we decided to be exclusive. Except, I thought being exclusive meant being devoted to each other and not sleeping around recreationally. He thought it meant me being out of a job. In truth, that was long enough ago that I could have packed up and done something else, but I didn't want to, and I resented him for asking."

Mike stopped to chew and swallow before adding, "When you were talking a moment ago, I was having flashbacks to that."

"I'm sorry."

"It's okay. You didn't know." Mike shot him a wry smile. "I've heard you're not supposed to bring up exes on the first date."

Josh shrugged. "I've seen you naked. I think we can bend some of the traditional dating rules."

"That we can. Which reminds me. I have a surprise for you."

"Oh?"

The waitress returned with their wine, poured it for them, and left.

"Perfect timing." Mike held up his glass. "I propose a toast."

"To what?" Josh clinked his glass against Mike's.

"To my new professional endeavors." Mike took a sip. "I spoke to Colette earlier today and told her I don't want to be in porn anymore."

Josh almost spit out the mouthful he'd taken. "You *what*?"

"Try not to shout, baby." His eyes sparkled with mischief. "We don't want anyone else to hear, right?"

Josh had to struggle to keep his voice down. "What do you mean you *quit*? I didn't ask you to."

"Yeah, and make no mistake, if you had, I probably would have called Colette right back and told her I changed my mind. I'm stubborn like that."

Josh set his glass down before he dropped it. "I don't understand. You said you'd never quit for someone else."

"What makes you think I quit because of you? That's kinda self-absorbed, don't you think?" He winked. "In truth, this has been a long time coming. Taking those two weeks off made me realize how tired I was. Tired of *everything*. I know it was stressful for you, but I'm grateful we had that scare. It gave me two things I needed: time and perspective. It's funny: I accused you of being a shooting star when I'm the one who burned out a long time ago."

"It wasn't all that stressful for me, if it helps. Or at least, I say that now that I know I'm negative."

Mike laughed. "I know how you feel."

"How'd Colette take the news?"

"Pretty well. She told me she'd never expected me to last this long, which was a hell of a backhanded compliment. She asked if I want to quit sex work altogether, and I said no. Murmur Inc. is like a second home to me. I have a whole foundation built there, and it'd be silly to give that up. She gave me a bunch of suggestions for other things I can do."

"Like what?"

"Modeling, for one. I've done nude work on and off in the past, and I can put a decent portfolio together. Also, it turns out Colette is opening some all-gender strip clubs in the city. The popularity of *Magic Mike*, among other things, created a demand for them. I figured I'll audition, since I love to dance." He nudged Josh's knee with his. "And I have a proposal for you, if you're up for it. It should be beneficial to us both."

"Oh?"

"Webcam channels featuring couples and groups make about twice as much as ones with single people. There's so much more you can offer to clients with multiple performers. I was thinking maybe I could guest star on your channel? It'd be an easy way to get paid for all the sex we're going to be having anyway."

Josh, who had managed to keep his hormones in check all throughout dinner, suddenly found himself salivating. "That sounds *amazing*. You're welcome anytime you like."

"I appreciate that, but for the record, it's still your channel. I'm not going to take over. I think maybe once a week or so we could give your clients a hell of a show. But the rest of the time, I want you all to myself."

Josh nodded. "I'm so down for that. Out of curiosity, are you gonna be in sex work forever, or are you going to look at other things?"

"I don't know. The biz has been good to me, and it's not going anywhere. Sex is one industry that thrives no matter what the economy is like. But I've been thinking about getting older and if I want to be that thirty- or forty- or fifty-year-old who's still putting on a show. The pressure to look a certain way is hard enough, and I'm young. How's it going to be when I'm going gray and have arthritis or whatever?"

"I'd still buy a lap dance from you." Josh gave him a cheeky smile.

Mike chuckled. "Sweet as that is, I want to keep my options open. I was thinking I might look into acting someday. I'm always saying that porn stars deserve Oscars for what they do. I'll still have to look a certain way, but no one will expect me to have washboard abs when I'm fifty."

"Aren't you worried people might recognize you from porn?"

"I don't plan to hide my past," Mike said with a shrug. "If that keeps me from getting jobs, then fuck 'em. Besides, people are always complaining about how liberal Hollywood is. I'm sure there are producers out there who are willing to hire an ex-porn star. And if that doesn't work out, I'll find something else. I could get some use out of my degree, for example."

"What's it in?"

"Marketing. I bet I'd be a good PR rep or something. God only knows I've spent the past three years marketing the hell out of myself to get where I am."

"How would you cite that on a résumé?" Josh tapped his chin. "'Extensive experience interacting with porn addicts on social media'?"

"You'd be surprised. Colette gives great references from what I hear, and she's not afraid to find creative ways to describe job roles. I heard that once a cam girl who was known for performing in elaborate outfits wanted to become a florist. Colette wrote her a recommendation letter in which she praised her 'impeccable taste, color choices, and unique aesthetics.'"

"Good to know! I might need that one day."

"Oh?" Mike raised an eyebrow.

"Well, yeah, I don't think I'm gonna run a cam channel for the rest of my life either."

"What do you plan to do, then?"

Josh took a sip of wine to wet his dry mouth. "I've been thinking about going back to school."

Mike was silent.

"I know, I was shocked too. I only ever got my AA, and I think it's because I wasn't mature enough for higher education. Well, that, and I was more interested in partying with my friends. It's funny, I remember sitting in my shitty room, thinking about my minimum-wage job and my routine life, and feeling like I was better than that. But now I know I never did anything to deserve better."

"What made you realize that?"

"I think you did. Watching you work your ass off. Hearing you talk about how difficult it was to become successful. I got into porn because I thought it was going to be easy, and I was wrong yet again. I expected things to get handed to me, and I shouldn't have. I've grown a lot since then, though. I think once I've saved up some tuition money, I could give it another go."

"If that's what you want, I'll support you." Mike leaned in like he was going to kiss him again.

Before he could, Genzo appeared to clear some of their empty plates. He looked between them and giggled. "We can move you two to a booth if you'd like. They're more *private*."

For the first time since Josh had met him, Mike blushed. "That won't be necessary."

"Lemme know if you change your mind."

As soon as he left, Mike turned back to Josh. "I have a question for you, if that's okay. A serious one."

"Shoot."

"How's this date going so far? Have I proven myself to you?"

"I think so. Provided you never, *ever* lie to me again, then I'd say we can leave the past behind." Josh cleared his throat and did his best official voice. "Mike Harwood, I forgive you. I don't think you meant any harm, and you did the two things everyone needs to do when they fuck up. You owned up to it, and you accepted responsibility."

"Thank you. That's a very mature way of looking at it. When I first met you, there were aspects of your immaturity that I was drawn to, but I must say, I think you've grown into someone I like even more." Mike brushed a strand of hair away from Josh's face. "Someone I find attractive inside and out."

That gave Josh an idea. "I have one more question myself."

"What's that?"

Josh fiddled with his glass, suddenly nervous. "You said one of the perks of you appearing on my cam channel would be getting paid for all the sex we're going to have, right?"

Mike's lips started to turn up. He must've sensed where Josh was going with this. "That's correct."

"Well . . ." Josh took a quick breath and looked up at him. "How much sex are we talking?"

Mike's little smile turned into his trademark wicked grin in a flash. "You tell me. There hasn't been a moment since I met you that I wasn't ready to go. I'm pretty sure I can deliver on all the toe-curling, world-rocking sex you can handle, and then some."

Arousal flooded into Josh with such force, it made him dizzy. "And if I said I wanted to get started on that right now?"

"I'd say 'check please.'" Mike leaned toward him and lowered his voice to the deep, dark tone Josh liked best. "I feel like I've been waiting for this my whole life. The chance to be with you the way I've wanted to from the moment we met. No cameras. No audience. No one to call cut right when it gets to the good part. This isn't going to be like anything we've done before. Are you ready for that?"

Josh could scarcely draw the breath he needed to reply. "Please."

CHAPTER 14

M ike had no idea how he got them from the restaurant to his apartment without breaking every traffic law California had, but the next thing he knew, he was fumbling to get his front door unlocked while Josh clung to him like a horny octopus.

"Can't wait to be with you." Josh's tongue brushed the shell of his ear. "Want you so bad." He was grinding his cock against Mike's ass, and his hands were *everywhere*. Pushing up Mike's shirt and delving into the front of his jeans. Mike had never really noticed the height advantage Josh had on him, but now that the man was splayed against his back, he felt every inch of it. In a good way.

Mike drew a ragged breath. "Much as I love your enthusiasm, if you don't let me get the door unlocked, we're never going to get inside."

"We could give your neighbors a show."

"Tempting, but I thought you were looking forward to finally being alone?"

That got Josh to back off. Marginally. He stopped grinding against Mike, at least, but he kept his arms wrapped around him. It was as if he thought Mike would disappear if he let him go.

But Mike had no intention of going anywhere except to the nearest flat surface. He'd waited a long time for this, and he intended to be *very* thorough.

He got the door unlocked and flung it open, hurrying inside. Josh followed after him, only to stop in the doorframe, eyes wide as they swept over the living room and up to the loft. "Holy shit. This place is *nice*."

"You can admire my décor after."

Josh's eyes snapped from the brick fireplace to Mike's face. An impish grin tugged at the corners of his mouth. "After?"

"You heard me." Mike grabbed him by the front of his shirt, yanking him inside and into a passionate kiss. Josh made a surprised, muffled sound and then softened like warm chocolate. Mike wrapped one arm around him while the other found the door and pushed it shut. Then he shoved Josh against it. Josh went back easily, without a hint of resistance. If it hurt when his back connected with the wood, he was too busy kissing Mike to complain.

Mike wasted no time taking Josh's wrists and pinning them up by his head. To Mike's delight, Josh seemed to like that. He'd been kissing him back fine before, but now he melted into it, opening not only his mouth but what felt to Mike like his whole body. He even widened his stance so they were the same height and Mike could fit their hips together.

Mike broke away with a gasp. "Remember the first time we kissed?" He sucked Josh's bottom lip into his mouth and nibbled on it. "Seems like forever ago."

"I can't believe we're the same people." Josh pushed against his hands, as if testing how pinned he was. "Feels totally different, being with you now."

Mike held him in place without breaking a sweat. "I dunno about that. You're still a brat."

Josh stopped struggling and grinned. "I can't make it too easy for you. What would be the fun in that?" He nipped playfully at Mike's lip.

"Want me to let you go?"

"Only if you promise to catch me again."

Mike released his wrists and grabbed a fistful of his shirt instead, hauling him into another kiss, one that deepened and then darkened. Josh didn't seem content with kissing any longer, though. He pushed at Mike's jacket, indicating that he wanted it off. Mike let go of Josh's shirt long enough for Josh to slide the jacket off his shoulders and discard it. When Josh reached for Mike's belt buckle, Mike captured his hands again.

"Let's take this to the bedroom, okay? If we get too carried away out here, I may decide the couch will do."

"I'm all right with the couch." Josh ran his tongue along his abused bottom lip.

This man knows exactly how to work me.

"Nice try, but we're having sex on a bed. Trust me, you're going to want to be comfortable."

Leaving their shoes and Mike's jacket by the door, Mike led the way through the apartment to his bedroom in the back. He kept his room neat and made his bed every morning, so when he opened the door, they were met with a presentable scene: white sheets, fluffy pillows, and tasteful furniture. No pile of laundry on the floor like in Josh's room.

Josh trailed a hand down the curve of Mike's back. "It's just how I pictured it."

"You've imagined what my bedroom looks like before?"

Josh's gaze fell to his toes. "Maybe once or twice."

Mike pulled Josh into his arms, pressing their foreheads together. "I like it a lot better with you in it. I'm happy you're finally here."

"Me too. I get the feeling I'm about to be a whole lot happier, though." Josh reached for the hem of his own shirt and lifted it teasingly up over his stomach. "Want another striptease like the one I gave you before? I've been practicing."

"Have you?"

"Of course. After I saw your moves at the club, I couldn't let you dance circles around me."

"Next time. There's a lot of new ground I want to cover." Mike peeled his shirt off and tossed it aside. The look on Josh's face as he drank him in made his blood hot. "Clothes off. Now."

Josh shivered, already moving to comply. "You're a little bossy in the bedroom, aren't you?"

Mike's pulse started to race as Josh pulled his shirt off and threw it next to Mike's on the floor. "Maybe a little."

"I was surprised by how much I liked it before." Josh started on his jeans, popping the button open with one hand while his eyes stayed fixed on Mike. "When we cammed together, and you told me how to touch myself."

Mike watched Josh undress, fighting a desire to pounce on him that grew with every item of clothing he removed. "I could do that again, but I'd much rather be the one touching you."

Josh unzipped his pants and hesitated halfway through the motion of pushing them down. "I like it when you take control, though. Can we have a little of both?"

Mike had been aroused since the restaurant, but that stroked something deep within him. He cocked his head to the side and smiled in a way that probably looked predatory. "Maybe if you ask nicely."

Josh licked his lips, green eyes shining behind lowered lashes. "Please."

Arousal, thick and intoxicating, sunk into Mike's very bones. He had to take a breath before he could speak again. "Strip down to your underwear and get on the bed."

"Fuck yeah." Josh had his pants off in three seconds flat and stepped backward to the bed, eyes never leaving Mike.

"On your knees."

Without hesitation, Josh climbed onto the bed and faced the headboard. He didn't peek behind him like Mike expected. Instead, he waited patiently for Mike to walk over and stand next to him. The urge to smack his ass was overwhelming, but Mike restrained himself. There would be plenty of time for that when he finally, *finally* had Josh naked and sprawled across his sheets. Where he belonged.

Mike didn't speak. He reached for his belt and undid it, letting the buckle make metal clicking sounds that were resonant in the silence. He'd noticed when they were in the bathroom at the club that Josh had seemed to react to the sound. Like last time, Josh started breathing faster as soon as he heard it. A quiver traveled down his bare back, arching his spine. It was beautiful and deeply sexy. Mike hadn't touched himself once, and yet every little reaction that rippled through Josh made him infinitesimally harder.

Much as Mike wanted to tease him, he was too turned on to draw this out. He hastily disrobed, and when he was naked, he reached out and traced a single finger down Josh's spine.

Josh inhaled sharply. The anticipation must have heightened his senses. Mike stopped when he reached the small of his back, splayed a hand across it, and then dipped it below the waistband of his underwear.

By the time Mike grabbed a handful of his ass, Josh was quivering. His back moved with his labored breaths like a rising and ebbing tide.

His whole body seemed tuned in to what Mike was doing, from his tense shoulders to his heated skin.

Mike worked his underwear down with one hand, a single inch at a time. He left it around his thighs and stood back to admire him. "You're beautiful."

Another tremor rippled through Josh. "Do something. The suspense is killing me."

Mike gave in and smacked him on the ass. "What's the magic word?"

"Abracadabra."

Chuckling, Mike slid his fingers into Josh's hair only to grip it and use it to haul him up onto his knees. Josh didn't resist; in fact, when Mike tightened his hold, Josh moaned. Mike said, "You're only punishing yourself. I can do this all night."

Josh made a helpless noise. "You wouldn't."

"Try me."

Josh's expression was priceless: a mixture of desire, petulance, and acceptance. "Please, Mike. I want you so badly."

"Much better."

Mike let go of Josh's hair and kneeled on the bed. He nestled up close to Josh, back to chest, and slid an arm around his waist. Josh leaned against his body, resting his head on Mike's shoulder, reaching up to touch Mike's hair, the nape of his neck, whatever bits of him he could reach. It was intimate and almost innocent, until Josh rocked his hips, rubbing Mike's cock with his ass. Mike indulged him, thrusting lightly between his cheeks. Josh made soft, pleasured noises that Mike could easily imagine becoming addicted to.

Much as he was enjoying the soft touches, the need for more was building in him, like a coil tensing to spring. He let go of Josh's waist. "Turn around. I want to see your face."

Josh shifted on the bed until they were facing each other. Mike was surprised to find him looking down, light eyelashes leaving shadows on his cheeks.

"Hey." Mike touched his chin, lifting it up. "You all right?"

Josh's eyes swept over his face before dipping down to his body. Mike swore he felt them trail down his chest, his sides, his hips, like Josh had actually touched him. "I feel like if I look at you, I'm gonna explode." He trailed a finger along Mike's collarbone. "One of these days I'm going to kiss every freckle on your body."

A different sort of arousal seeped into Mike, something warm and sweet like honey. "Better get started. There are a lot of them."

"This one's my favorite." Josh brushed a finger against the corner of Mike's mouth, where he happened to know he had a freckle that was almost on his lip. Josh followed the touch with his own mouth. "It was the first thing I notice about you. The second I saw it, I knew I wanted to kiss it." And he did, softly and with so much reverence, it made Mike ache.

He'd had a lot of sex in his life. In every position imaginable, with toys and props and some of the world's most beautiful people, but Mike had never felt so engaged by a partner.

He turned his head a fraction, and their lips met. He kissed Josh with deliberation, with all the exhilarating emotion that was simmering in him. Josh must have sensed it, because he sunk into the kiss like Mike was air and he couldn't breathe without him.

Within seconds, it grew heated. Mike found himself pushing Josh back onto the bed, climbing on top of him, slotting their bodies together so he could feel every inch of him at once. There wasn't a part of Josh he didn't want to touch, and he couldn't wait to feel him inside and out.

Josh pulled his underwear all the way off and wrapped his legs around him. When their groins came together—hot and velvety soft—Mike's desire came to a boil.

He broke the kiss with a gasp. "Stay right there." He disentangled himself and reached for the nightstand. Before he could do more than open the bottom drawer, something warm pressed against his back.

"I told you to stay put," he said without an ounce of venom.

"I couldn't." Josh slid his arms around him and nosed the back of Mike's neck. "You were too far away."

"Keep acting up, and I'll smack your ass again."

"Mmm." Josh nibbled on his earlobe. "You've given me the perfect motivation."

Grabbing a condom and a bottle of lube, Mike placed them within reach, turned around, and picked Josh up by the waist, only to toss him back onto the mattress. Josh giggled until Mike pounced on him, covering Josh's mouth with his. Then his laughter morphed into moans as Mike slipped a hand between them and found his cock, palming it. Josh convulsed under him, arching his hips up into the touch. Mike expertly stroked him with one hand while the other reached for the lube.

When he had it, he sat up and silenced Josh's whine of protest by holding it where Josh could see it. "You all right with bottoming this time?"

"If I said no, would you let me top?"

"Yes."

The look on Josh's face was so priceless, Mike wanted to frame it and hang it over his mantle.

"Seriously?"

"Of course. You don't think I'm gonna top *every* time, do you?"

"But you said . . . when we met, you were all—"

Mike shook his head. "Sean Hardwood is a career power top. Mike Harwood is a little more flexible. A little, mind. I'm talking special occasions. I think tonight qualifies."

Josh's eyes darted between him and the lube before he blew out a breath. "Rain check. I want you to fuck me."

Mike salivated. "Are you sure?" He wasn't asking because he doubted Josh's sincerity. He wanted to hear him say it again.

Josh came through in a big way. "Yes, Mike. Fuck me. Please."

It was like obscene music to Mike's ears. He tossed the bottle of lube at Josh. It landed on his chest with a soft sound. "Get ready."

Josh glanced down at it. "I thought you said you wanted to 'spend hours fucking me with your fingers.'"

"I do, and at some point, I will, but I've had enough foreplay for now. After all that backtalk, you're in for a hard and dirty fuck."

Josh's hand blurred, he grabbed the bottle so fast. Mike watched in satisfaction as he uncapped it, lubed up his fingers, and slipped one into himself with enough enthusiasm to make Mike's cock twitch with envy.

He added a second finger and then seemed to find the right spot. He threw his head back with a gasp while pre-come appeared at the head of his dick. The sight was mesmerizing and spurred Mike into action. He had the condom open and on in three quick movements.

Josh opened a bleary eye. "How do you want me?" His thighs were spread wide, and he now had three fingers moving shallowly in and out of his hole. He shivered and shut his eyes again, possibly from the pleasure that was making his hips arch off the bed, or possibly from the sweat starting to drip down his face.

"Christ. How you are right now is perfect. So sexy."

Josh made a helpless noise and fucked himself a little harder. Mike was really going to have to ask him about that whole praise-kink thing later.

"I mean it, Josh. I feel like I could come from watching you like this, so desperate and beautiful." He kneeled between Josh's legs and bent down to nuzzle his neck. "You think you're ready enough?"

With a whine, Josh pulled his fingers out of himself. "Yeah. And if I'm not, I bet I'll like it anyway. What was that you said at the club? You wanted to feel me clenching around your cock?"

It was Mike's turn to whine as he took himself in hand and pressed the head of his cock against Josh's hole. "Good memory."

"It's hard to forget an image that hot." Josh rolled his hips, breaching himself. "I doubt I'll ever forget this."

Mike pushed in slowly. He managed to pop the head in before Josh clenched and he had to stop. "All right?"

"Yeah." Josh was panting, eyes lidded. "More."

"You gotta relax."

Josh grabbed on to his shoulders and seemed to use those as an anchor. After a breath, he unclenched. Before Mike could stop himself, he slipped into him by another two inches. *Fuck, that's good.*

It was so hard to stop with Josh so pliant and inviting beneath him, but through great exertion, he took it slow. Josh still had his shoulders in a death grip. He waited until Josh relaxed again before thrusting about three-quarters of the way in.

"Holy shit." Josh sucked in a breath. "I feel so full. That was it, right?"

"It can be. I don't have to go all the way. Or we can stop altogether."

"Don't you fucking dare." Josh spread his legs farther apart. "I can take it. I wanna take it."

Mike exhaled and rested his sweaty brow against Josh's. "I'm not strong enough to resist if you say it's okay. You need to mean it, because I want to fuck you with everything I have."

As if to prove his point, Josh moved his hips like he intended to have the rest whether Mike gave it to him or not. "I mean it. Please, Mike. I want it."

Mike groaned and with one smooth movement sunk into Josh until he couldn't anymore. Josh cried out, and for a horrified second, Mike thought it was too much, but then his cry morphed into a moan. "Oh God, move. Please move. I need it."

"Take a breath, and—"

Josh kissed him so hard, Mike felt teeth. He hooked a leg around his waist, and with Mike fully seated inside him, it felt like he was closing the last connection that kept their bodies apart. He spoke against his lips: "Mike. Fuck me."

Mike's resolve splintered. He pulled out of Josh by a few inches and slid back in. His pace was slow but deliberate, and Josh shuddered beneath him. There were so many sensations—the smell of Josh's skin and sweat, their slick bodies, Josh's hands and legs anchoring him even as he wanted to lose himself in the deep thrum of pleasure resonating through him.

He scraped together enough cohesion to ask, "How does it feel?"

"It burns," Josh said, "but it's a good burn. Just on the right side of pain, and I feel so *full*. I didn't think I'd like it, but . . ." Mike thrust all the way into him again, and Josh made a garbled noise. "Shit, yeah. Bury yourself in me."

Mike pulled out again, almost all the way, and thrust hard back in. "Like that?"

Josh's head fell back against the bed. "Yes, so good. Feels so good."

Mike increased his pace, and Josh's voice rose in volume. It had been so long since Mike had heard someone be genuinely vocal in bed, it sent a hot burst of pleasure through him. "*You* feel good, Josh. So tight and hot."

"Fuck yeah." Josh groaned and tightened his legs around him. "Tell me how good I'm doing. Tell me how well I'm taking your cock."

Praise kink confirmed.

"You're doing great, baby. I love watching you take my cock. You look so hot. Tell me what feels good." Mike changed his angle and tried a series of short, shallow thrusts.

Josh shook his head. "Not that."

"How about this?" Mike put his hands under Josh's hips, lifting him up, and changed his rhythm to long, deep, rocking motions.

"That's good." Josh wriggled under him like he was searching for something. "I think I can make it better if— Oh. *Oh*. Do that again."

Mike had added a grinding motion to the end of his last thrust. He pushed in again and repeated the movement. He was rewarded by Josh jolting as if he'd been shocked. "Mike, oh God. That's it."

"Hold on. I think I know what you need." Mike sunk deeply into him and ground his hips in slow, wide circles.

Josh *lost* it. He threw his arms over Mike's shoulders and dug his nails into Mike's back, moaning louder than before. He arched up off the bed like he was trying to draw Mike deeper into him. "Mike, please, don't stop. Need this. Need you."

Mike could listen to him all night, but the coil that had begun winding in him earlier had tightened to critical levels. Pretty soon, it was going to spring, and he could only imagine how powerful the force behind it would be. "Are you close?"

Josh nodded, eyes shut and mouth slack. His hair was dark with sweat, and a full-body flush had heated his skin. He looked lewd and beautiful at the same time. His hips made little stuttering motions in time with Mike's thrusts. Not enough to upset Mike's rhythm, but it made him aware of Josh's cock wedged between their stomachs, sliding easily thanks to sweat and pre-come.

Mike reached between them and wrapped a hand around it. It was like he'd touched Josh with a live wire. Josh spasmed and canted up, sliding his cock between Mike's fingers. Mike didn't need any more encouragement. Without stopping the slow grind that had brought Josh to the edge, Mike pumped him with all the finesse he could manage. Josh only made it through a few jerky strokes, and then he came unraveled as if Mike had pulled on a loose thread.

Despite being so vocal earlier, Josh's orgasm was quiet. Wordless. Like the breath had been stolen from his lungs. His muscles seized up, locking him with his neck thrown back and his legs still tight around Mike's waist.

It was one of the most purely erotic things Mike had ever witnessed, and while Josh was swept up in the throes, he switched from grinding to fucking him in earnest. Half a dozen thrusts later, the world blackened, and deep, raw pleasure burst through him. He came with a shout that was muffled by Josh's neck, though he had no memory of burying his face there. He sensed nothing but the salt of Josh's sweat on his lips and the heat that seemed to envelop him.

He had no idea how long it took him to come down, but when he did Josh was panting.

"Damn," he said, eyes open but glassy.

"Same." Mike eased himself gently out of Josh and rolled over. The sheets were cool against his hot skin, but Josh was warm next to him. Mike was exhausted and sweaty and needed to throw the condom away, but an earthquake couldn't have moved him in this moment.

For a full minute, they both stared at the ceiling, breathing hard. Mike was debating if he had the energy to lift his head and put it on a pillow when Josh shifted. He flopped onto his side, eyes unfocused in Mike's general direction, and smiled. "Hey."

Mike smiled back. "I must have done a good job. This is the quietest you've ever been."

To his surprise, Josh's gaze dropped to the bed in a shy way. It was uncharacteristic to say the least.

Mike was suddenly wide-awake. "Everything all right?"

"Yeah, I'm great."

Mike studied him. He knew for a fact Josh wasn't that good of an actor, but it still seemed like there was something he wasn't saying. "Was it something I did? If I hurt you, you gotta tell me."

"No!" Josh snuggled up to his side. "No, everything was great. That was—" he whistled "—the hottest sex I've ever had. But I was thinking it was . . . I dunno how to describe it. Intimate, I guess? I don't know if it felt that way for you."

Mike reached out and touched his cheek. "It did."

Josh bit his lip. "I've never had sex like that before."

"Me neither. In a good way?"

"Definitely."

"Good. I'll be right back, okay?" Mike got up and made his way to the bathroom. Once there, he disposed of the condom, grabbed two hand towels, and wet one of them. A shower would be better, but if he was too tired for that, he was willing to bet Josh was as well. He made his way back to the bed and handed the wet towel to Josh. "Wanna clean up?"

"Thank you."

While Josh mopped himself up, Mike wiped most of the sweat off his face and chest. A glance in the mirror told him his hair was dark with it, and as he turned around, he had some delightful claw marks on his back from Josh's nails. He was so going to Instagram those later. It'd cheer up his fans after he broke the news of his retirement to them.

When Josh had finished, Mike threw the towels in his laundry basket and slipped back onto the bed. He pulled Josh to his side, kissing his sweaty temple. "Hey, handsome."

Josh let out a contented breath, closing his eyes. "Can I sleep here tonight?"

"No, I'm gonna kick you out." He kissed his temple again. "Of course you can."

"Good."

They lapsed into silence. Mike had started to drift off—still naked and on top of the sheets—when Josh shifted. "Can we talk? Or are you too tired?"

Mike cracked an eye open and found Josh watching him from a few inches away. "I think I can manage that. For a few minutes, at least. What's up?"

"We agreed before that we'd see how the first date went before we talked about the future. Well, it's been an unofficial date, an official one, and some pretty spectacular sex. I was wondering where you're at."

Josh seemed calm, for once. Mike would have thought this would be the sort of subject that would make him babble, but his face was relaxed. He looked like he could wait all night for Mike to respond.

Mike grinned. "You wanna define the relationship?"

"We don't have to go that far. I don't think there's any question that we're gonna keep seeing each other. I think I'm still reeling from the intensity of the sex we had. It'd be nice to know if we're in the same place or not. You might not want to jump into something monogamous while you're changing careers and thinking about the future."

Mike sat up a bit. "What about you? You're only twenty-one. You should be out living it up. Partying with your friends."

Josh laughed. "You make it sound like you're ancient or something. And nah, I've done my fair share of partying, and I never was one to play the field. I have enough trouble keeping my mouth shut around one guy. I would never be able to juggle side relationships."

"Good to know. I told you before that I haven't slept with anyone else since you. Have you?"

"Recreationally or professionally?"

Mike raised a brow, and Josh giggled.

"I'm kidding. You're the last for me as well. But that's not unusual for me. My sex life wasn't exactly teeming before we met."

"It's unusual for me. At the height of my career, I probably had three or four sexual partners a week. Now I've had one in the past month."

Josh frowned. "Is that a bad thing?"

"It's neither good nor bad. It's merely a thing. I've never cared about my number. But I do care about you." Mike nudged Josh's cheek with his nose. "I'm happy to be exclusive, if that's what you want."

"Is it what *you* want, though?"

Mike matched Josh's pose, propping his head up on his hand. "It might be a little early to say this, but since we're on the subject, I haven't felt this way about someone in a long time. The first time I met you, I knew there was something different about you. It took me a while to admit it, but it gripped me and wouldn't let go."

"Do you know what that 'something' was?"

"It's hard to put into words. You were so *yourself*, and no matter how much I tried to brush you off or keep things professional, I couldn't. I would like nothing more than to be your boyfriend, but if you just want to be exclusive, that's fine. I can be patient."

Josh's smile was radiant. "'Boyfriends' sounds wonderful to me. Let's wait until after the third date to make it official, though. That's supposed to be the big one."

"Deal." Mike yawned. "I dunno about you, but I don't think I can keep my eyes open another minute."

"Same. Want me to get the lights?"

"I got it." Mike rolled out of bed, ignoring the delicious soreness in his muscles, and clicked off the overhead light. He and Josh dove under the covers, fumbled for a position that worked for both of them, and fell asleep in a tangle of limbs.

Mike didn't remember much of what he dreamed, but he remembered looking out toward something—the future, maybe—and seeing nothing but blue skies, golden sunlight, and beautiful green eyes.

CHAPTER 15

One Year Later

Josh had barely logged in to his webcam channel before the comments came flooding in.

"All right, all right, you vultures," he joked, checking his appearance in the little window that displayed his camera feed. His freshly washed face was visible, along with glimpses of the bedroom around him. "I'm sorry I was gone for a few days, but Boyfriend took me to the beach for a long weekend."

Welcome back, Bret!

u look like u got some sun

Is Boyfriend gonna join us today?

Josh craned his neck until he could see past his laptop. The door to the bathroom was cracked, and the sound of water emanated from the shower. He flopped onto his stomach, kicking his feet up so they were visible above his head. "Maybe. But then, he also said he's gonna need to shower for a year to get all the sand out from everywhere. He calls it 'nature's glitter.' Once it's on you, it's there forever."

u should help him

Get in there with him. Xx

"What, am I not enough for you guys anymore?" Josh's tone was playful. After a whole year of running one of Murmur Inc.'s most popular gay cam channels, he knew there were plenty of people who logged in just to see him. Not that "Boyfriend" didn't give him a noticeable boost in ratings.

A request for a private show popped up. Josh read the description of what the guy wanted—some foot fetish stuff; that was what he got for kicking up his heels—and hit the Reject button. He wasn't in the mood for that right now.

That was possibly the biggest change that had occurred since he'd started making a name for himself in the cam world. Back in the day, he would have taken whatever requests came his way, so long as the person could pay. Now that he had a core following, he could pick and choose what shows he wanted to do.

Out of the sea of messages scrolling past in the chat box, Josh spotted one from a regular, a middle-aged Cincinnati man who went by the handle "Spirk5ever": *How's school going?*

"School's fine, Spirk." Josh nodded toward a pile of textbooks visible on the dresser behind him. "I did better on my midterm than I thought I would. The professor must like me or something."

"Or all that studying you did paid off." The door to the bathroom opened, and Mike emerged from a cloud of steam. His wet red hair looked like a pile of scraggly autumn leaves on top of his head. Not that Josh was paying much attention to that, considering Mike was wearing nothing but a towel wrapped around his waist. Little beads of water were trailing down his abs, and his skin was flushed from the heat of the shower.

Josh swallowed. *Gorgeous.*

He cleared his throat. "Things just got a whole lot hotter, everyone. It's Boyfriend."

The stream of messages doubled in rate. Josh sat up and patted the bed next to him, grinning at Mike. "Come say hi, my love."

Mike kneeled on the bed and crawled into frame long enough to give Josh a firm, breathtaking kiss, before he headed over to the closet. The brief appearance sent requests for private shows popping up all over the screen like sprouts bursting out of the soil.

"I'll be right back, everyone." Josh winked at his webcam. "Let me have a chat with Boyfriend. Maybe I can talk him into a show."

He muted the mic but left the camera running. Mike was out of frame, so all they would see was Josh talking to the left.

"Feel better now that you've showered?"

"Oh yeah." Mike stretched his arms above his head and gave a luxurious groan. His shoulders, which were always dark with freckles, had a distinct pink tinge. "I swear, all that sun did me in. I never should have let you talk me into playing beach volleyball with those college kids. I'm an old man."

"If you're an old man, then I guess I have a thing for that. What's the opposite of a cradle robber?"

Mike stuck his tongue out at him. "I expected you to burn worse than me. But here you are, all tan and golden like a damn movie star. It's not fair."

"I offered to rub sunscreen on you every hour." Josh wet his lips. "Believe me, it would have been my pleasure."

"It wouldn't have helped. Sunburns are a redhead's lot in life. Also, are you actually flirting with me, or do you want to rile me up so I'll do a show with you?"

"The answer is always I'm flirting with you."

"Well, after a year of dating, I think it's safe to say I'm yours." Mike riffled through the closet, and, appearing unsatisfied, pulled open the top drawer of the dresser instead. "Have you seen my favorite shirt?"

"It's in the laundry, remember? You're lucky I moved in, or you'd never be able to find anything."

Mike selected what Josh had learned were his version of lying-around-the-house clothes: boxers and a black Gucci T-shirt. That was right. The man even shelled out for his *T-shirts*. Josh had gotten him to calm down about his wardrobe a bit, but he still insisted on sleeping in clothes that had a higher thread count than their sheets.

When Mike had finished dressing, he sauntered back over to Josh's side. "I'm lucky you moved in for a lot more reasons than that."

"I know." Josh beamed. "I was being modest."

Mike laughed. "If that's your version of modesty, it's no wonder I thought you were such a cocky brat when I first met you."

"Slander!" He jerked his chin at the screen. "We have our pick of show requests if you're up for it."

"I dunno." Mike knelt on the bed again, this time situating himself behind Josh so he could fold him into his arms. "We only got back this morning. Can't we enjoy some alone time before we titillate your legions of fans?"

"Mmm." Josh leaned back, resting his head on Mike's shoulder. "I suppose we should while we can. I have an evening class later, and you have that audition tomorrow. Oh, that reminds me." Josh tapped the button to turn the mic back on. "Good news, everyone. Boyfriend landed a role in a local play. He's gonna be the next big Hollywood star."

There was a sprinkle of congratulations among all the requests for them to take their shirts off.

"That's a bit of an exaggeration, baby. I'm playing Coffee Patron #2, and I have one line."

"I know, but I was at your dress rehearsal, and the way you asked for skim milk was so *moving*. Some big movie execs are gonna be banging down our door any day now."

Mike clenched his lips shut like he was holding back laughter. "Let's start with theater for now and see where it goes. But your faith in me is heartwarming."

"Of course. I'm your biggest fan." Josh muted the mic again. "For now, at least."

"And my biggest patron." Mike nosed his hair. "I still can't believe you donated all that money to my acting troupe."

"It was the least I could do. When I decided to go back to school, you paid my first semester's tuition. I dunno if I could have done it without you. And if it weren't for you, there's no way my channel would be pulling in the money that it is."

"We'll call it a joint effort, then." Mike started kissing his face, sending sparks down his spine. "You smell good."

"That's usually my line." Mike nibbled on his neck, and Josh gasped. "*Ah.*"

"I might be up for a show after all."

"You sure?" Josh smiled. "We can still make it a private affair."

"I'd hate to let down your fans. Besides, we had plenty of alone time in our hotel room. And in the hot tub. And in that cove we found. And on the beach next to the fire we built that one night."

"Totally worth getting sand everywhere." Josh chuckled. "In case I didn't tell you enough before, happy anniversary."

"Happy anniversary, baby. Can't believe it's been a year already."

"Me neither. A wonderful year I wouldn't trade for anything." His finger was poised over the unmute button. "You ready?"

"Just one more thing while they can't hear us." Mike turned Josh's face to the side until they were looking each other in the eye. "I love you, Josh."

Even with everything that had changed in the past year, and how far they'd come together, Josh's heart still fluttered every time Mike said those three words. "I love you too."

"All right." Mike's grin, as devilish and playful as ever, swept across his handsome face. "Let's show them how it's done."

Explore more of the *Murmur Inc.* series at:
riptidepublishing.com/titles/universe/murmur-inc

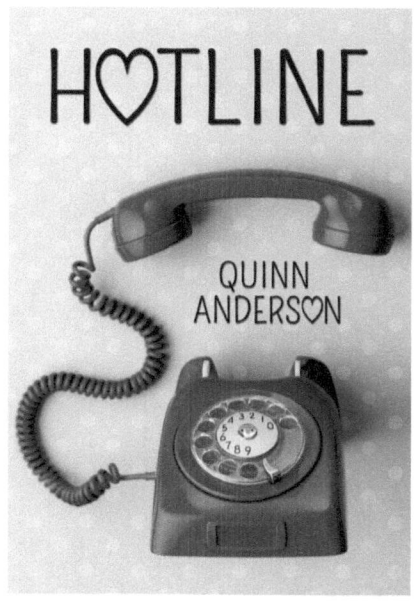

Dear Reader,

Thank you for reading Quinn Anderson's *Cam Boy*!

We know your time is precious and you have many, many entertainment options, so it means a lot that you've chosen to spend your time reading. We really hope you enjoyed it.

We'd be honored if you'd consider posting a review—good or bad—on sites like **Amazon, Barnes & Noble, Kobo, Goodreads, Twitter, Facebook, Tumblr,** and your blog or website. We'd also be honored if you told your friends and family about this book. Word of mouth is a book's lifeblood!

For more information on upcoming releases, author interviews, blog tours, contests, giveaways, and more, please sign up for our weekly, spam-free newsletter and visit us around the web:

Newsletter: tinyurl.com/RiptideSignup
Twitter: twitter.com/RiptideBooks
Facebook: facebook.com/RiptidePublishing
Goodreads: tinyurl.com/RiptideOnGoodreads
Tumblr: riptidepublishing.tumblr.com

Thank you so much for Reading the Rainbow!

RiptidePublishing.com

ALSO BY
QUINN ANDERS♡N

ABOUT
THE AUTH♡R

Quinn Anderson is an alumna of the University of Dublin in Ireland and has a master's degree in psychology. She wrote her dissertation on sexuality in popular literature and continues to explore evolving themes in erotica in her professional life.

A nerd extraordinaire, she was raised on an unhealthy diet of video games, anime, pop culture, and comics from infancy. Her girlfriend swears her sense of humor is just one big Buffy reference. She stays true to her nerd roots in writing and in life, and frequently draws inspiration from her many fandoms, which include Yuri on Ice, Harry Potter, Star Wars, Buffy, and more. Growing up, while most of her friends were fighting evil by moonlight, Anderson was kamehameha-ing her way through all the shounen anime she could get her hands on. You will often find her interacting with fellow fans online and offline via conventions and Tumblr, and she is happy to talk about anything from nerd life to writing tips. She has attended conventions on three separate continents and now considers herself a career geek. She advises anyone who attends pop culture events in the UK to watch out for Weeping Angels, as they are everywhere. If you're at an event, and you see a 6'2" redhead wandering around with a vague look on her face, that's probably her.

Her favorite authors include J.K. Rowling, Gail Carson Levine, Libba Bray, and Tamora Pierce. When she's not writing, she enjoys traveling, cooking, spending too much time on the internet, playing fetch with her cat, screwing the rules, watching Markiplier play games she's too scared to play herself, and catching 'em all.

Connect with Quinn:
Facebook: facebook.com/AuthorQuinnAnderson
Twitter: @QuinnAndersonXO
Email: quinnandersonwrites@gmail.com

Enjoy more stories like
Cam Boy
at RiptidePublishing.com!

Dead Ringer
ISBN: 978-1-62649-338-4

Apple Polisher
ISBN: 978-1-62649-035-2

Earn Bonus Bucks!
Earn 1 Bonus Buck for each dollar you spend. Find out how at
RiptidePublishing.com/news/bonus-bucks.

Win Free Ebooks for a Year!
Pre-order coming soon titles directly through our site and you'll
receive one entry into a drawing for a chance to win free books for
a year! Get the details at RiptidePublishing.com/contests.